The Opera Ghost Lives

Ann M. Kraft

HIS PUB G
The Publishing Group

www.hispubg.com
A division of HISpecialists, llc

Published by HIS Publishing Group,
a Division of Human Improvement Specialists, llc
Contact: info@hispubg.com

First printing, revised edition

Library of Congress Control Number: 2011926651

ISBN-13: 978-0-615-47138-9
ISBN-10: 0-615-47138-2

Printed and bound in the United States of America

Dedication

To my Mom and Dad:
Thank you for loving me for who I am and
knowing what I could accomplish.

Acknowledgments

    I'd like to thank my husband Curtis and our daughter Emily for their encouragement, support and love. I never would have been able to follow my dream had both of you not wanted to follow along with me. To my family and friends that have supported me along this journey, I say thank you for your prayers, your love and believing in me.

    To Gaston Leroux, the author of *The Phantom of the Opera*, I give my thanks and gratitude for giving us all such a wonderful book of characters on which to draw upon for inspiration, insight into the human soul and the quest for obtaining what all of us desire.....to be loved.

    Finally and foremost, to God, the Savior of my life, I give my humble thanks for filling me with the desire to do what I love to do.....write.

Contents

An Opportunity

A messenger rang the doorbell of the small but adequate home of Gaston Girault. Gaston's wife, Louise opened the door and politely took the envelope from the messenger, thanked him and closed the door behind her.

"Who was at the door?" asked a young inquisitive voice.

"It was a messenger with a letter for your father."

"May I take it to him? Please? Please?" plead the young girl's voice.

"Yes dear, you may take it to him. He's in his study."

Amalie was a young girl of sixteen. Her eyes were brown and shimmered like rare black opals. Her hair was deep brown and to her shoulders. It had no curl but a slight wave that made it look as if it were always in motion even when she was still. As she opened the door to her father's study, she tiptoed so that he would not hear her enter the room. She glided across the floor without making a sound and then placed the letter on his desk.

"Amalie, you're getting quite good at sneaking up on your father. I didn't hear *or* see you come in. I'll have to be extra careful when I'm hiding your birthday gift this year. You're almost certain to catch me in the act without my knowing." He laughed and gently pulled his daughter to his side.

"What do you bring to me today?"

"It's a letter from the city I suspect," replied Amalie in her best detective's voice.

"Open it Father. Open it. You shouldn't find it so easy to keep me in suspense.

You know how I love a good mystery and we haven't received a note from the city in months."

Gaston drew his letter opener and opened it. He read it quietly to himself, then after great consideration decided to reveal it to his curious daughter.

"What does it say?" she exclaimed impatiently.

Gaston read aloud.

> *M. Girault,*
> *My name is M. Charles Benoit and I am writing to you because of our great need of an engineer and architect. The cellars at the bakery that falls in the shadows of the great Opera House are in need of inspection and possible repair. There are passageways that may have been damaged during the war and the owner of the bakery has asked that I find a suitable architectural engineer to provide sound counsel on this matter.*
> *Since you are known to be one of the best architects and engineers in France, I should be pleased if you would accept this position. If you are at all obliged to take this offer please send word to my office in Paris. Your wages will be discussed at our first meeting if you choose to accept.*
> *Sincerely,*
> *M. Benoit*

Scratching his chin and then looking into his daughter's brown eyes he folded the letter and placed it in the top drawer of his desk.

"What do you think, Amalie? Should I accept this position? I'll probably have to stay in the city for a month or possibly two which will probably lead to you and your mother joining me in Paris for at least a week or two of my employment."

Amalie glowed with excitement and threw her arms around her father's neck, kissing his cheek.

"I take it that you are in agreement of my acceptance of this position?" Gaston playfully laughed at his daughter's response to his proposition.

"I will speak to your mother at once to see if she is in agreement with our plans."

"Oh, you know that Mother will agree. She loves to go into Paris as much as I. I'm just disappointed that the Paris Opera House isn't finished being built yet or we'd be able to attend an opera while we were there. Promise me that someday when it's finished, we'll go."

"We will, I promise."

She turned to leave her father's study, sung a few notes, took a bow as her father applauded and exited through the door that was partially ajar from her secretive entrance.

Structurally Sound

O nce in Paris, Gaston set about his duties as Master Architect and Chief Mechanical and Structural Engineer for the owner of the bakery, who was in fact M. Benoit. He had felt that if a bakery owner had approached the famed and renowned M. Girault about his cellar problems that he might have been turned away. Fortunately for M. Benoit, M. Girault had already known the identity of M. Benoit and was more than happy to accommodate a fellow businessman in his quest to make certain his investment did not literally collapse out from under him.

Gaston's first duty of his new contract was to do a thorough inspection and mapping of the passageways, cellars and storage areas that were beneath the bakery. He often did his inspections alone and wasn't seen for hours at a time once he got started. He was very meticulous in his recording of the inadequacies he found in the structure and marked the areas that were in question with a small tack that held a bright red ribbon. He did this so that he would be able to return to the places he had inspected enabling him to create a master map of all the sites that needed work.

It was right at dusk and the bakery had closed when Gaston ventured down into the cellars to continue his inspection of two particular passageways. He found that it was easier to work when M. Benoit was not constantly interrupting him with question after question. This caused delays and tired him of climbing up and down the passageways through the three levels of cellars. He had arrived at the conclusion that his work would best be served if done after the bakery was closed. While checking all of the places he'd marked he noticed that one of his markers did not hold his ribbon. He dropped to his knees and began looking for it with his lantern perched next to him. He was astonished not to find his marker but a small light coming from the bottom of a brick from which the mortar had come loose. He took his pen and pushed it into the hole, scraping the mortar away and loosening the brick. He removed it and peered inside.

The late hour made it impossible to find anyone to tell of his discovery, so he decided to return to the first level cellar to retrieve his pick hammer and begin exposing what lay behind the brick wall.

When he returned with his small pick he noticed that the brick had been put back into place. He thought....... did I put it back? Perhaps I did. Although it puzzled him, he continued to take his small pick and pull away at the mortar and remove brick after brick until there was an opening big enough for him to pull his small but muscular stature through. He no longer saw the light and pulled his lantern into the passageway. Scrambling to his feet he felt a cold rush of air across his face. He held his lantern up next to his eyes while turning to his right where he noticed the passageway went up a few steps and then abruptly came to an end.

"I guess I shall go down," mumbled Gaston out loud as he turned around and went down the stairway. He came to a small landing where he found a large rock sitting alone and looking quite out of place. To his left there was a tunnel and to his right there appeared to be the beginnings of new tunnel. He turned to his right and followed the freshly excavated tunnel. He was only about one hundred steps into it when a portion of the passageway above his head started to crumble. Small crumbs of rock sprinkled upon his head and as he tried to outrun his fate, the passageway collapsed, knocking him to the ground. He was covered from the top of his chest to his knees with rocks and in the confusion of the event his lantern had been tossed violently striking him in the head, leaving a large cut on his forehead. He lay unconscious and bleeding in the dark.

Delivered by the Devil

Gaston woke to find himself in a strange place. He was lying on a bed with a small table next to it. The bed was dressed in very fine linens and a beautiful lace canopy hung overhead. For a brief moment he thought that he was dreaming. Then he heard a voice like he'd never heard before. The voice was singing and it was accompanied by the music of an organ. The voice poured out its drink of melody. It was intoxicating to his senses and seduced his ears while hypnotizing his mind. Pleasure was all he could feel even though he knew his body was injured. He tried to rise from his bed so that he could find the person that the voice belonged to but his head and chest were bound so tightly with bandages, and his legs felt to be filled with the heaviest of stones that even though his brain was sending the message to rise, his body did not obey its commands. All he could do was listen and return to his slumber.

An hour had passed. He was still sleeping but he was soon to be awakened by a very unfamiliar voice.

"M. Girault, are you comfortable?" a low voice inquired as he touched him on his bare shoulder. Gaston's eyes began to open slowly as he turned his head toward the voice and replied "Where am I and who are you?"

"M. Girault, I asked if you're comfortable. After you answer my question, I'll answer yours."

"Yes, I am. Now will you please tell me where I am and who you are?" he gasped as his breathing was slightly shallow and labored.

"Who I am is not important. What's important is that you somehow have found a way into my home which no one has ever entered. I'd like to know by what method you have discovered such an entrance. I'd also like to know what you were planning on doing." The voice was careful not to face M. Girault. He moved about the small room with his back always to his guest making sure his face was not seen.

Gaston, still gasping and without hesitation, replied to the voice, "I was inspecting the structure of the bakery......next door and came upon a loose brick....which led me to your corridors. The last thing I recall.....is a few small grains of sand and then.... pebbles shifting from above me.....then I awoke here."

The faceless voice was surprised by the honesty of the man that lay before him. Although the details of his story matched the scene that he had come upon when he had found him, he still didn't trust his words. For all he knew, this was a clever plan to infiltrate and evict him from his home. But then how could that be? No one knew he was there, at least he didn't think so until now.

"I honestly didn't know anyone was down here but I'm glad that you were or I may not be alive." Gaston was gaining his lung capacity and was not breathing so heavily now. "And as soon as I can gain my strength, I shall be on my way," he stated very firmly as he tried to rise again from the bed.

As the faceless voice turned toward him he grabbed his shoulder to help him up and then asked, "And why do you think that I'll let you leave? Do you think that I should trust that you won't tell all that you know to those around you? Oh, M. Girault, I don't believe that you'll be leaving here today or any other day."

Gaston looked up to see a man, who he guessed was in his twenties staring him in the face. However, where a face should have been there was not one; there was only a smooth white mask. It covered the entirety of his face leaving holes only for his mouth, nose and eyes. The sight of this startled him and he fell back onto the bed.

"Does my face or lack of one frighten you M. Girault? "

"Yes...I mean no. It's just that your voice did not lead me to believe I would be greeted by a masked face."

"Then it does frighten you."

"Not at all," he said sincerely.

"Then you must be the bravest man I've ever met. Most men shudder at my masked face and you stand here telling me that you aren't scared at all." He walked around the room with his hand on his chin and if his face could've been seen it would have revealed a pensive look. M. Girault was no ordinary man which he already knew but it wasn't only his ideas about how to build things that were unusual; it was becoming obvious that all of his thinking was unlike anyone he had ever known. The faceless voice stood at the end of the bed facing Gaston; his eyes staring at him through the mask.

"What you would like me to believe is that you're not the least bit worried that your life is in danger; that you don't fear someone who has this odd appearance." He paused and then continued. "You must think that I'm completely without intelligence if you think that I believe you."

"I would never assume the aptitude of someone's intelligence from their appearance. The only reason I believe that I'm in no danger is because I can't believe that you would harm someone whose life you have just saved. However, I can't be certain because I don't know you but fretting over what my fate is to be wouldn't serve any purpose at all, now would it?"

"I suppose not but that's it, now isn't it? That is the real problem. You don't know me so you really don't know what I will do. However, I'm certain that if you knew who you were dealing with, you *would* be afraid," the faceless voice replied. He believed with great certainty M. Girault would show some kind of hesitance or reservations.

"Are you a criminal and that is why you hide your face or is it that your face is truly so unattractive that you don't want it to be seen?"

Gaston's host began to pace around the small room. His words struck the very core of his existence. "How dare you speak to me as if you know anything about me or the reasons I live in the shadows. You know nothing of the torment that this face has caused me. It draws the fear of all that come in contact with it. My own mother wouldn't accept a kiss from my lips. I was her child and even *she* couldn't love me or my face. My mask would be handed to me quickly if she ever saw that I had removed it."

Gaston sat at the edge of the bed still trying to get up. It was evident that this young man had been badly scarred by his own mother's rejection of him. He motioned to the faceless voice to come closer to him. "Please, come help me." He paused for a few seconds to catch his breath and then asked, "Why would anyone be afraid of someone who had such compassion for a stranger who was in need? You obviously haven't lost all of your faith in mankind or you would have left me there to die, would you have not?"

Gaston's question burned in his mind. His reluctance to see him as anything other than evil was puzzling to him. He wasn't sure what this stranger's game was or even if it were a game but he definitely didn't like that nothing appeared to change the opinion this he had of him. His optimism and faith that he wouldn't take his life was peculiar and he couldn't trust it. The faceless voice moved toward Gaston to help him stand and replied with a superior air, "Rescuing you was more of a survival instinct so that I could re-brick the wall that you entered through so that no one would know where you had gone. It was more about *my* survival than yours." Gaston gently grabbed the hand and shoulder of his host as he struggled to gain his balance.

"You could have bricked up the wall without saving me. You rescuing me had nothing to do with your survival. No, I think that you are a decent man, a man of good character, who has found it easier to hide than to put his trust in others."

"If I showed you what was behind this mask, I doubt that you would trust me. Character isn't what people see first when they are looking to trust someone. They only see what is on the outside not what truly makes a man who he is. Their eyes are all they see with and in doing so they reject what their hearts may tell them. I don't believe that you would be any different."

"You cut me, my friend. It wounds me that you take me for a man that judges one only by their outer appearances. I would think that since you know my name that you would at least have made yourself aware of *my* character." Gaston took a few steps away from his unlikely helper, turned to face him and said to him with sincerity, "It makes no difference to me what lies behind your mask. Your actions have shown me what is in your heart and for that I'm grateful. Whatever your secret is, it will always be safe with me. I have nothing to gain by exposing it. Apparently the horror of your own face has convinced you that you must hide away from the world and I shall respect that."

The faceless voice, determined to prove that this man was only lavishing him with kind words to trick him into letting him go, turned to M. Girault and slowly removed his mask. "Is this the face of a man you would trust or a monster?" he asked.

His face was indeed horrific. Only the right side was disfigured leaving his left side unscathed by whatever tragedy had been born to the other side of his face. The skin on the right side of his nose was transparent which made visible the cavity that creates the opening of the nose. The right corner of his top lip was slightly pulled tight making it thin and almost invisible. The skin was rippled along the side of his ear which ran down his right cheek stopping right above his cheek bone. Ridges and raised lumps outlined the top right portion of his scalp which kept his long wispy dark brown hair from being tame. His right eye had no visible eyebrow and was inset deeper into his skull than his left. His skin was reddish in color and resembled flesh that had been scarred from a burn.

He paused for a moment to observe his rescuer and as he tried to keep his composure at the ghastly sight before him, he found that he was drawn to his eyes. They were clear blue like a thin piece of ice and sparkled in the light like sunlight dancing on a lake in the summer. As he looked into his eyes he noticed the sadness of past rejections but as he peered deeper, he could sense the heart of a child; innocent and longing to trust. There was no monster living beneath the disfigured face. There was only a man that longed to be loved for who he was and what he could accomplish. As long as he focused on his eyes, the monster never appeared to him.

"A man," said Gaston as he grabbed his new friend's shoulder and looked him right in the eyes. "Only a man would be brave enough to reveal a secret so personal to a complete stranger. Only a trustworthy man would save a stranger's life. I have met no man braver than you, Monsieur. If you wish to continue to conceal your face it is entirely up to you but you need not hide it for my sake. Your face causes me no terror."

The faceless voice put his mask on the table and then sat on the edge of the bed with his face in his hands. He had never had anyone speak to him with such understanding and compassion. Tears flowed down his cheeks. He was confused and uncertain. Could the words this man spoke be true? Was M. Girault trying to trick him so that he would let him go? While his mind told him of the many reasons that this man's words shouldn't be trusted, his heart wanted to believe. Gaston placed his hand on his head and gently stroked his hair.

"Have I said something to upset you young man? I was merely answering your question. I didn't intend to upset you."

After regaining his composure he looked up at Gaston and answered, "I want to believe that you are being honest with me but I don't trust you. On the other hand, if you are telling the truth, you have given me hope that there is at least one person that can see me and not my affliction. But then again how do I know that you are telling me the truth. After all, I have already told you that I have no intentions of letting you go. I find it hard to trust the words of a man who is either blind or truly *can't* see the monster that I am since it is so obvious, or he lies about what he really sees to better his own situation."

"I wouldn't lie to save myself especially if my lie wounded an already suffering soul. I only speak the truth and my truth comes from personal experiences. I have found that even in the most beautiful of bodies a monster can exist. It usually masks its dark and twisted soul in such a disguise so that no will suspect that it is there." Gaston paused to catch his breath. "I may see an imperfect face but I haven't witnessed any actions that would prove to me that you possess a dark and twisted soul."

"I thank you M. Girault for your kind words but I still don't know how I'll be able to release you. If your words were meant to be the key to your freedom then I regret to inform you that your freedom is still in jeopardy. I can't have you running off to expose me and my home to those who have no compassion or understanding for my hidden existence. I don't know if you are telling the truth and I'm not willing to take the risk. The only truth I know is that I don't trust you."

Gaston sat back down on the bed. He was feeling tired and the pain in his chest was returning. He knew that he was not physically well enough to leave without help so concluded that he could either be this man's willing guest or his unwilling victim, so he made a decision, hoping that it would prove to be the right one.

"I shall stay with you as long as I need to in order to earn your trust. As I always tell my daughter, trust is to be earned and not given and a lie separates friends just as truth bonds them forever." He paused again to catch his breath. "I have but one request and that is for a message to be sent to my employer and to my wife and daughter as to a reason for my absence. My family was to be joining me in Paris soon and I shouldn't want them to get word that I have disappeared."

The faceless voice was shocked at the suggestion of M. Girault. Either his mind was taking leave of him or he was truly sincere that he would stay in order to gain the trust of his captor. He was not sure if he liked the suggestion but in light of all that had transpired he didn't see that he had much of a choice. However, he decided to try one last time to break the confidence of this man that so willingly volunteered to stay with him.

"I will accept your offer but if you don't earn my trust then you'll have to remain here with me and never leave." The faceless voice thought with great certainty that this would bring the man to beg for him to release him. He was wrong. He decided to put his faith in God that night. Although he didn't know with any certainty that this young man wouldn't keep him there forever, he had to trust that there was a reason he'd met him. He knew that if he changed his mind now, that earning this man's trust would be nearly impossible. So instead, without hesitation or doubts, he agreed to the terms but added one more request.

"I should also like to know the name of my rescuer since it has been decided that I will be your guest. You do have a name, don't you?" Gaston curiously inquired.

"Yes, of course, I have a name. I've never had much use for it but if you must know, my name is Erik."

"Just Erik? Do you not have a surname that I shall call you by Monsieur, as I am known as M. Girault?"

"I don't recall ever having use for a surname but if you insist on knowing my proper name, it too shall be earned as well as your trust," Erik replied as he walked out of the small room.

Gaston said a prayer and thanked God for sending an angel of mercy to rescue him from an almost certain death. He was not afraid of who or what this young man was or may have done. There was something about him that drew Gaston to him, something that he couldn't explain. As he lay there the room filled with the same hypnotic and intoxicating sound of Erik's voice that had greeted him. It was soothing and calming to Gaston. So he shut his eyes and let the music take away the pain once more. Then after a few minutes, Gaston, without fear or anxiousness about what was to become of him, fell fast asleep.

An Angel in a Disguise

$\mathcal{A}$ s the search party closed in on the abandoned lair of the Opera Ghost, Erik exited through a passageway that was hidden by a secret door that he had constructed many years before; never believing he'd ever use it. His heart continued to break, even though he knew that letting Christine flee with her beloved Raoul three weeks prior was the right thing to do. Even though she had chosen to stay there with him he knew that she'd always long to be with Raoul. No, the deception had to end and his life had to move forward. He could no longer hang on to the dream that had turned into a nightmare.

He was not afraid of leaving his home for he had come and gone many times before for short periods of time. However, this time he'd be leaving for good, never to return. He had never been afraid of anything except not being loved for himself and although Christine seemed to have proven that it was possible with the acceptance of a kiss from him; he knew deep inside that true love of a physical nature would always be out of his reach.

The true test of Christine's love was to be if she kept her promise; the promise that only he and his friend, the Persian knew about. She had promised to come back to bury him with the gold ring he had given to her. He had arranged that after the Persian received several items from him that he was to place a public announcement of his death in the paper. The receiving of the items would notify the Persian that he was dead and the announcement would notify Christine of the same. He waited five days for her return but she never came. He believed it was Raoul that had kept her from coming. He knew that he had not trusted his words when he told them he was dying. Raoul's instincts to distrust him were right. He had no intentions of dying. He had actually planned to kidnap her once again, this time knowing that her return would prove that she truly loved him. He'd never know for certain whether it was Christine's or Raoul's decision that had kept her from coming to him but the truth became clearer every day that passed and she didn't reappear. It was clear now that she had made her grand gesture only to save her lover's life from his wicked and destructive hands. He had hoped that her love would be the key to unlocking him from the prison that his life had become but it would seem that love of any kind would remain a dream that would never become a reality.

It was to his advantage that no one was to know that she hadn't returned or that there had been any arrangement at all; it gave him the tools he needed to create the illusion that he was dead. In order to carry out such a plan he took one of his earlier victims decomposing bodies, placed a gold ring on its finger and laid it to rest in an open coffin. This was the coffin in which he had slept. He left this coffin, not in his lake house but near the well where he had first brought Christine to his house. Only the Persian would think to look there and he wouldn't do so anytime soon, if he were to look at all. It wasn't a common place that others would happen upon by chance during a search. It would be months, possibly years before they would find his cleverly placed decoy.

Once the Persian felt that enough time had passed, he thought that sharing what he knew with the investigators of Mademoiselle Daaé's disappearance to be harmless for he believed Erik was dead. Erik, however, was very much alive and preparing to make his departure from the lake house. It was unexpected that what had been revealed to the investigators of how the two lovers and Erik were intertwined would lead to irrational actions by those that knew the singer; forcing him to leave unexpectedly.

Even though the Persian had explained how he knew that Erik was dead, a mob of unbelieving, outraged players and patrons from the Opera House had decided to venture late this particular evening down into the five floors of cellars to seek out the hideous creature that had kidnapped their precious singer only a month ago. Even if they only found him dead, it would be better than having to go on believing he hadn't really been there at all. Proof was what they needed and vengeance was what they wanted. He knew if he didn't leave immediately those that found him whether he was guilty or not would certainly thrust their own justice upon him.

He had lived in the belly of the Opera House cellars for so long that it would be strange to venture past the walls that kept him safe and yet a prisoner at the same time. He had thought that perhaps he *should* take his own life but he knew that he'd be confirmed dead soon enough and then no one would ever come looking for him again. Christine's acceptance of a kiss had given him false hope and his happiness quickly turned to sadness as he stumbled up the stairs of his escape route.

Knowing that her love was fleeting and not eternal turned his sadness to rage. He began cursing his existence and begging God for mercy, for it was at this moment he gained a conscience and realized that all of the wicked acts and deceptions he had played upon the innocent people of the Opera House were all in vain. The love he sought had still not been returned nor was it within reach. Manipulation, fear and trickery did not prove formidable methods of acquiring the love he so desperately longed for all of his life. In the end it had only proved that no one would really love him and if they did they would never stay with him until his death. Anyone that stayed would be committing themselves to a life of seclusion and alienation as he had done all of these years. He charged down the passageway toward his exit, venting his anger and rage.

"God, why haven't you sent me to your hell where all of the other demons like me live? I deserve no better fate than they for I have forced hell upon those that were to be part of your heaven and I shall surely burn for eternity. I'll gladly go now if it will spare me the pain of my heartbreak." He grabbed his head and slowly fell onto a large stone that was on a landing near a drainage grate. His heart was racing along with his mind. He wanted desperately to be spared the pain that he knew all too well was his own infliction. Had he never tried to make her love him, he would never have had reason to ever feel the loss and grief with which her rejection plagued him. However, there was no use dwelling on what he couldn't change. It was done and now he had to live with the consequences.

As he caught his breath and sat upon the rock, he heard a faint melody. At first, he thought it was his mind longing for the past; replaying the music that he had once intoxicated himself with to keep him from his loneliness. The voice continued to sing. It was moving closer and he was compelled to savor its richness and delicate sound. The angelic melody was coming from the direction of the drainage grate. The voice didn't seem familiar but there was something about the manner in which it delivered its song that made his mind take leave and focus only on the voice ignoring the sounds of the angry mob that could possibly surround him soon if they found their way into the lake house. The voice's song reminded him of his first love….music; a love that never betrayed him or abandoned him. Then he wondered… could this voice be Christine's? Had she finally come to him? The voice began to grow faint and then there was silence.

He grabbed the grate and peered through the iron hoping to see someone or to hear the melody again. There was nothing but silence. Drawing back from the iron grate, disappointed and believing himself to have dreamed it, he began to make his way toward the entrance of the next passageway that was to lead to his final destination....freedom. "I have to make it to the upper landing so that I may be free from this prison of memories that destroys me from the inside," he mumbled aloud as if hearing his words would give him strength and purpose to continue.

"Your exit has been compromised M. Opera Ghost. If you want your freedom from this prison I'll show you the way," a soft angelic voice announced.

Without question to who or where the voice originated he hesitated only for a moment and then with the curiosity that even a cat would not have dared possess in this situation, he inquired, " How is it that you know my exit is compromised?"

"I know, because I'm the one who compromised it."

"Why then, would you come to rescue me if you had sent others to destroy me?" He roared as he grabbed the iron grate and fell to his knees.

"It is not I that has come to rescue you but an angel of mercy. He has sent me to bring you to safety away from those that would do you harm."

"Show yourself, angel of mercy. I shall be the judge if you are merciful or not. Mercy would be death and yet you have come to save me from that fate."

"I am not the angel of mercy M. Opera Ghost, you are."

He was growing tired of the riddles and became very enraged at the angelic voice. "Stop speaking to me in your ridiculous riddles and tell me who you are and who sent you."

"You called for me, did you not when you asked God to have mercy on your soul for your treacherous deeds? That is why I'm here. God is showing you mercy as you have done at least once in your life M. Opera Ghost. We don't have time for this folly in which we are partaking, so I must compel you to remove yourself from the grate and I will show you your freedom."

Erik, without question released his grip from the iron grate and stepped back. Within seconds the grate began to move downward into the water and the water receded and a stone step was revealed.

"Come quickly, before we are discovered."

He stepped into the passageway and the water began to rise and the grate was back in place as if nothing had ever shifted from its foundation. As he stood on the step, a stairway that could not be seen from his original location outside of the drainage grate was revealed as he looked up.

"Come to the second landing. There you'll find what you left behind and a change of attire that will be suitable for making a departure that will leave you unnoticed."

He climbed the stairway to the second landing and there he found a peculiar note attached to the bundle of clothes he was to change into.

> *Opera Ghost,*
> *Please find that your disguise is in order but please do not wear the mask. The eye patch, false hair and nose should serve you well as the cloak and hat you wear will hide any imperfections from prying eyes. Answers to your questions will come in time. Explanations will be at your will as soon as you are safe.*
> *Angel in a Disguise*

After reading the note Erik was more intrigued and began to feel like a prisoner not of his own making but one of someone else's intervention. If he had had more time to analyze the situation he may have questioned why he would be so easily influenced to follow along with a plan he had not devised but the voice demanded haste and he succumbed to its demands. He quickly changed his attire and tucked the mask, that although looked familiar was not quite as his once was, into the small leather satchel that was to be part of his disguise. Oddly even though he had despised looking into mirrors all of his life, at this moment he wished he had one in front of him so that he could be sure his disguise was presented perfectly.

"Are you presentable M. Opera Ghost?" whispered the angelic voice. "Yes," he replied. "Now what do you want me to do?"

"There is a small hole in the wall where you are standing. Take the tip of your walking stick and place it inside the hole, turn it to the right and push. A door should present itself. I shouldn't have to tell you what to do from there."

Erik did as he was told and as he walked through the door a shadowy figure draped in a black hooded cloak stood in front of him. He walked up to the figure and then made sure that his cloak collar was up high enough so that prying eyes could not see. The hooded figure floated past him removed his walking stick from the door and closed the opening so that it could and would not be detected.

"Here is your walking stick M. Opera Ghost. I hope that your disguise is to your liking."

"It's fine. Where are we?" Erik's tone had changed from agitation to boyish charm with a hint of inquisition.

"We are in the storage room of the bakery next door to the Opera House."

"How did you get into the bakery?"

"The same way I came in, through the door," and before he could ask how she had acquired a key to the bakery, the hooded figure put her finger to his lips and whispered in his ear," There is no time to explain but answers you will have soon enough." She carefully removed her finger from his lips and spoke her plan to him. "My coach is out front. You and I shall blend in with the patrons leaving the Opera House and board my coach."

"I would like to know who it is I'm creating deception and lies with tonight," he stated as he adjusted his eye patch. "I shall not have you referring to me as M. Opera Ghost all night so I will tell you the name that I have taken."

"Your name is Erik Geraurd sir," the hooded figure whispered. As she pulled off her hood to reveal her face, she gently spoke, "and I am Amalie Girault." She opened the bakery door and said as she closed it behind them, "We must hurry to the coach and then your questions may be answered."

Erik took her arm and they crossed the street to her coach.

The Subtle Inquisition

"Mademoiselle, there you are. I was worried that you were a victim of that terrible mob but I did not dare leave my post for fear that you may return and need to flee this place to the safety of your estate."

"Chester, you are such a dear to worry about me. I was so lucky as to come upon one of my father's dear friends and he was kind enough to escort me to safety. He'll be riding home with me as I am not quite myself after such an ordeal as this."

"Yes, Mademoiselle, I'm sure it has been quite an eventful evening. One no one will ever forget."

"Chester, forgive my manners, this is M. Geraurd. M. Geraurd, this is Chester, my driver."

Chester tipped his hat and replied, "It's a pleasure to meet you sir."

"I assure you good sir, the pleasure is all mine," Erik tipped his hat in kind toward Chester.

As Chester retrieved the foot stool and opened the door to the coach, Erik noticed the rapport that Amalie had with her driver. She didn't speak to him as a servant but as a daughter might speak to her father or to a close friend. Erik had never seen such relations between a servant and his superior but it was clear that if she was who he thought she was she wasn't going to be like anyone else he had met.

Erik's observation was abruptly interrupted when she grasped his hand and squeezed it gently. She leaned over and whispered, "The trip to safety will be a long journey into the countryside away from prying eyes and suspicion. If you have questions, now is the time to ask."

Erik was quite surprised how comfortable she was around him. There was no fear in her eyes, nor were there any questions she seemed to need answered by him. She had knowledge about him that no stranger would ever have known. She knew of his need to hide himself and yet was not afraid that she may catch a glimpse of the disfigured horror that lay behind his disguise. She always made eye contact with him and never ventured to pull away in horror when he touched her arm or hand. Although he was certain he knew who she was, he had never met her. It was merely the name that he recognized.

He took her hand and held it as he looked in her eyes. "I know who you are and I'm indebted to you. Your father spoke of you often. M. Girault didn't lie when he spoke of your beauty and your fiery spirit. However, he did not mention that you had a voice that could make the angels in heaven jealous."

She smiled a slight smile at his compliments but did not relish in his praises.

"How *is* your father, Amalie?" he inquired.

"He died three years ago." Amalie sighed and gently pulled her hand away from Erik's grasp.

"I'm sorry to hear of it. Please accept my condolences. M. Girault was a very fine man and a pioneer in his field. I'm sure he prospered from his innovations and ideas. May I be so bold as to ask how M. Girault came to pass away?"

"It does not take boldness to ask a question to which one already knows the answer." She glared at him from across the coach as her words seared like fire to the ears of her companion.

"How should I know how your father came to leave you? I never had the pleasure of meeting your father in person. We only corresponded by messenger and never received any word that he had passed." He glanced out the window with the hopes that she couldn't hear the deception in the words he spoke.

"Why do you insist on lying to me? I guess it's possible that you had no knowledge of how my father died but you most certainly had met him."

"I don't know why you accuse me of deception. Why would I withhold my meeting your father in person? What purpose would that serve?"

She sat quietly and did not respond for several minutes. The moonlight that would shine inside the coach for brief intervals made visible the tears that were falling onto her cheek.

"My father died from an injury that did not heal properly many years ago. He had been sick with a fever and was having violent coughing fits. He became panicked one evening when he couldn't breathe well. I was told by his doctor he had pneumonia but upon further examination it was found that he had a cracked rib which had punctured his lung. There wasn't anything that could be done for him. He was dying. And while he was dying the only thing he concerned himself with was your safety. He worried that he wouldn't be able to help you when you needed him most. That is when he told me of his arrangements for you."

At that moment Erik knew that his dark secrets had at last been brought to light. His eyes darted back and forth as he rung his hands. He wondered how much she knew. What did she know and was what she knew lies or truth? Erik wasn't willing to give up anything and would continue to pretend that he was innocent until she revealed the secrets to verify his proof of guilt.

As he offered her his handkerchief, he took her hand in his and said in his most charming of voices, "Why would your father have been thinking of me?"

She took the handkerchief, wiped her eyes and gazed out the window of the coach into the moonlight. "I'm not as foolish as you may believe me to be M. Geraurd. I won't tell you why because you know why as well as I do. Maybe someday when we have earned one another's trust we'll be able to compare our evidence and you'll be caught in your lies."

He had met many an adversary but none so quick to pounce as Amalie Girault. She was spirited and intelligent exactly as her father had described her and apparently just as capable at playing games as he. He smiled at his unexpected adversary, laughed a soft laugh and adjusted his eye patch.

"I, in no way believe you to be foolish. You're obviously a very intelligent and skilled woman or I wouldn't be with you now creating the deceptions and lies we have conjured this evening. I'm puzzled by your response and I've no doubt that it's possible that I may be guilty of what you accuse me. However, until we have *earned* each other's trust I believe that neither of us will get our answers to this query, at least not tonight."

She passed a slight smile and a faint laugh at what he had stated so eloquently. She turned her head from the window, leaned toward him and replied, "My dear companion, remember that trust is earned, not given, just as lies separate friends and truth bonds them forever." Then she adjusted her position in her seat and went back to gazing at the moon that bounced in and out of view with each pass of a tree.

A Man's Character

Their journey took the remainder of the evening and consumed the daylight of the following day. It was dusk when the coach came to a gradual stop in front of the Girault chateau which was nestled in the wooded countryside outside the small village of Trie-Chateau. Chester climbed down from his seat, pulled the stool down and opened the coach door.

"You're home Mademoiselle Girault. I trust that the ride was not too rough?

"Chester the ride was fine and you may retire the horses for the evening."

"Will you be staying on at the house tonight M. Geraurd?" Chester asked quite boldly as if he was protecting the honor of his own daughter.

Erik looked at Amalie and she returned the glance. Before she could reply with a lie of her own, Erik calmly replied to the question. "I'll only be staying for a short time until my coach arrives. I only came to see that Mademoiselle Girault made it home safely and to keep her company. My coach should be here in a few hours. I assure you that I'd never do anything to put Mademoiselle Girault's honor into question."

Chester nodded his head and tipped his hat toward M. Geraurd.

"Good night Mademoiselle," Chester said in a low voice that was filled with skepticism about where M. Geraurd would be for the rest of the evening.

She leaned forward and kissed the old man on the cheek. "Good night Chester. Thank you for worrying about my honor but I promise you that M. Geraurd is not someone you need to distrust." She said this knowing that she didn't trust him either but was willing to play this game in order to carry out her father's wishes. "Tell Meg I'm sorry you were gone so long. Take tomorrow to yourself and spend some time with her." As she finished these words she took his left hand and in it she placed 30 francs. "Have a good tomorrow."

Chester looked at the money in his hand and then back at Amalie. "You are too generous. I can't accept this."

"You can and you will. There will be no more discussion about it." She took his right hand which bore only a thumb and an index finger, placed it over his left and spoke softly to him, "You have earned more than your wages while being in my service. You have earned my respect and my friendship. It's a gift. Now be on your way so that we may all get indoors where there is warmth."

Chester thanked her again for her kindness as he climbed to his seat on the coach and drove out of sight.

There was that strange rapport between them again. Erik could not quite understand it. It shouldn't have bothered him so much but it gnawed away at his sensibilities like a beaver gnaws at a log. It struck him as so odd that he had to keep himself from inquiring as to why they were so friendly. Her comments of earning trust came back to him. It was a familiar taunt that he recognized. It seemed that the tables had been turned and it would be he who had to earn the trust of a woman not much unlike her father. In keeping with trying to obtain this goal he thought it better not to pry too quickly into matters that did not concern him; at least not yet.

His thoughts were soon interrupted by Amalie touching his arm and coaxing him to follow her to the door of the house.

"Let's get inside where we may warm ourselves."

He followed her into the modest house and removed his cloak and assisted Amalie in removing hers. She hung them in the coat closet and then motioned him to follow her. She led him into her father's study and walked over to her father's desk. She opened one of the drawers, pulled out a stack of papers that were bundled together and handed them to him.

"My father wished for you to have these. He said that he had made a promise to you and that you would know what to do with them."

He took the papers from her small delicate hand. It was a bundle of all the letters that Erik had once written to him. It surprised him that Gaston had kept all of them. Erik fumbled through them looking for something that Gaston had told him he would leave for him. Of course, he never believed that this moment would ever come or that Gaston had really meant to keep his promise. Nevertheless he continued to look through the stack of papers. His fingers came to a stop and then he pulled out an envelope that had a small red wax seal on it that had not been broken. Erik opened it immediately and read it quietly.

My dear friend Erik,

If you are reading this letter in my study, then know that you are safe. The promise that I made to you all those years ago has been kept. I found it necessary in my feeble condition to share the promise I made to you with my loving daughter, Amalie. I hope that someday you will forgive me for this. My making her privy to the promise was not meant to be a part of any deception. It was only so that my promise to you could be carried out in your time of great need. She knows of your secret that you keep behind your mask. I felt it necessary to reprise her of your secret so that she would understand the nature of the disguise for your escape if an escape was needed.

Please trust my daughter, for as I cared a great deal for you, so shall she. Present to her the man that I grew to trust and I assure you that you will earn her trust and loyalty as well. If you find that you are not happy with the arrangements I have made for you, please feel free to return to a life that you choose. My hope is that you will live your life and not just have life.

With great friendship and admiration,

M. Gaston Girault

He folded the letter, tucked it back into the stack of papers, pushed them into the satchel and walked toward the door. Amalie did not speak a word as she sat in her father's chair behind the desk. Erik stood facing the door with his hand on the doorknob. His first thoughts were to leave but then he decided it would be premature to leave before finding out how Gaston had planned on keeping his promise. He was disappointed that his friend of many years had divulged his most intimate secret, and not to just anyone but to his daughter; a woman whose intellect paralleled his own and whose beauty although not stunning would still turn the heads of many men. How could he have given his secret away so easily? It was almost certain that she would only pity him and never truly see him for who he was. The real test of her loyalty to her father's plans would be if she could withstand the sight of his secret as her father had. No woman, other than Christine Daaé had ever been able to look at him and not turn away in fear or disgust. Even now Erik doubted that she had done it out of love for him, but for Raoul. He took his hand from the door and faced Amalie.

"What are we to do now, Amalie? Your father wrote of arrangements that he had made for me."

She rose from the chair, walked over to Erik, looked into his eyes and replied, "Yes, I will tell you of the arrangements Father made for you...... in the morning. The hour is late and I'm very tired. We shall retire for the evening and begin again in the morning."

She began her exit out of the study and Erik grabbed her gently by the arm stopping her.

"I promised Chester that I wouldn't bring dishonor to you. Do you plan for me to stay alone with you in the house tonight or is your mother here?"

Amalie answered with impatience and agitation in her voice, "My mother died six years ago. She was not ill and I don't wish to discuss the circumstances in which she left us, so please do not ask. I'm alone in this house and that is how I wish it to be. I have only two servants and although they live on the property they don't live in the house with me. Chester is one of them and his wife Meg is the other. She comes only on Mondays and if I need her any other day, I need only ask her to come. Chester comes in the mornings to tend to the horses except on Sundays." She stopped for a moment and then Erik was about to speak when she interrupted him. " And if you're wondering why they don't live with me, then I must tell you that it was Father's belief that everyone should have their own home, which is why they live in the small house that my father had built for them."

Erik was startled by her agitated response. Her fiery spirit and aggressiveness aroused something in him that he had not intended to feel. He liked how she carried herself and that she was not afraid to speak her mind. She treated him as he assumed she would have treated anyone else. She didn't seem to care if he liked her or not and that was a welcomed challenge. Fear wouldn't drive this woman to be his friend. He would definitely have to earn her friendship along with her trust.

He gently turned her so that he could see her face which was flush with red; an obvious indicator of her discontent. "I did not intend to upset you with my inquiry. I was merely reminding you that I made a promise to Chester and I intend to keep it, as I do all of my promises." Erik softly replied with his deep soothing voice. "If it is your wish for me to stay here until the morning, I'll do as you ask."

She freed herself from his gentle grip, walked through the foyer and into the great room where the staircase made its ascension to the upper floor where her room awaited her.

"It is not I that asks any of this of you. It was my father's wish that you stay here. He was not worried about the impropriety that it could cause me. He was a man that believed in doing the right thing no matter what social rules he had to break to do it. But of course, you know that better than I, after all he referred to you as one of his most trusted friends. If anyone would have seen you they would have wondered if his faculties were intact." She began to walk slowly up the stairs. "I don't say this to be cruel or to suggest that he was wrong to be your friend; I am merely stating it as fact. If it wasn't the truth then we, M. Geraurd, wouldn't be standing in this room together now."

Her comments wounded him but he knew that she was right. The world had never showed much compassion or understanding toward him. There were a few people that had deemed his life worth saving and he'd never forget them. However, most people put their judgments upon him strictly because of his outer appearance totally ignoring that he was human and had a heart, a mind, a soul that needed to be accepted as all humans do. It was Gaston's unexpected friendship that had changed his mind about how people could possibly see him. But with her honest words she made him realize that Gaston was probably the only person that would ever see him as a man and not a monster.

He followed her up the stairs and into the hall that presented three doors; one at the end of the hall to the left, one at the end of the hall to the right and one in the center of the hallway.

"Do you believe as your father did or do you believe as society does that someone such as I should be locked away out of the view of others?" he asked, curious to hear her response.

"You will come to find that my beliefs are much as my father's. We didn't always agree on everything but on the most important things in life we rarely ever parted thought."

He asked the question again. "Do you believe that someone such as me belongs locked away just because of my appearance?"

She walked toward the door at the end of the hall to her left. She opened the door, entered the room, turned on the light and walked over to the window. He assumed that he was to follow her, so he did. She looked out of the window into the black night where the moon cast strange shadows from the trees.

"Erik, I cannot harm or discriminate against a person that has an outer appearance that displeases the senses of some when that person could not control how it was formed in the womb of its mother." She turned to face him. "To display any prejudice against those that may have a flaw or imperfection upon them without knowledge of their character would be criminal. My father believed that to be true and I would have to agree with him."

Her words fell like gentle rain upon his face; rinsing away the uncertainty that he had first felt when he knew his secret had been exposed. He was assured now that she would not pity him, but would give him a chance to show her that his trust could be earned....... and given. He would do his best to live up to her father's description of him as one of his most trusted friends. Shedding the past would be hard. His tendencies to act first and ask questions later would have to be buried deep down inside him, possibly discarded. There was no need to assume the worst about Amalie. She presented no threat to him or his wellbeing. However, he believed that letting his guard down too much might lead him into an easily laid trap and he didn't want to seem too eager to succumb to the whims of a beautiful woman and her dead father's plans for him.

He looked in the mirror of the dressing table at his face. He adjusted his false nose and eye patch and smoothed his hair piece.

"Amalie, I'm pleased that you believe as your father. If you didn't it would make our meeting not as pleasant as it has been. It must have been hard to lose him. He was a great man. I never knew anyone like him.....until now."

She turned from the window. "This is where you will stay. I hope that it suits you. You will find adequate attire in the armoire and the dresser. If you find yourself in need of anything else my room is at the other end of the hall. Please knock and wait for my answer before you enter."

She exited the room, walked down the hall into her room and closed the door behind her. He stood looking down the hall at her closed door for a moment, and then gently shut his door. He removed his disguise and then opened the satchel to take a look at the mask that Gaston had made for him. It really wasn't much of a mask at all. It was made of leather that had been dyed a flesh color to give the appearance of skin. He examined it further and then placed it on his face. It covered the right portion of his forehead, came down around the eye only covering the skin on and above the cheek bone. It went down over the right side of his nose just enough to cover the transparency of the skin that revealed the dark cavity. He looked in the mirror and admired Gaston's gift. It was strange to see his face without the mask he once wore. It would take some getting used to but he liked the new design of his mask. It made him feel more human and look more like a man and not a monster.

After he took it off he placed it on the nightstand next to the bed and then he fumbled through the drawers of the dresser for something to wear. He found several night shirts and decided on one that was a little longer than the others. It was a very cold evening and it had been years since he had slept in a bed with all of the comforts this one presented.

He replayed her words in his head, over and over again. "A man's character is what he is judged by," he whispered aloud. His character had never been an issue in which he had concerned himself. He hadn't relied on his character to gain friends or enemies, his disfigured face had always been the catalyst that sent people running far from him. No one ever took enough time to find out his true character which unfortunately had caused him to assume the worst about everyone. His past presented many reasons for his character to be in question but he was certain she didn't have any knowledge of his prior indiscretions. He leaned over to turn off the lamp and rolled back into the center of the bed. Pulling the blanket up over his chest he closed his eyes and drifted off to sleep.

Although the hour was late Amalie readied herself for bed as she usually did. She changed into her nightgown and robe and then sat down at her dressing table. With brush in hand she began to count out the number of strokes to her hair until she reached twenty-five. Her mother had brushed her hair in the same manner since she was five years old. She missed her mother and wished that she was there to help share the burden of this task that her father had made her promise to keep. She was not afraid of her task or Erik and the secrets he thought to be hidden from her. Her father had taught her that a man's character and actions were more important than his appearance and she truly believed this too. However, before her father died he didn't know what terrible acts Erik would commit in the Opera House. Not knowing would have been better for Amalie as well, but it was at her own hands that she knew the deeds of her house guest. She would have to figure out a way to see past all of it and try to see the man that her father had described to her. She often wondered what had happened to Erik to make him change so drastically. Her father's description of him was not at all the man she had come to know in the past few years. She would give him a chance because that was the right thing to do and her father would want it that way. However, proceeding with caution was the best way to keep from getting snared in one of his traps.

After brushing her hair, she tucked herself into her warm bed and fell asleep.

An Arrangement

ne morning came too soon for Amalie. She pulled the covers over her head as the sun peaked through a small crack in the drapes. The trip home had exhausted her and all she wanted to do was lay in bed even if she wasn't going to be sleeping. Her guest was probably still asleep anyway and why should she risk waking him. She had almost convinced herself to stay put when she heard a soft knock on the door.

"Amalie, are you awake?" Erik asked quietly.

She rose from her warm refuge and frantically pulled her robe onto her chilled body. On the way to open the door she stopped to check her face and hair in the mirror. It wasn't the best she had looked but vanity wasn't one of her concerns, if anything she was more worried that someone would think she was a woman without any intellect. She reached the door and opened it to find Erik fully dressed and affixed to his face was his newly crafted mask that her father had made for him.

She didn't notice the gasp she let out at his appearance. However, she did not gasp out of fear or disgust but out of surprise at how attractive he was. The mask her father had made for him concealed his birthmark well but revealed his attractive features on the other side of his face. She had obviously not taken notice of them the day before due to the fact that she had her mind on completing her task.

"Are you all right?" inquired Erik.

"Yes, I'm fine. I wasn't ready to be up at this early hour after being up so late." She pulled the top of her robe up and closed it tightly around her neck. "Did you need something, Erik? Was your room adequate for the night?"

"Yes, it was quite adequate. I haven't slept so peacefully in years. I came to ask if you would care to join me for breakfast. I have prepared some eggs, bread and bacon. I was going to squeeze some oranges for juice but there weren't any in the fruit basket. Milk is all I could find."

"An Opera Ghost that makes breakfast." She giggled. "My father told me that you had many talents but he never mentioned you being

able to cook. Give me time to dress and I shall be down to join you."
She wanted so much to loath this man but he was making it very hard
for her to see the dark side in him that she knew existed.

"I'll see you downstairs in the formal dining room then. I promise
you won't be disappointed," he replied.

He walked down the hall and turned to go down the staircase. He
had promised himself that he wouldn't go down the path he had with
Christine. He would be himself and not manipulate or use trickery to
gain her trust. He wanted her to reveal to him what her father had told
her about their friendship but he knew that she wasn't going to give
up the information very easily. He concluded that this was a woman
of strong mind and will. She wouldn't be easily persuaded, seduced
by his hypnotic voice or his tricks and manipulation. No, she was an
adversary of the best kind....she was a challenge and challenges had to
be met with *new* strategies.

The table was set for two and he found two candlesticks to set onto
the table that seated eight. They would only dine at the end of the table;
she at the seat of honor and he to her left so he could enter and exit to
the kitchen for anything they might need. Erik was a romantic at heart.
It didn't matter that he wasn't trying to win the love of this particular
woman, he always felt compelled to do more than was required when
a woman was in his presence. It was probably because he was continu-
ously trying to win the affections of his mother who could barely stand to
glance at him and ignored him unless he was doting on her every whim.

She entered the room without him noticing her. She watched him
as he fussed and rearranged the placement of the candlesticks. She was
flattered by the attention he was giving his presentation. Not even she
would have fussed over such things.

He raised his head to see her standing at the opposite end of the
room. She was dressed in a beautiful sky blue riding dress and was
clinching her gloves, riding crop and bonnet in her hands. Surprised
that she had not alerted him to her entry he simply said, "Do you make
it a habit of sneaking up on everyone or only me?"

"It was a game my father and I played. I was always better at it than he."

"I guess I will watch myself around you. You're as quiet as a mouse
and...." Before he could get the rest of his words out she finished his
sentence. ".....And as light as the Opera Ghost." She laughed at her
words and walked toward Erik who was now standing behind the chair
he had pulled out for her.

"You are making fun of me," he replied with a light-hearted grin on
his face.

"Oh no, I should never make fun of you, Erik. However, knowing all that I know of the Opera Ghost's mischief in the Opera House, I would assume that you must be fairly light on your feet."

"I don't wish to talk about the past this morning. I'm only interested in the future and the arrangements that your father made for me," he abruptly and sternly remarked while seating himself at the table.

She sensed that she had struck a nerve in him. It either made him reflect poorly upon his days at the Opera House, striking guilt into his heart or made him want to avoid it in order to keep her from finding out the details of his past which unfortunately she already knew.

"The table looks really nice. You didn't have to do so much for breakfast. I usually eat at the small work table in the kitchen and when it's warm outside I eat out on the terrace with Sampson."

Erik's curiosity was roused. "Who is Sampson? Is he your suitor?"

Amalie laughed.

"What is so funny?" he demanded.

After catching her breath she replied, "Sampson is not my suitor, he is my tomcat. I'm surprised he hasn't made an appearance at the back of the house this morning. He likes to eat bacon from my hand."

"I think he was here this morning. I heard a sound that sounded a lot like scratching but I thought it was the sound of the bacon cooking. If I had known I would have tended to his needs. Forgive me?"

"There's nothing to forgive. Sampson is quite the mouser and he'll be back later if he is not successful catching his first meal of the day." She placed her napkin on her plate and rose from the table. "It was delicious. I'll clear the table and wash the dishes then we can discuss Father's arrangements."

He was amazed that there was not a hint of awkwardness between them. It was as if they had met before and were getting reacquainted even though he knew very little about her and she seemed to know much more about him. He found that she was not as formal as most would have assumed she should be in the presence of a man. Most women would have waited for the gentleman to leave the table first, allowing them to pull their chairs out to help them exit from dining. This would have bothered him if he hadn't known her father. He was never one for the pretentious confines of social etiquette. He was a free spirit and lived by his own rules, much like he did. It was his misfortune that his rules were not only looked down upon by society but could be considered criminal in many aspects.

She cleared the table and washed the dishes while he took a towel and dried them. The light conversation continued with him inquiring,

"What do you do all day alone in this house? Certainly you must venture out to the village and visit friends." He was trying to be subtle in his fact finding but she knew what his game was and avoided divulging too much information.

"I read a lot. I find that an education is more important than self-indulgent, vain hobbies such as voice lessons and ballet." She hoped to rouse some animosity in him with her comments.

"I suppose it is all relevant for what a person has grown a passion. What would this world be if we all were intellectual and none artistic?" He asked while continuing to dry a plate. "And was it not your harmonious voice I heard in the stairway last night," he said with arrogance in his voice.

"Yes, it was," she said in a very matter of fact tone.

"I think that you're a hypocrite, Mademoiselle Girault."

She glared at him with disapproval of his words in her eyes. He could tell he had angered her with his comments.

"I'm not a hypocrite Monsieur Geraurd. I've never indulged in formal voice lessons or vain public displays of my vocal capacity." She stopped washing the dishes and turned toward him. "Whatever musical talents I possess were given to me by God and I only sing when I feel like it. I don't sing to receive accolades from anyone. I sing purely for my own enjoyment," she snapped at him.

"You have such passion about a talent for which you don't see much need. I believe you have many secrets that you don't wish me to reveal."

"You, Monsieur are one to speak of secrets. I believe you've many more secrets than I to conceal. The most obvious one stares at me now." Before she knew she had made her thoughts audible she had wished she could take them back.

He quickly walked out of the room and into the foyer. He was hurt by her coldness and lack of sensitivity. He went to the closet to retrieve his cloak and hat. As he put them on, she came walking into the room and planted herself in his path.

"Forgive me, Monsieur. My words did not come out the way I had intended."

"Perhaps it is time that we parted ways. I am sure your father's arrangements for me were very well intentioned but I cannot stay where insults are passed out like candy to a small child."

He was toying with his hostess. Yes, he'd promised himself that he would not engage in manipulation and trickery anymore but this was too much fun. He had no intentions of leaving since he had nowhere to go but he wanted to see how far she would go to keep him there or if she would try at all.

He finished putting his cloak on, fixed his hat in the mirror and started toward the door pivoting around her well-proportioned shape.

"Please let me explain my words. Father would never forgive me if you left here without so much as hearing of his arrangements for you," she pleaded with him as she tried again to place herself in his path.

"I'll listen to your explanation but it doesn't mean that I won't leave."

She felt sick to her stomach and wanted to let him walk out the door but she knew she couldn't. She paused for a moment to gather her thoughts and then put her hand on his face; the portion which was not concealed by the mask. He was startled by her gesture. No one had ever dared touch his face before. Her hands felt soft against his skin. It almost made him forget what they were discussing.

"I didn't mean that your face was a secret or that you hide it because you have secrets." She began rambling and stumbling over her words in her attempt to try to make right what had come out so wrong. "I don't know why you conceal it. Your face is no secret to me. You have no need to hide your disfigurement from me. My father described to me the condition of your face and I'm convinced that I should be able to bear the sight of it," she explained trying not to let him hear the anxiousness in her voice.

He quickly removed her hand from his face. "Why would you want to look upon such a sight? Do you wish to turn all of your pleasant dreams into nightmares?" he asked with clear agitation in his voice.

"I doubt your flaws are as hellish as you claim. If my father was able to see you without your mask and not have nightmares, why shouldn't I?" she demanded as she stepped closer to him.

"*You* are not your father. We have only met and I remember you saying that trust had to be earned not given. I don't believe a night of creating deception is a reason for me to give you the privilege of sharing my deepest most personal secret."

She moved closer to the door and leaned against it creating a barricade with her body. Her head hanging as she looked at the floor.

She was humbled by his words and knew she had been wrong to assume she had any right to ask this of him. "You're right. I haven't known you long enough to ask this of you. Please forgive my boldness."

"There is nothing to forgive. You have spoken from your heart and you shouldn't apologize for doing so." He picked her small chin up with his hand so that he could look into her eyes. "You must promise me that you'll never try to remove my mask from my face, Amalie. You mean well but I don't know when I'll be able to trust anyone again with the secret pain that my distortion inflicts upon me and those who gaze upon it."

She removed his hand from her chin. "Why would I take something that was not freely given to me? I'm offended that you think such a selfish act would ever come from me. I hope someday you won't have the inclination to let such horrible thoughts of me enter your mind."

He wondered how he was thrust into being the villain in this conversation; a villain that needed to repent and apologize for similar thoughts of his accuser. She was indeed very good at turning things to her advantage. He would have to keep his guard up and his wits about him less she entangle him again.

He removed his cloak and in his most gentile voice gave her what she wanted: an apology.

"I didn't intend to offend you. I don't know you very well and it is my mistake to have assumed that you could ever be capable of such an act. I beg your forgiveness."

She looked into his icy blue eyes and with profound conviction stated, "I never said I wasn't capable. We are *all* capable of many things that are dark and self-serving. I simply choose not to do them."

He knew that she was baiting him to reply so that the conversation would continue. He consciously chose to let it commence to be revisited another day. He stood in silence as she took his cloak from him, hung it in the closet and put his hat back on the shelf above the rack where the cloaks and coats hung. She shut the closet door and stood smiling at him.

"So, I guess this means you'll be staying?"

"I suppose I am. I don't know how I could tear myself away from someone so charming," he said with sarcasm in his voice.

She was not offended by his sarcasm. She found it refreshing to have someone to verbally spar with like she used to with her father. Although she was not completely comfortable with this mysterious man staying with her, she was determined to trust her father's judgment. It was hard to believe that she would finally have someone else in the house. That is if he decided to accept the arrangements that her father had made for him.

She walked to the door of her father's study and opened the door. The room was flooded with sunlight which revealed a room much bigger than it had appeared last night in the dimness of the lamps. Her father's desk was to the left of the entrance and placed strategically in front of the large windows where the light was brighter. Two chairs faced the desk. Bookshelves filled with an assortment of books on subjects such as architecture, engineering, literature, philosophy and geography lined the outer walls of the room. Two large chairs faced opposite of each other with a small table centered between them in the middle of the room. She was glad to be in this room again. It made her feel safe and secure even though she was feeling anything but that at the moment.

"Erik," she shouted. "Come join me in the study."

He entered the room like an actor first appearing on stage. His presence was commanding and not easily ignored. He walked over to where she was seated in her father's chair behind the desk.

"Please have a seat and I shall enlighten you," she smiled and beamed with enthusiasm. "Now it is time to reveal the arrangements my father made for you. I believe the promise he made was to be there in your time of need and to help you realize God's purpose for your life. Is this the promise he made to you, Erik?" Her tone had become very businesslike and formal.

"Yes, that is the promise he made me." He walked over, took a seat and sat back with his legs crossed waiting for the unveiling.

Amalie removed a black leather case that was tied shut with leather straps from the bottom right desk drawer and handed it to him.

"What is this?" He untied the straps and unfolded the case. There were stacks of papers with drawings, hand written lists of building materials and two envelopes that were sealed shut. On the outside of one of the envelopes it read "Open in Six Months" and then the other read "Open in One Year."

"It is the arrangement that my father made for you."

"I don't understand. This is only a stack of old drawings and lists. What does this have to do with me?"

He looked at the papers again and still could not figure what any of it had to do with the promise Gaston had made to him. She rose to her feet, walked around to the front of the desk and leaned against the corner.

"Are you a good rider?"

He was still trying to decipher the stack of papers in front of him so he didn't hear her question.

"I said, are you a good rider?"

"What does that have to do with what we are involved in at this moment?" he snapped without realizing his tone.

"Everything!" she said not bothered by his disposition. "Bind up the papers while I get our riding crops and gloves. You may use my father's. I think he would like that. Bring the papers in the satchel I gave to you last night and meet me in the kitchen by the back entrance.

He was completely confused now. No one had ever been able to confuse him or out smart him. He was known to be better at creating confusion than anyone, but he was starting to see that this woman and her father were very good at the games in which he thought he was the master. It was difficult to be in an environment that he wasn't familiar with and didn't have much control over. However, it did have its advantages. Being in his friend's home made him feel safe and it was a place where he didn't have to constantly look over his shoulder wondering if someone was going to discover his whereabouts. The house gave him a sense of peace that he had never felt before. It was strange that spending one night there would make him feel this way but he was glad that it did. He had always wanted to live where other people lived; in a house. He wasn't sure that he would be staying but even having one night was better than not having any at all.

He did as he was told. He could have resisted but didn't see the point. He knew that his headstrong hostess would eventually get her way and he would end up looking like the villain again. He went up the stairs into his room, retrieved the satchel and placed the papers into it. What did it all mean? Why was it necessary to go for a ride? This was pure madness. Nothing made any sense. He took his cloak from the closet and walked to the kitchen. There he stood looking out the kitchen window while he waited for Amalie. A small cry came from outside that peaked Erik's curiosity. He opened the door to find a sleek, black cat staring at him.

"Ah, you must be Sampson. No luck finding a mouse this morning?"

Sampson looked at this strange face that was speaking to him. Sampson hesitated and then slowly walked into the kitchen. Erik bent over to pet him and Sampson met his hand with the top of his head.

"You are a very friendly cat. However, I think you are only being nice so that I'll find you something to eat. I don't blame you," he whispered. "I would do the same thing."

Amalie had entered the room once again undetected. She watched as Erik, someone who had taken the lives of many with his own hands, was reduced to a childlike state. He scratched Sampson's fur under his neck and continued to talk sweetly to him.

"Oh, you really like that, don't you? Would you like me to get you a bowl of milk?" As he raised his head he saw her standing at the entrance into the kitchen, smiling.

Embarrassed and a little annoyed that she had managed to sneak up on him again without him noticing, he rose to his feet.

"Sampson was at the back door....I let him in....he looked hungry," his words tripped out of his slightly distorted mouth.

"I see. I will get the milk." She pulled a bottle from the icebox, poured it into a bowl and set it on the floor. "Come here Sampson," she called to the black cat that was purring wildly from the neck rub. Sampson ran quickly to the bowl bumping it, almost tipping it over.

"I have seen just about everything now. How did you teach him to do that?"

"He has always come to me when I've called him by his name. He's done it ever since he was a kitten. I think he wanted to be a dog but he will have to settle on being a cat; a very smart cat."

They both gave him a soft rub on his back. She picked up the bowl of milk and set it outside along with Sampson as they exited the house through the back entrance.

At the stables, they prepared the horses for the ride. The horses were both black with a white diamond shape running down their faces between their eyes to the tips of their nostrils. One had a white band right above its left front hoof. This horse was her favorite and his name was Jasper. He was a gift from her father a year before he died. The other horse was named Shadow for obvious reasons. He was quite spirited and she didn't like riding him very much because he would sometimes get the notion to stop and not move. He was a stubborn horse but very quick on his feet. Her father would joke that Shadow's father must have been a mule.

He walked over to help her up onto her horse but before he was halfway there she was sitting atop Jasper adjusting her gloves and reins. It was obvious that she was an experienced rider. The abilities that she possessed seemed to be endless. He mounted Shadow, adjusted his cloak, gloves and reins. Jasper trotted up to Shadow, Amalie smiled and asked, "Are you ready?"

"It would be nice to know what I'm supposed to be ready for Amalie."

"You'll soon find out. If you can keep up," she challenged. She cracked her crop against the flank of Jasper and he tore out with rapid speed. Erik cracked his crop and away they went.

"Where are you taking me?" he shouted to her as he caught up to her and she began to reduce Jasper's speed to a trot.

"I'm taking you to your arrangement, Erik. I thought that it would be easier to explain if you could see it."

"Your riddles are very childish. I wish you would tell me."

"I could….but I won't. That's the kind of person that I am. If you want to know what my father arranged for you, it is best seen and not told."

"I guess I'll have to trust you on this even though I think you have gone quite mad."

"You are one to talk of madness."

"What do you mean, Amalie?" Erik knew she was hiding something. She knew more about him than she was letting on or she wouldn't continue to make these elusive but accurate accusations. But how could she know anything about his recent madness, she wasn't there to witness any of it. If she was, he would have known, wouldn't he?

"I would think you are quite mad for allowing a total stranger to coax you into a coach in the middle of the night, going to an undisclosed location and trusting that your life was not in danger, when you knew nothing about them. That is what I mean, Erik," she stated frankly.

His paranoid thoughts had been silenced by her response. They rode for what seemed like forever but it was about five minutes. They came to a small clearing nestled in the center of the most beautiful oak and chestnut trees. The clearing was not flat. It had a rolling hill that protruded just enough above the ground so that you couldn't see what was on the other side. She climbed down from Jasper and Erik followed.

"That was a short ride," he laughed. "Was it really necessary to ride the horses out here?"

"Yes, it was necessary," she snidely remarked. "They need their exercise and this has the greenest grass. I always bring them to graze here."

"What are *we* doing here?"

"My father was quite taken by your architectural capabilities. I never understood why he would ride out here and be gone for hours. Then one day I followed him." She stopped talking and then led him into a small wooded area beyond the clearing. She removed some brush that had been strategically laid across a mound covered with grass and greenery revealing an opening into a tunnel. She walked a few feet inside, grabbed two lamps, lit them and handed one to Erik. She walked over to the wall of the cave and ran her hand down the side of a protruding rock. Slowly a door that looked like the cave walls appeared. She pushed it open and began walking down the tunnel that led to a passageway that was wide enough for two people to walk beside each other. Erik followed.

"I watched him go in and out of this cave for five months. I finally grew tired of his absence at the house and confessed that I had been watching him. That is when he told me about a great architect and engineer he had met in Paris during the time he was working in the bakery. He spoke of secret passages and fantastic hidden doors. I began to help him with designing and constructing a hidden door to the cave. We worked for almost a year trying to perfect it. He swore me to secrecy and made me promise to never tell anyone what he had told me about you. He never spoke your name until he was certain he was dying."

They came to another door at the end of the passageway. She pulled a key from inside the wrist of her glove and handed it to Erik.

"Here, you open the door." She handed him the key. "After all this is your arrangement and your future if you choose it."

He placed it in the lock and turned it. He took a deep breath and then walked inside. He looked around the dark hole and saw nothing but a dark, hollowed out shell. It was a cave. It appeared to be about 112 square meters and the clearance was approximately four meters at its highest peak, two meters at it's lowest. There were stacks of building materials lined against the walls and a large barrel full of water with a ladle. The walls were rugged stone and had flecks that sparkled in them. He walked around inspecting and touching the walls. He then noticed a fairly large opening that was not visible from a distance. It was large enough for two men to walk through.

"Where does this lead?" he said as he pointed to the opening.

"That is the natural cavern in which Father found this cave. Years ago when Father was building the stable he was out walking past the tree line and his foot went straight through the ground. He noticed that it never hit anything underneath, it just dangled there. He never told any of us but I suspect curiosity got the better of him. He later told me that he pulled the grass and dirt out from around the hole to see if there was anything down here. He thought it was an old well. Fortunately for you he was wrong."

She leaned up against the pile of lumber, rubbing her arms with her hands to chase the chill away. She continued. "As he went deeper into the hole he found that it leveled out about a man's height down. And it went from a hole into a long tunnel where the walls were rock not dirt; definitely not made by a gopher or other burrowing animal."

"But where does it lead?" Erik asked impatiently.

"Follow me and I'll show you." She picked up her lantern and proceeded into the tunnel.

The tunnel went to the left, straightened out and then wound around to the right. They walked a good distance and then the walls of the tunnel suddenly changed from stone to dirt as it wound again to the left. They walked in silence down the long winding tunnel until they came to another door. She pulled another key from the wrist of her glove, placed it in the lock and then gently pushed the door open. It opened into a room that had not been completed but looked to be a cellar. On the opposite side of the room there was a wooden staircase that led to a door in the ceiling. She walked up the stairs that had been crafted by her father, standing five steps shy of the top and while grabbing the looped rope that was in the place of a door knob, pushed open the door. She held the rope tightly as the door went up and then to her left. She set it down gently so it did not make a loud thud. It opened up into a small room that had no special features at all.

"Where are we?" Erik asked as he closed the door.

"Have patience....you will see." She went to the wall directly in front of her, ran her fingers along the molding and then a click was heard and a door opened. She motioned for him to follow her and as they went through the door they found themselves back in the study.

"How clever," he grinned while rubbing his chin. He inspected the door, trying to locate the mechanism that kept the door hidden.

"Your father had a good memory. It seems he improved upon my design." Erik said while he continued to run his hands around the door. "It's obvious that the tunnel that adjoins the house to the original cavern was manmade. Did your father dig the tunnel that connected them?"

"Yes, it took him many years but he did and it was easy to do since the house already had the cellar it was easy for him to dig through the walls and create a passageway out of the house. It isn't that far from where he fell into the hole. It was only 45 meters or less. He would go into his study and lock the door and we never knew he wasn't in there. The door to the cellar was in the study but no one ever went down there because it was never completed. About six months after he got back from Paris he had removed the door and built a bookshelf into the wall. I never knew it was a secret door until years later. He never told me why he never finished the cellar but it doesn't matter now."

"Your father was a peculiar man; full of questions and dreams like a child. It really hurt me when the letters stopped coming. That is when....." and he suddenly stopped talking.

"That is when what?" Amalie inquired. She was hoping for a confession or a revelation of some kind from her complex guest. She would not get it.

"Nothing, it isn't important." Quickly changing the subject Erik turned to Amalie. "I think we should probably go back to the cave and retrieve the horses."

"Yes, that is probably a good idea. I wouldn't want them to wander off. The grass will only keep them occupied for so long."

They closed up the study, entered the tunnel and returned to the cave. She went to check on the horses leaving Erik alone in the cave. He walked around and took note of all that his friend Gaston had left him. He opened the satchel, pulled out the leather case, untied the straps and began going through the papers again. This time he was careful to go through them one by one; examining each drawing, each diagram in a meticulous manner. Amalie returned and stood beside him looking at the drawings too.

"Amalie, I still don't understand what all of this means. What does this cave, these drawings and all of these stacks of lumber have to do with me?" he asked very confused and wondering how this was supposed to fulfill the promise Gaston had made to him.

"This is your arrangement. Father wanted you to finish his dream for him. He wanted you to complete his hidden room. He loved your house on the lake beneath the Opera House. He said it was the most ingenious creation he had ever laid eyes upon."

"I don't want to re-create that prison!" He exclaimed with rage. "Why would he want me to do that? He knew how much I wanted my freedom; to not have to hide myself from the world."

She put her hand on his shoulder, gently turning him around so that she could see his face.

"Father didn't want you to be a prisoner. He wanted you to be safe from those who would harm you. He didn't want you to build a replica of your lake house; this is supposed to help you find God's purpose for your life." He looked at her very puzzled and still rather confused. She continued with her explanation. "He said that you would understand why he gave you this task. Something about giving back to God the gifts that He had given to you." She stood quietly for a moment waiting for Erik to respond.

"Yes, your father told me that God had given me my gifts and that I should use them to do God's work. I assume that building this room is supposed to make me see what God's purpose is for my life?" He walked around the lumber, sliding his hands over the top of it. "He was determined to make me see that God had not abandoned me. Your father's faith was very strong; I only wished that I could have understood why."

She walked over to him, stood in front of him and spoke sincerely. "My father's faith was strong and his belief was that everyone possesses a special gift from God, especially you Erik. I think that is why he wanted you to construct this room of tranquility. He referred to it as this many times before he died. He said coming down into this cold empty cave always gave him a sense of peace. It was a place where he could be alone to think and to converse with God without interruption."

He walked back over to the drawings he had laid on the stack of lumber. He picked up a couple of the pages, scanning them as if he had missed something. "This looks quite simple which is odd for something Gaston would have designed, but maybe simple was what he wanted. However, it appears that one of the drawings is missing. The largest room doesn't look to have been completed." He looked at Amalie. "Did he give it to you?"

"No, he said that all you needed would be in this stack of papers." Amalie replied.

"I'll look through them more carefully at a later date. I'm sure I have overlooked them." He smiled at Amalie.

"I'm going to assume that since you'll be looking at them later that it means you'll be staying." She was feeling sick to her stomach again. She was nervous that he would walk away from it all and her father's promise would not be fulfilled. She really didn't care if he stayed or went. It made no difference to her. Her life would continue as it always had and she would be fine, but the thought of her father's last request not being honored would tear her apart. She would always blame herself for not trying harder to convince Erik that he needed to stay.

"Yes, Amalie, I'll stay and construct this room. It's obvious that this was very important to him. He has kept the first part of his promise that he made to me and in return I feel obligated to do that which your father has asked of me. Whether or not this will reveal God's purpose for my life will be up to God I suppose. Your father was always more concerned about my salvation than I was but it occurs to me that he may have had good reason to be concerned considering…." Erik cut his own words short and began gathering the papers. He put them back into the leather case, then into the satchel.

Considering what, Amalie thought. She decided that she had the answer to that question already and it was best not to make an issue of it at this particular moment. Things were going well and she saw no need to cause problems between them.

"Are you ready to go back to the house, Amalie?"

"Yes, we should go. I'm sure the horses have eaten enough today."

Troubles

*I*t had been almost three weeks since Erik's arrival. Although Amalie did not trust him, she did not fear him either. Her father had taught her to never judge anyone quickly even if she did know things about them that could easily persuade her to do so. His rule of judgment came with how he was treated by the person, not by how others may have been treated by them. In most cases that would have seemed like a plausible argument but when the person in question was suspected of murdering people, she would have thought her father would have changed his mind; he didn't.

Erik usually rose between the hours of five and six in the morning in order to have his breakfast alone. He liked to get an early start on his work in the cave. Amalie would rise shortly after he had left each morning and they usually would not cross paths until dinner time which was when she would take him something to eat. She often wondered why he always ate breakfast by himself but it wasn't that important to see him every moment of the day so it didn't bother her that he did. She figured it was probably best that they had their moments alone since they were obviously going to be living in the same house for quite some time.

Amalie had told him the conditions of his occupancy when he had decided to stay. He was always to make sure his room was made to appear as if no one lived in it. He was to stay hidden if he saw that company had come and was not to leave the property unless she was told where he was going and why. These were actually only partially her conditions. The latter was her father's since he wanted to make sure that Erik was kept safe and knowing where he was at all times would make that easier for his daughter. Erik surprisingly agreed without hesitation. She didn't know why but concluded that it must be because there was not anywhere else for a homeless opera ghost to go.

It was late in the afternoon on a cold February day and Amalie had just settled into her father's study. She would go there in the afternoons to read her Bible and then afterwards she would read her medical books. Reading her Bible relaxed her, giving her peace and guidance to do what God would want her to do. She had just finished reading one of her favorite passages from the book of Isaiah when she heard a hard knock on the front door. It startled her so much that she dropped her Bible into her lap. Who could that be, she thought. She wasn't expecting anyone. She rose from her chair, walked out of the study, closing the doors tightly behind her. She went to the door, straightened her dress, took a deep breath and then opened the door slowly. Outside the door stood two men, one in a dark suit and the other in an official Magistrate's uniform.

"Good afternoon, Mademoiselle Girault. May we have a word with you?" the man in the uniform asked. She couldn't understand why they would want to speak with her but she dared not refuse them. "Why certainly. Please come in." She opened up the door so that they could pass through and then showed them into the sitting room which was to the left of the foyer.

"I am M. Claude Ferrot and I'm with the Inspector Magistrate's Office from Paris and this is my associate M. Bernard Chantel. We have come to ask you a few questions about what you may know of the events that took place in the cellars of the Opera House a few weeks ago." Amalie's heart began to race and her palms began to moisten. "I don't understand," she said calmly, 'I have been to the Opera House but I don't have any knowledge of any events that took place in the cellars; unless you count the rumors about the Opera Ghost who supposedly lives there. That is the only thing I know about the cellars of the Opera House."

"Were you not there the night that the mob invaded the cellars?" M. Ferrot asked. "Yes, I was but I was there to see the opera. I did not join the mob afterward. I don't believe in ghosts only coincidences." She informed the two men with very little emotion.

M. Ferrot motioned to his associate and then M. Chantel walked over to Amalie and pulled an object out of his leather case. It was wrapped in a piece of cloth. He laid it on the coffee table that was in the center of the room and unfolded the cloth. Inside the cloth was a small pick hammer. Amalie recognized it immediately. It was her father's. She tried to hide the fact that she had recognized it but it was too late, M. Ferrot could tell by the raising of her eyebrow the she recognized it.

"It is obvious from the look on your face Mademoiselle that you have seen this object before now." He paused for her response but she said nothing. "Can you tell me why you recognize it?" He asked with a harsh tone. She still said nothing.

"Mademoiselle, I encourage you to answer my questions here or I will be forced to take you back to Paris with me and you'll be made to answer them there." His voice became louder. "I promise that the questioning won't be as pleasant as this."

She could tell that she was testing his patience and decided that she needed to say something. "It was my father's. At least it looks like one my father had many years ago before he lost it while he was doing some work at the bakery near the Opera House in Paris." She started to pick it up to get a better look at it and then M. Chantel picked it up, "Please Mademoiselle, allow me." He picked it up and showed it to her. "What is it that you are hoping to find on it?" M. Chantel asked.

"My father's pick hammer had his name engraved on the handle." Amalie looked at it as closely as she could without touching it. She was not having any luck finding his name. M. Chantel turned it over onto the opposite side, revealing the name Gaston Girault.

She didn't know what to do. She walked to the window that looked out into the flower garden that was in the front of the house. She was thinking at that moment that she wished she had never let Erik come stay with her.

"Mademoiselle, are you alright?" M. Ferrot asked her, hoping to see some emotion that might help in their investigation. Calmly she answered, "How is it that you have come to be in possession of my father's hammer? He lost it over sixteen years ago."

"We found it in the cellars of the Opera House along with some other items that this alleged Opera Ghost left behind. Although we have yet to find any evidence of an actual house or living quarters, there were a few things found in some of the tunnels."

"Did this Opera Ghost use it on one of the alleged victims, is that why you are here?"

"No Mademoiselle, it doesn't appear that there is any reason to believe it was used for anything but for that which it was designed." M. Ferrot stated.

"Well, isn't it obvious that this Opera Ghost must have stolen it from my father? Neither my father nor I have ever been in the cellars of the Opera House, that can be the only reasonable explanation for it having been there," she insisted.

"Yes, Mademoiselle that is what we believed to have happened also, we only needed you to verify what we had assumed and for you to make a positive identification of the hammer. You may keep it if you like. We will no longer need it." He handed it to her. "However, we still need to clear up the matter of your attendance at the opera of the evening in question."

She was not worried. She had planned her rescue so well that not even the Inspector Magistrate's men would be able to put her in the cellars that evening. "What do you mean M. Ferrot?" she asked in her most innocent of voices.

"It seems that many of the opera patrons that night saw you enter but none of them saw you leave when it was over."

"That is easily explained M. Ferrot. I left the opera early. I was recovering from a cold that I had earlier during the week. I had actually thought about not attending but the opera always makes me feel better, so I went. During the final act I began to feel tired and since I had already seen this particular opera twice, I decided to leave early." She was very convincing and left no reason for suspicion by her interrogators.

"And where did you go, after you left the Opera House, Mademoiselle?" M. Ferrot thought that he would certainly catch her in a lie.

"I went for a short walk down by the bakery to clear my head and that is where my coach picked me up. You may ask my driver, Chester if you like. He has gone home for the day but he arrives early every morning if you wish to speak with him." Her words were presented with such conviction that M. Ferrot could not find any reason not to believe her.

Amalie was very curious to know what she was supposedly doing in the cellars that evening. She couldn't resist asking; so she did. "M. Ferrot why is it that you think I may have been down in the cellars that particular evening and what crime am I allegedly supposed to have committed?" M. Ferrot was surprised by her question because it wasn't often that anyone dared to question him. However, considering the circumstances he welcomed the opportunity to clarify the purpose of their visit. "Mademoiselle, there are no crimes in which you are suspected of committing. We are verifying the whereabouts of everyone that had tickets to the opera that night. The managers of the Opera House asked us to conduct a thorough investigation into the escapades of the Opera Ghost that the mob seemed to believe was still there. It sounds rather absurd but a man who claimed to know as fact that the Opera Ghost lived in the cellars came forward three weeks after Mademoiselle Daaé's disappearance. He spoke of many things that sounded like fiction. We believed the man was not in his own mind but nevertheless we had to follow up on every clue and piece of information that may have any ties to the evening in question. That is why we came to see you." He began walking toward the front door and then turned to Amalie. "It's obvious to us now that there was a man living there or your father's hammer wouldn't have been among the few things we found in the tunnels. This Opera Ghost left quite a collection of odd things in many different places of the cellars. You are the only person that we have been able to identify as the original owner of any of these items."

"Thank you, M. Ferrot, M. Chantel for returning my father's hammer to me." She held it in the cloth they had brought it in and clung tightly to it. "As you may know he died a few years ago and he had always regretted not finding it. He was an architect and engineer and this was one of his very first tools. My mother bought it for him when he began building our house." Her eyes began to tear up. "It means a lot to have it back."

"We are glad that we could return it to you." M. Ferrot said as he put his hat on.

"We must be getting along now. We're sorry to have taken up so much of your time Mademoiselle." M. Chantel said apologetically. "I don't believe that we'll ever have a need to speak with you again about this matter but if you should think of anything that would help us with our investigation please don't hesitate to send word to us."

"I'll do that M. Ferrot. Thank you again for returning my father's hammer." Amalie shook his hand, then leaned forward and kissed his cheek. "You have no idea how much it means to me to have it back." M. Ferrot was blushing at her gesture. "It was our pleasure, take care Mademoiselle Girault." She opened the door and the two gentlemen walked out.

Amalie walked into the sitting room, pulled the drapes to where they were almost shut and watched them as they boarded their coach and left. She was relieved that they were gone. She turned around ready to go into the great room and Erik was standing behind her. His presence startled her which caused her to let out a loud gasp. "Erik, you really shouldn't sneak up on me like that."

"Now you know how I feel when you do that to me." Erik said with a light chuckle. "What may I ask has made you so tense this afternoon? What is so interesting outside?" he asked while looking over her shoulder trying to see.

"I just had the most interesting visit from the Inspector Magistrate's Office in Paris. M. Ferrot and M. Chantel were inquiring about my whereabouts of the night the mob stormed the Opera House cellars." She held the small hammer tighter inside its wrappings, making sure that Erik could not see it.

"Why would they come here? Did someone see us?" His curiosity was turning to fear quickly.

"No, Erik. No one saw us. That was the problem." She passed him and walked into the great room and stood beside the fireplace and Erik followed. She grabbed the poker to stir the embers and then turned to face Erik. His curiosity was now peaked which she could see on his face. She began to speak but was stopped by another question from Erik. "What do you mean, that was the problem? Please explain yourself Amalie."

"No one saw me leave. They were here to verify that I had gone to the opera and wanted to know why no one had seen me leave afterward." She explained.

"What did you tell them?" Erik moved closer to her, now noticing that she was holding something in her hands.

"I told them that I was not feeling well so I left early. I took a walk out to the bakery and then Chester picked me up." She said very crossly to him. "I was glad that not all of what happened that night had to be revealed. It is bad enough that I have had to lie more than once to keep you safe, but the fact that lying comes quite easily for me now turns my stomach."

He could see that she was upset about what she had just gone through and her principles once again being put in a compromised position in order to help him from being discovered. "Sometimes deception is necessary Amalie." He walked over and sat down on the large sofa that faced the fireplace. "Thank you for being so discrete. I'm sorry that you've found yourself in a situation where it has become necessary so often. However, that's the life that I've had to live in order to survive."

"No, Erik. It was not necessary in order for you to live. You've always had a choice," she replied with an arrogant tone.

Her words angered him but he didn't let her see it. She had no idea what she was talking about. She had never had to live in fear of being brutally beaten, jailed or even murdered just because of her appearance. No, she was quite naïve about the life that he had led and the choices she spoke of were the idealistic dreams of someone who had never had to live in fear of what she had being taken away from her.

"And you had a choice too, Amalie. However, you chose deception and don't say it was for me, it was really to save yourself." He said haughtily. She turned her head to face the fireplace. She knew that he was telling the truth. She had in fact lied to save her own neck and he was a benefactor of her deceit. "That may be true Erik but I wouldn't have had to lie to even save myself if you weren't living here."

"This is true. However, you chose to have me stay here and in doing so you accepted the challenges that choice would present." He walked over to the fireplace to warm his hands. She replied, "That may be so but we both know that this was Father's doing and I'm only doing as he asked. I don't feel that I had a choice." He quickly responded to her words. "Exactly Amalie, sometimes other people make choices for us and then we have to live with the consequences of those choices. Just as you felt that the only choice you had was to lie because of the situation before you; that is how I've had to live my whole life as well; making choices in circumstances others have created."

She realized that his view on this particular situation was correct. She did in fact inherit a situation that she had not chosen for herself. She was at the mercy of her father's request. She was irritated that he was able to find fault with her perceptions, bringing them into the light, revealing the fallacy behind her thought process. There was only one other person that was ever able to do that to her; her father. She remained silent, staring into the fire.

He stood quietly next to her, waiting for the sound of her voice to fill the air. He was sure that she would at least attempt to put him in his place, which she often did when they would speak. Her intelligence was exceptional but she lacked compassion at times. He could tell that she was a person who saw things as black and white with no shades of grey ever being allowed to muddle up her perfect picture. From the moment that he figured this out about her he had decided that it was his responsibility to point out the grey areas which in turn would cause Amalie to retreat into silence. He grew tired of the silence and spoke as he playfully tapped her on the shoulder.

"What are you thinking Mademoiselle?" He waited for a smile or any kind of response but received nothing from her. "I'm sorry if I have offended you with my observations but I feel that you must be told the truth. Life's choices don't come with simple answers all of the time." He waited again and still she said nothing. "I'm sorry that you had to lie but if it's any consolation it only means that I'm indebted to you even more now. Your kindness will not go without a reward."

She finally tired of his speech and began walking toward the staircase. When she reached the staircase, she turned to Erik who was watching her walk away from him and said, "My kindness whether rewarded or not will always be given to you. You're right about choices not being simple and my choosing to have you stay here was one of the hardest things I've ever had to do. I'm sure you see no difficulty in that decision because you have only benefitted from it. However, I have had to make sacrifices and decisions that you'll never know about just to bring you here. I'm also certain that you would consider these very small compared to the decisions you've had to make in your life but nonetheless I've had to make them and some of them have caused me great distress; causing me to question my own character."

She began to walk up the staircase. Erik, who had already begun walking toward her while she spoke, picked up his pace and grabbed her hand as it slid across the banister. His grasp stopped her from progressing up the stairs.

"Amalie, I have no doubt that your bringing me here was a difficult decision for you. After all, I'm practically a stranger. In the past few weeks I have often wondered why you would take such a risk and I have yet to find an answer that makes any sense." He led her back down the stairs as he spoke to her, bringing her face to face with him. "You're an extraordinary woman and I'm glad that your father's request became your decision. I'll do my best to make sure that it is not one that you'll regret." He squeezed her hand then continued to hold it. "I'll never know what it took to bring me here but I do know that I am grateful that you did."

She wanted to believe that he was sincere but she had seen him too many times in the cellars of the Opera House working his charms on those who didn't know any better than to believe him. Tonight she would give him the benefit of the doubts that she had swirling around in her head. She had never seen him this humble and there was something in the way that he looked at her that convinced her that his sincerity was authentic.

"I'm glad I did too, Erik. I'm sorry for taking my frustrations out on you tonight. You didn't ask for this situation any more than I did. I guess our loyalty to my father has brought us to a place that neither of us expected to be now." She took a step up, pulling her hand away from his as she held tightly to the hammer that Erik had fortunately not inquired about in her other hand. "That being said, I don't see the need to dwell on the matter. The original plans may not have been ours but we did make the decisions that led to us being here together. We will both have to find a way to make the best of it." She continued walking up the stairs and made it to her door. Erik didn't follow her. He stood at the bottom of the staircase watching her.

After she reached her door she went into her room closing the door behind her. She went over to her armoire and pulled out one of the drawers and placed her father's hammer underneath a stack of freshly pressed scarves. She needed to make sure that Erik would never be able to find it. Her father had always told her and Mother that he had lost it and she never questioned that until now. How did it wind up with Erik?

Had Father left it there by accident or had Erik stolen it from him making him believe that he had lost it? Amalie had many questions about this new link to her father. Somehow she would find out the truth but for now she just wanted to make sure that it was safe and out of sight.

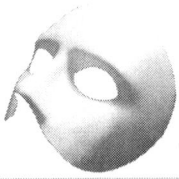

Secrets

It had been four months since the unexpected visitors had come to the Girault home. During that time Amalie and Erik had settled most of their differences and found some common ground on which to build some kind of mutually respectful relationship. Their days would play out as they always did. Erik would work in the cave until it was dark only seeing Amalie during supper now. He knew he didn't have to work so much but he found that the work was therapeutic; using his hands for creation instead of destruction.

Amalie continued to go about her routine as usual; reading her books, riding her horse and occasionally going into the village for food and other supplies. She also spent her days going back and forth from the house to the cave checking on Erik, bringing him meals and fresh water. Chester would tend to the horses in the stable every day and Meg would come to the house once a week helping with laundry and other chores, on Mondays, as was the agreement. Neither of them ever noticed that there was anyone else living on the property.

On a beautiful Monday morning Amalie went out to the stable to saddle Jasper for her daily ride. There she happened upon Chester, who had decided to get an early start on his duties of cleaning the stalls, grooming the horses and maintaining the coach.

"Good morning, Chester!" Amalie chimed with her melodic voice. "I didn't expect to see you here so early."

"Oh, I decided that I should get an early start today. Meg wants to go into the village this afternoon so I brought her with me. She needed to get an early start too. Didn't she come to the door?"

Panic struck in Amalie's heart. She wasn't sure if Erik had already left to go to the cave this morning. Of course, this was one of many Mondays that Meg had come to clean and he had not been found in his room but Meg usually didn't come until mid-morning.

"Yes, I let her in. The lie came out before she could stop it. Her mind raced with thoughts about what would happen if Erik was discovered.

How would she explain? What would they think of her? What would they do to him?

Calmly she told Chester, "I don't like these riding gloves. Would you be a dear and saddle Jasper for me while I go back to the house to fetch my other pair?"

"Yes, Mademoiselle, it would be my pleasure."

Amalie walked quickly back to the house. She ran to the front door, found it locked and Meg was not standing outside waiting. She went up the stairs and down the hall to Erik's room. It was empty. Amalie scurried down the stairs hunting for Meg. She was in the study, dusting the bookshelves, when Amalie found her.

"Meg! You are early this morning." Amalie felt her heart racing. "Yes, Mademoiselle, Chester and I are planning an afternoon in the village. I was wondering where you were. You unlocked the door and then just disappeared into thin air."

Amalie felt her heart beating faster now. How do I explain this? Unfortunately for Meg, Amalie had become an excellent creator of deception.

"Oh, I wasn't completely dressed when I heard your knock. I ran down the stairs, unlocked the door and then hurried back up to finish dressing. I'm sorry I didn't stay to say good morning but I was hoping to get a ride in before the sun became too warm."

"You're forgiven, Mademoiselle. I too am anxious to get things done early today. It looks to be a beautiful day. I would like to enjoy as much of it as I can." Meg continued with her dusting.

"I'm going for my ride now, Meg. I should only be an hour." Amalie shouted from the great room.

"Enjoy your ride dear."

Amalie exited the house and returned to the stable where Jasper was saddled and ready. She thanked him, mounted and then rode out to the clearing. She grabbed a lantern and entered the passageway to the cave. Erik had finished building all of the outer walls and was now working on the interior walls that would separate the room into one large room and two smaller rooms. She found him consulting the pages of her father's designs. She watched him for a moment, again unnoticed. Finally, she spoke.

"Good morning, Erik." She said softly so as not to startle him.

"You *must* stop doing that Amalie. You know how much I despise you sneaking up on me."

"I'm sorry Erik. Some habits are hard to break." She shrugged her shoulders and set her lantern down on a pile of lumber.

"Meg is in the house cleaning. Did you unlock the door for her?" She inquired with an accusing tone.

"I did," he replied as he continued to consult the drawings.

"What if you would've been seen? You could have ruined everything," she spouted angrily as she walked over to him.

"Amalie you have obviously forgotten that I have hidden myself from mortal eyes for many years. I'm very good at being a ghost." He took her by the hand and led her into one of the separate rooms.

"There is nothing to worry about. Meg doesn't suspect anything." He assured her.

"I was already at the stables when Chester informed me that she was at the house. I made up a silly lie about my gloves and went back to the house." She was still very anxious. She released her hand from his and began pacing.

"Luckily, she went right to work and didn't bother looking for me in any of the rooms. I told her that I had unlocked the door and ran back upstairs to finish dressing." She paused to catch her breath since she was speaking so quickly as if she needed to hurry up and confess her deception to someone.

"Meg didn't see through my lie and went about her duties." She was quite spent after speaking and found a barrel to sit on.

"I never want that to happen again Erik. If the door is locked leave it alone. I want you to be safe and if you are found here no one will believe that we are just friends. They will assume we are lovers committing many acts against God's laws. The secret of your birthmark and who and what you were and did before you came to live here will be investigated. Our reputations will not survive it." She continued to speak as in a state of panic. It was as if her mind was expelling every thought she had whether it needed to be heard or not.

He gently took her by the shoulders and stared into her eyes. His instinct was to fly into a rage demanding that she leave him alone. Instead he touched her hair with his right hand and lifted her chin with his other.

"Amalie, you must not worry about such things. I won't live in fear of what others think about me and you shouldn't either. Your father never did. However, if it pleases you, I won't unlock the door again for Meg. She can wait patiently outside if you've gone for your ride. I'm glad that you care so much about what happens to me but I'm very careful." He dropped his hand from her chin, placing it on her shoulder. "I'm glad that you think of me as your friend. I have waited a long time to here you say that." She stood up and began to walk out of the small room in which he had taken her.

"Amalie, is something wrong?"

"I'm fine. You're right. I shouldn't worry so much about what other people think," she said with sadness in her voice. "What a disappointment I have become to my father," she said as tears streamed down her face.

"How can you say that? Your father would be proud of all of the things you've done." He offered her one of his rags. She took it and dried the tears from her eyes. "I don't know anyone who would have taken me in just because their father told them to, especially considering my appearance. You could've refused him but instead you honored him. Amalie, I'm certain that your father wouldn't consider you a disappointment....more of a blessing."

"I suppose you're right. I only wish the world could see you as my father did so that you wouldn't have to stay hidden."

The fact that she left herself out of that statement bothered him. Did she *not* see him as her father did? Why would she consciously omit herself? Erik wanted to know and thought that maybe now she would tell him if he asked. He knew that he would be taking a great risk if he asked her but he needed to know.

"Do *you* not see me as your father did?" He waited attentively for her response.

She wanted very much to tell him what she knew about his past but she feared that he would despise her forever. She had never really thought that it would matter what he thought about her; but now it did. She had thought about revealing what she knew about his past many times but as the days and months went by she had begun to like him and realized that nothing good would come of it. She was beginning to see that the person he was then was definitely not the person that he presented to her now. Perhaps change was possible but trusting in that change was something she wasn't ready to do just yet.

"If I told you the truth you would surely hate me." She continued to walk toward the tunnel that exited out of the cave to the clearing. "I really must get back to the house. Meg will wonder where I am."

He wanted to know what she meant but saw that she couldn't bring herself to tell him. Trying to force her would only drive her deeper into her silence.

"When you're ready, you'll tell me." He said very compassionately to her. She nodded her head.

"Will I see you for supper tonight? You shouldn't take all of your meals alone down here." She smiled a crooked smile.

"I will do as you request. Shall I dress for the occasion?" He said playfully.

Her eyes lit up like a thousand candles. It had been a long time since she had entertained in the house or had a reason to wear one of the evening gowns she had in her armoire.

"That's a grand idea. I will see you at half past six and don't keep me waiting," she laughed.

"Mademoiselle, I would not dare keep a woman of your beauty and charm waiting." He said as he bowed with his arm across his waist. "I shall see you at supper."

He watched her as she exited the cave. He was glad that he hadn't tried to force her to tell him what she clearly wasn't willing to tell freely. He had learned something during the past few months about respecting other people's feelings. Mostly it was just recognizing that they had them. He had grown so accustomed to the world not showing him any consideration for his that he had assumed that he should do the same. No one had ever cared about his feelings; that is until he met Gaston. He taught him about what true friendship was and how to be a friend. Amalie was a lot like her father in that way. She definitely knew how to be a friend; even if she wasn't particularly fond of someone he could tell that she would never intentionally hurt them. The fact that she wanted to spare *his* feelings almost brought him to tears. Someone considering his feelings was as foreign to him as true love. No, he would wait. He was certain that his patience would pay off and she would tell him her secrets someday.

The hours had passed quickly and it was soon time for supper. Erik entered the dining room. He was dressed in a black tailcoat, a black brocade vest with gold accents, a white ascot tie and black trousers. His boots were black and shined like onyx. Amalie had set the table with her mother's finest china, silver, crystal wine glasses, linen cloths and a candelabrum was placed in the center of the table.

He walked around the table looking at the dishes that she had prepared. There was a roasted chicken which was seasoned with rosemary, fresh green beans, fresh rolls and a bottle of red wine chilling in an ice bucket. The aroma made his mouth water. It was definitely better than eating a cold piece of ham on bread in the confines of the cave.

He began pacing back and forth; growing more and more impatient waiting for his dining companion to join him. He checked his watch. It was three minutes past the time she had designated for supper. She was late. He had made up his mind that he would go check on her when she entered the room. She was a vision. He'd never seen her look so lovely. Her hair was pulled up off of her shoulders, allowing only a few strands that curled to frame her picturesque face. She wore a royal blue gown that had small puffed sleeves that hung slightly off her shoulders leaving them bare, her blue suede gloves covered most of her arms and the bodice was cinched in at her waist. The design of the gown accentuated her hour glass figure. He felt his heart beating faster inside his chest. He was used to seeing her in every day clothes and only on occasion would she dress up for church services on Sunday but he had never seen her shimmer as bright as a star in the darkness. She lit up the room like the sun and her smile carried its warmth to his heart. He knew he shouldn't allow himself to feel anything for her but it was hard not to when she looked as beautiful as she did at this moment.

"You look stunning," he said to her as he met her at the entrance to the dining room.

"Thank you. You look very nice too." He was quite striking for a man in his late forties even with his face partially concealed. He offered her his arm and asked, "Shall we?" She put her hand on top of his as he walked her to her chair. He seated her and then himself.

"If you don't mind Erik, I'd like you to say the prayer this evening."

"I have no objections but I haven't prayed in many years," he informed her.

"I don't think God will hold it against you," she cheerfully replied.

He took a deep breath and thought a moment. He tried to remember what Gaston would pray before they ate together hoping it would sound as eloquent coming from him. After gathering his thoughts he prayed: "Lord, let us be truly thankful for the food that we are about to receive. Let it nourish our bodies in order to do your work. Please keep Amalie safe as she has kept me safe. Amen."

She felt her eyes watering and quickly took her napkin and dabbed the tears from the corners of her eyes. She suddenly felt guilty for not trusting him. She was overwhelmed by his words; words that showed a much different person than the one she was trying so hard to put out of her mind. The man seated next to her had shown that he was caring, giving and dare she say loving. Could he really know what love was after all she had seen him do in the name of love? She wanted to believe it was possible but there was always that voice in her head telling her she shouldn't.

"Was my prayer so bad that it brought you to tears?" He jokingly asked her.

"No. It was very sweet. I don't think anyone has ever put me in a supper prayer before."

He began to pour the wine.

"I told you it had been some time since I had prayed and when I did it was never in public. I didn't promise it would be a proper prayer."

"You did fine and I think I like being part of a supper prayer." She smiled a flirtatious smile at him. "Would you like to cut the chicken or shall I?"

She held out the carving fork and knife for him to take. He graciously took it from her petite hands and began carving. He placed a few slices of breast meat on her plate. She served the green beans and the rolls and then they began to eat. The conversation was mostly about the meal and the work he was doing in the cave. She even laughed about the events that had happened earlier during the day concerning Meg. They finished their supper and cleared the table together. She suggested leaving the dishes for the morning and he was in agreement.

"Shall we retire for the evening?" he asked as he walked with her arm around his to the bottom of the staircase.

"It's early, Erik. Come with me. I want to show you something." She led him to two doors that were always locked in which he had never seen anyone, not even Amalie enter or leave through. She went over to the table that was outside the doors of the drawing room, pulled a drawer open and took out a key. She placed the key in the lock and turned it until it clicked. Leaving the key in the door she turned the knob and opened the double doors to the room.

As they entered the room the large rock fireplace that was directly opposite the doors caught his attention. Gaston's use of the rock was quite unique and the mantle was adorned with family pictures and figurines. It reminded him of the things he had collected on his adventures when he was a much younger man. Inside the room there were exquisite golden drapes that flowed all the way to the floor and beautiful tapestries that were imported from foreign lands. There were two small sofas one framed with two small end tables; one to the left and the other to the right. There was one high backed chair that was upholstered with the finest fabrics from Paris and an oval coffee table was centered among them. Bookshelves with books about music, art and medicine towered against the walls on one side of the room and in the right corner there was a large object covered with a sheet of fabric.

"Why haven't you ever showed me this room?" he asked as his eyes scanned the bookshelves until they landed on a book with sheet music in it. He pulled it down and began rummaging through it like he was looking for something he had once lost.

"I wasn't ready to share this room with anyone. I didn't even let my father come in here after my mother died." She walked to the object that was covered with the sheet. "My mother and I loved to come in here after supper. It was a place of laughter, joy and love. When she died all of that seemed to go with her."

"So what has changed, Amalie?" he asked still fumbling through the music book.

"I met you." Her eyes met his from across the room.

"Well, yes, I could see how that could change some things, actually many things but how did that change how you felt about keeping this room locked up?"

"Meeting you made me realize that I can't lock my memories away inside a room in order to preserve them. It's not the room that keeps the memories of my mother alive, only I can do that. She loved me and she loved this room. The times we shared in this room meant a lot to us both. I realized after meeting you that locking your most precious items away isn't always the best thing to do." She was almost blushing at her own words. She hadn't meant it to come out the way it did but then again maybe she did. Being around him every day for the last few months had let her see a part of him that had been almost absent during the time that she had witnessed his destruction and deception at the opera house. Amalie had begun to see how charming he was and how much they had in common. He had, in fact, been a very good friend to her these past months; a friend like none she had ever known. She was willing to forget everything she knew about his past some days but then other days her curiosity needed to be satisfied. She desired to know what drove him to do the things that he had done.

"I'm glad that you've opened this room. It's a magnificent room and these books of music are fascinating." He walked over to her and showed her a piece that he had often played down in the cellars at his lake house. "This is a wonderful piece of music. I thought you said you didn't take lessons, so why do you have all of these books about music?"

She grabbed the sheet and pulled it quickly, revealing a grand piano. The ebony shined as the light hit it.

"This is why, Erik."

His face beamed with delight as he ran his fingers over the silhouette of the piano.

"It's beautiful, Amalie. Do you play?"

"Sadly I do not. That was my mother's favorite past time. She would play and...."

Erik interrupted, "You would sing." Amalie quickly responded. "Sometimes I would sing but only for Mother and Father; most of the time I would sit and listen to her play. She was an exceptional pianist."

She quickly put the focus back onto him. "My father said that you were quite an accomplished musician. Would you mind playing something for me?"

He didn't know what to say. It had been months since he'd sat in front of a piano. His hands had done nothing but manual labor since he'd left the opera house and he never dreamed he'd play again. Although he loved music, it held some terrible memories for him. He looked at the lovely face of his hostess and couldn't refuse her this one request. After all she had shown him trust on some small level when she opened the room to share it with him.

"It's been a while since I have played but I'll do my best for you, Amalie." He walked over to the small wooden bench, placed the sheets of music on the stand and pulled the cover back from the keys. He took a deep breath, then placed his fingers gently onto the keys and began to play. He had picked a piece that her mother had played many times but it never sounded quite as sharp and crisp as it did at the fingertips of M. Geraurd. He continued to play as she became entranced by the music. She felt as if she was floating and then the music stopped. He turned around to find her almost in a trance upon the sofa. He quickly began playing a piece that he knew she'd feel compelled to sing. He could only hope that he was right. After all, he was quite good at using music to hypnotize his audience. He wanted to hear her voice again. He wanted it to rise and become a part of the air that he breathed. The sound of the notes from the piano had suddenly taken him back to his old world of manipulation. It was all too easy for him to fall prey to its seduction.

She rose from the sofa, walked over to the piano and stood facing him. For a moment, he thought he had failed but then there was a note, then another exiting her perfectly shaped mouth and they floated into his ears. She began to sing. The words of the song encompassed the room and flooded his senses. Her voice was pure perfection; even better than Christine's. She had demonstrated in her singing what he had once taught Christine and delivered her performance to a level of perfection that he had always hoped Christine would reach but never did. That was the familiarity he had heard in her voice the evening of his rescue. How was it possible that this beautiful creature had learned musical techniques if she'd never had formal lessons? There was a piece of this puzzle that was missing.

When he finished playing he clapped for her and cheered, "Brava, Mademoiselle, Brava!"

Catching her breath she curtsied and said, "Thank you!"

Trying to catch her in the moment of adoration, he made a statement that would change everything.

"You sing very well. You have a well-trained voice. I've never heard a voice sing with such great attention to the sound of each note and the emotion of the music. Not just the words."

His praise was welcomed by her being that she had never received such accolades for her singing. Caught up in the moment she replied with words she had not intended to say.

"I can't take all of the credit. I had a great teacher." She felt the color rush from her face instantly. She covered her mouth with both of her hands; trying to put the words back into her mouth.

He rose to his feet quickly and stood directly in front of her. He pulled her hands away from her mouth, wringing her wrists tightly with his hands.

"So, you're not only a hypocrite, but you're a liar too! Was it not *you* that claimed to have never had a lesson? Why lie to me about having a voice teacher?" He had let the music and the moment transform him back into the role he had played deep down in the cellars; a victim of betrayal and a deliverer of pain. His anger grew and it was turning to rage quickly. He pushed her up against the piano still tightly gripping her wrists, demanding to know why she had to lie to him. She began to cry and screamed at him, "Let go of me! You're hurting me! I didn't lie to you. I've never had a formal voice lesson in my life." She struggled to free herself but was unsuccessful.

"But you just said that you had a teacher. Give me your teacher's name. Why is it so important that it be kept a secret from me?" He shook her hands again which shook her entire small frame. Tears were rolling quickly down her face and since she feared that he may go too far as he had with so many of his other victims, she blurted out her secret, "My teacher was you, Erik......it was you!"

Her words were the key that unlocked the shackles of his hands from her wrist. He dropped his grip and stepped backward a few steps. He held his head with his hands and turned back to face her.

"How is that possible? Why are you telling me things that I don't understand? How could *I* have been your teacher?" His mind was rewinding his past looking for any glimpse of her in it and she was not there.

Her fear had now turned to rage over the brief assault in which she had just fell victim. She spoke to him with venom seeping from her words.

She walked up to him, without a hint of fear and looked straight into his eyes. "It's possible because I was there! There in the cellars of the Paris Opera House, watching and hearing everything you said and did. I'm not the only deceiver in this room."

He realized in an instant that Amalie, if she was telling the truth, had seen some of the most horrific things he had ever done. He knew now that he would always be seen as a monster in her eyes. This was the reason she had omitted herself from the hopes of others seeing him like her father had. She had seen too much of the darkness that overtook him and her father had never witnessed it; therefore he would've never seen him as she regrettably had.

He backed her into a wall, grabbed her face with his hand and asked, "How is it that you were able to enter without being noticed? You must tell me Amalie." He glared into her eyes.

She had decided that she wouldn't be his victim. She would have to act quickly before he was able to restrain her again. She pulled her hands up in front of her and with all of the strength she could muster, she pushed him in the chest, shoving him backward; knocking him off balance. He stumbled a few steps back and the small end table caught him in the back of the knees which upended him. He landed on his back but not before hitting his head on the coffee table. He lay there, bleeding and unconscious. She stood looking at him with tears rolling down her face, shocked at the sight that was in front of her.

She ran to him, hoping that she had not killed him. She knew she was capable of murder but had never thought she could ever actually carry it out. She had to get that thought out of her head. This was an accident. She removed her gloves and ripped a piece of fabric from her petticoat and applied pressure to the left side of his head. She had to get the bleeding to stop. The cut was not deep but it was producing a lot of blood. She knew that flesh wounds on the head would bleed a lot but were not life threatening. She needed to stop the bleeding. She ripped a few more pieces from her petticoat and tied them around his head. She put a pillow from one of the sofas under his head and gently ran her hand down the unmasked side of his face.

"Erik," she whispered, 'Erik, are you alright? Please say something. I don't even care if it is something cruel, just say something," she pleaded.

The guilt of her actions weighed heavily on her. She cried even harder than before when he had been holding her wrist. "Please wake up, Erik. I'm sorry that I didn't tell you everything. I wanted to give you the benefit of the doubt. I didn't want to believe that you were that dark, hellish creature. I wanted to see you as my father saw you; as a friend."

She buried her face in his chest, sobbing uncontrollably. She felt something touch her hair. It was his hand. She rose up and saw that his eyes were open. She put her blood stained hand on his cheek.

"Oh, thank God! You're awake. I thought I had killed you," she nervously laughed while still crying.

He put his hand on her cheek. "Am I badly injured?"

"You have a long, but not deep cut on the left side of your head and a large bump. I think you'll be fine but I'd like to get you upstairs to your bed so I can clean it up and put a proper bandage on it."

"Amalie?"

"Yes, Erik?

"Could I stay here on the floor for a moment? I'm not feeling well." He said grabbing his forehead with his right hand.

"Yes, you may stay here. I'll go upstairs to get the bandages and some clean towels. I will be back quickly."

After she left the room he managed to sit up; propping himself against one of the sofas before she arrived with the bandages and towels. He was examining his wound with his fingers to verify his doctor's assessment. She was correct. There was a cut in his skin as long as his index finger. The place where he had been laying was covered with blood. Her mother's favorite room now looked like a crime scene.

She quickly entered the room with her supplies and upon entry noticed him sitting upright.

"You must be feeling better." She knelt beside him and after she took his make-shift bandages off, began cleaning his wound. "After I clean this up I will fill a towel with ice for you to put on the bump to keep the swelling down."

"You would make a fine doctor, Amalie."

"I'm surprised you didn't say nurse," she said playfully.

"Well, you'd make a fine nurse too but seeing as how your father told me of your ambitions to study medicine at a university, I assumed the obvious career choice would be a doctor," he chuckled back at her, wincing as the vibration of his laugh caused his head to throb.

Silence fell on the room as she continued to wrap the clean bandages around his head. He had not noticed that his hair piece was no longer intact and the hair that was born to him was visible along with a portion of his disfigurement. She didn't gasp or cringe at the sight of this; she just continued to treat his wound. His hair was a rich dark brown and although sparse in places was shiny and had the look of silk. It was long and flowed to the nape of his neck.

"Do you think you can make it to your room?" she asked as she packed up her supplies.

"I should help you clean this mess up. Look at what I've done to your mother's room," he said expressing his remorse for the earlier events of the evening.

"Don't be ridiculous. You're injured and I won't let you take all of the blame for the condition of this room. I believe the blame rest more on me than you." She walked over to the blood stained rug and began dabbing her wet towel on the fibers, trying to remove as much of the blood as she could.

"I want to stay down here until you finish. It will make me feel better knowing that I didn't abandon you." He traced the path of the bandages around his head.

"I'll get your towel with the ice. You can nurse your bump while I clean this up." She left the room and returned with his towel full of ice. As she handed it to him he took her left hand in his and kissed it. She was moved by the gesture and felt tears swelling in her eyes.

"Thank you, Amalie."

"You're welcome, Erik. You would've done the same for me." She squeezed his hand and smiled at him.

"That's not true," he said in a very sad tone. "I don't know that I would've done the same."

She took his imperfect face in her hands as she knelt beside him.

"You may not believe that you would have, but I do." She stood up, walked back to the place where she was cleaning and continued her work.

"How can you be so sure?" He asked with a bewildered face.

She kept cleaning the rug. "I can be sure because of my father." She turned her head and smiled at him.

She had waited for this moment to come for a long time; the moment that Erik would know that she knew about how he had saved her father's life all those years ago. It couldn't have been timed more perfectly had she planned it herself. He would now have to come clean, just as she did earlier. She just hoped that it wouldn't end with anymore blood being shed, especially hers.

"What do you mean, Amalie?" He tried to put the revealing of his and her father's relationship back onto her.

She immediately stopped cleaning and sat back on her heels. She smiled her best smile and looked directly at him.

"Now Erik, I have told you once before that I'm not as foolish as you'd like me to be. Don't pretend that you don't know why I'd be sure you would rescue me in my time of need." She went back to her work which was almost complete and continued her conversation. "I don't know why you insist on keeping something secret which is really not a secret at all."

"Well, if it isn't a secret', he bantered, 'then why can't *you* talk about it?"

"Oh, I could but I would like to hear your version of the story," she wittingly challenged.

"Why does my account of what happened between your father and I mean so much to you?" He curiously inquired as she finished putting her cleaning supplies up and readied to carry them to the kitchen.

"It just does. It's very hard to explain and I believe you'd think that I am a silly woman if I told you." She walked out of the room to unburden herself from her load of bloody towels.

He tried to make it to his feet but only succeeded at seating himself on the sofa. Everything in the room began to spin and then he passed out.

She returned to the room to find an unconscious Erik face down on the sofa. She rushed to him, pulled him up by his shoulders and in a panic stricken voice tried to rouse him by calling his name. He came to his senses slowly but fully.

"What happened?" she asked.

"I tried to stand up and then everything started to spin. I don't remember anything else," he said as he rubbed the back of his head.

"You stood up too quickly. I told you that I'd help you to your room. Why couldn't you just wait?" she scolded.

She put his left arm over her shoulder, putting her right arm around his waist and lifted his medium but well-built frame up off of the sofa. He was taller than she, so helping him was a challenge. She liked challenges though and refused to let him see that the weight of his stature was more than she could easily carry. They made it to the top of the staircase. She was visibly exhausted.

"Do you need to rest?" he asked.

As she took a deep breath she responded, "No, I'm fine. We're almost there."

"You're a stubborn woman." He stopped walking. "*I* need to rest." He looked down at her and she looked up at him. They both smiled at each other and then after a minute or two began walking again and entered Erik's room. She lowered him to a sitting position on the end of the bed. She walked to the top of the bed and turned down his covers, fluffed his pillow and turned on the lamp. He surprised her when she turned around to find him standing by himself, looking in the mirror at his bandages.

"Where is my hair piece?" he asked her without any emotion.

"I put it to soak in a bowl in the kitchen. It had some blood on it." She stood as still as a statue waiting for his response. Hoping it wouldn't turn into another dual of words. She knew how much he didn't want her to see his disfigurement. She feared seeing even the smallest portion of it would condemn her.

He thought about what she had seen and how she said nothing about it to him. She never shrieked in disgust or turned her eyes from her task. She had tended to his wound as if his disfigurement never existed. This gave him great joy but still couldn't find the strength to reveal the entirety of his secret that he kept beneath the mask. After a long period of silence he finally spoke.

"Thank you, Amalie. I appreciate your thoughtfulness. When do you think I can have it back?"

She walked up behind him. He could see her reflection in the mirror next to his.

"I can have it ready before you wake tomorrow. I know you may not believe me, but I prefer your natural hair. It brings out the blue in your eyes." She smiled and ran her hand down the back of his head stroking his soft hair.

"Your words are kind but I prefer my hair piece.....at least for now." He turned to look at her. "I want you to know that I'm sorry for my behavior tonight." He took her by the hands and looked at her wrists. They had a purplish ring around them. They were badly bruised. "Does it hurt Amalie? Tears began to stream down his face.

"A little, but I'll be fine. I'm more concerned about your head than I am my wrists." She took the handkerchief out of his pocket and soaked up the tears from his eye. "I wasn't without blame tonight. Your injury is my fault."

Erik nodded. "Yes, but I provoked you."

She assisted him to his bed. She seated him and helped him remove his boots.

"Let's not waste anymore words on this. The past is the past and that is where it should stay." She stood up, went to the armoire and removed a nightshirt. She laid it next to him. "I'll let you dress for bed while I tend to the towels downstairs. I'll check on you in a few minutes." She brushed her hand across the top of his leg and turned to exit the room.

"Amalie?"

"Yes Erik?"

"Tomorrow I'll tell you about what happened between me and your father."

She gave him a smile. "Thank you, Erik. That would mean a lot to me." She was almost out of the room and she spun around and said, "And since we are confessing our secrets, I'll tell you how I was able to get into the cellars." She closed the door behind her, not wanting him to have time to respond.

He changed his clothes and climbed under the covers. He couldn't help but wonder how he could he have missed a secret passageway into the cellars. He thought he knew where every tunnel, canal, crawl space and passageway was located in the cellars. How could *she* have known how to enter into his lake house? He needed to stop thinking about it. She would tell him tomorrow and hopefully he would learn just what she'd seen and heard while hiding in the cellars.

He'd finally fallen asleep when she entered his room to check on him. She noticed that he had not removed his mask. How uncomfortable that must be she thought. She touched him on his shoulder and whispered, "Erik? Erik? Can you hear me?" He groaned a deep groan and then opened his eyes. "Yes Amalie, what is it?" She leaned over and whispered softly into his ear, "I just wanted to tell you that your hair piece is on your dresser. I also wanted to say good night and to thank you for an evening I'll never forget." He smiled at her. "I won't check on you again until morning, so you may remove your mask when I leave. I'll knock on the door and wait for your answer before I enter tomorrow morning. You won't be working at the cave the rest of the week. You need your rest."

He nodded a sleepy nod and she exited the room.

Confessions of a Ghost

She woke the next morning before the sun rose to get an early start on her chores. She dressed and walked downstairs quietly so she wouldn't disturb Erik. The events of the previous evening had left both of them in a state of emotional exhaustion along with some physical discomforts; his head and her wrists. They'd both recover from their injuries but their lives together would never be the same for in those tumultuous hours they learned a great deal about on another's character and capabilities.

She gathered the towels covered in blood stains and tried without success to empty them of their blemishes. She thought it was better that no one ever see them to question who or why so she built a fire in the fireplace in the great room and burned them. The damage to the rug in the drawing room would be more difficult to conceal. She decided to roll it up and put it in the hidden room behind the secret door that led to the cellar. It would never be discovered there.

Hours passed and she had put in a full day of chores. Amalie, realizing that the sun had already risen at least an hour earlier, began making breakfast for her injured guest and for herself. Sampson had already come and gone for his morning milk but not without leaving a special deceased gift for her on the back stoop. It was rather disgusting but she knew Sampson meant well. It was his unique way of saying "thank you" to her. After preparing breakfast she placed a glass of milk, silverware, a plate of eggs, bacon, a slice of bread and a napkin onto a bed tray. She finished eating her breakfast quickly and hurried up the stairs to Erik's room. Balancing the tray with one hand she knocked on his door with the other. His low gentle voice broke through the door.

"You may come in."

She turned the knob and walked across the room to the side of his bed.

"Good morning. I hope your head is feeling better." She placed the tray over his legs. "After you have your breakfast I'll change the bandages and check your wound."

He rolled his eyes at her. "You really don't have to fuss over me. I think I can change the bandages myself." He took a bite of his eggs and bacon. "Thank you for breakfast. It's delicious."

"You're welcome and I *will* change your bandages after you're done." She gave him a motherly look. He didn't argue with her because he knew it would just be a waste of time. After living in with her the past few months, he had learned that if she wanted to do something it was best to let her. She was very head strong and confident in her abilities. He liked that about her…. most of the time. However, there were times he wished that she would let her guard down and let someone do things for her.

While he ate breakfast she busied herself opening the drapes that covered the large windows in his room. The view from his room was very scenic. There were trees and rolling hills in the foreground and tall mountains in the distance encircled by blue skies and brilliant white clouds. The sun was shining a pathway into the room. It was late spring and although the early mornings and late evenings were cool, the days were warm; calling all creatures out of their homes to frolic in the splendor of nature. She cleared the tray from the bed, changed his bandages and laid out his attire for the day. He watched her closely while she fluttered around the room like a mother hen tending her chicks.

"Amalie, you'll be exhausted before noon if you don't stop fussing over me," he scolded. "You must come and sit down." He lightly patted the bed.

She looked at him and rolled her eyes. She picked up the tray and as she exited the room she replied, "I will stop when I'm done. Now, get dressed. I'll be back up in a few minutes to check on you." She scurried down the hall leaving his door half-way opened.

She returned twenty minutes later to find that he wasn't in his room. The clothes that she had laid out were gone, the bed was made and the room tidy. Where had he gone? She looked in her room, thinking that he may have gone looking for her, but he wasn't there. She thought that he might be in the study but he wasn't in there either. Then she heard music…..and a voice that sounded like a cellos strings being played; low and calming. He was in the drawing room. She walked over to the doors and crept in so that she wouldn't disturb him. He sat with perfect posture, fingers draped over the keys of the piano and eyes closed. He was absorbed into the music that he played and sang. Strangely there was something different about his appearance and Amalie, after a few minutes of observation, realized that he had not put on the hair piece. Only his bandages covered the flaws of his scalp while the mask covered the rest of his secret.

She sat quietly on the sofa and as the music and the sound of his voice relaxed her, she fell asleep. He continued to play and sing for at least an hour without noticing she was there. He finished, closed the cover onto the piano keys and rose to his feet. It was then that he noticed her fast asleep on the sofa. She had done too much this particular morning and it had finally taken its toll on her. He found a small crocheted blanket that had been left on the back of the chair and placed it across her. "Sweet dreams," he whispered as he exited the room.

While she slept he passed the time by looking through the books in her father's study and reviewing the drawings that were his guide to building the room in the cave. He enjoyed being in Gaston's study. It made him feel like his friend had not left him at all. He would often speak out loud as if he were speaking to Gaston. He found that this helped him think and come up with solutions to the problems that some of Gaston's architectural plans were giving him. Sometimes he could hear his friend's voice guiding him even though he knew he wasn't there.

It was now four in the afternoon and Amalie had risen from her long nap. With a hint of drowsiness in her body movement she entered the study. "Erik, why did you let me sleep?" She yawned and then stretched her arms above her head. "Now I'm behind in my chores."

He walked over to her and put his hand on her right shoulder. "You needed to rest. You worry about me too much. I'm fine."

She put her hand on *his* right shoulder. "That's obvious from the performance you gave this morning at the piano. By the way, it was wonderful. I should have you play every day now that you're here."

"Nothing would give me greater pleasure, Amalie." He took her hand from his shoulder and held it in his.

She felt herself blushing but she didn't know why. His eyes seemed to be bluer and his charm was beginning to penetrate the walls she had thrown up against him but she couldn't think about that right now. She had things to do.

"Have you eaten since breakfast?" she asked him as she walked toward the kitchen.

"Yes. Sampson and I shared a piece of ham and I ate an apple too."

"That's not much of a meal but at least you had company," she laughed.

"Sampson is a good companion. He doesn't complain and he doesn't try to dominate the conversation." They both laughed. When their laughter subsided she began preparing things for supper. He sat on a chair in the kitchen keeping her company and occasionally offering assistance. She finished cooking; they ate supper and then retired to the drawing room.

They faced each other as they sat quietly on the sofa. She didn't know whether to ask him to tell her the story about him and her father or if she should wait until he offered to tell her. However, she didn't have to wait very long before he spoke. He hadn't told anyone except the Persian about Gaston and he was ready to tell his story.

"I suppose it's time for me to confess the secrets of my friendship with your father." He looked into her kind eyes and began telling his story. He told her how he had found her father lying unconscious and bleeding in a hidden passageway and then took him into his lake house to take care of him. He also told her how he had tried to scare him with his disfigured face and how her father never once turned away from him but instead consoled him; showing him compassion and understanding.

"Your father was the one that offered to stay until I gained his trust. He was never in any danger, Amalie. I wanted so much to become someone other than the person I'd been and helping your father gave me that chance. Instead of taking a life, I was saving one," he said with great sincerity.

"What do you mean by taking a life?" she asked with some hesitation in her voice.

He could sense the concern in her voice but felt that if he was really going to change and put his past behind him he needed to tell her everything.

"Please forgive me Amalie for what I'm about to tell you. Before I met your father my life was very different. My own mother and father didn't want me since the day I was born. So I ran away. I found myself among the gypsies selling my hideous face to entertain the curiosity of those that had never seen such a sight. I was mocked and scorned to the point that I didn't even love myself anymore. In my quest to be needed and wanted I took the position of an assassin. I was revered as one of the best and it made me feel important until one day when I was no longer needed. Those I had served decided that I knew too much, therefore I was to be the hunted and no longer the hunter. I was saved by a good man and afterward I found myself at the Paris Opera House. I had time to reflect upon where my life had gone and I wanted no more to do with death. Sometimes death does come with a purpose and to those who deserve it but I no longer wanted to be the instrument in which other men chose to send them to their graves."

She sat in silence and turned away from him. Instead, her eyes were fixed on her shoes.

"Amalie, please say something. I can't change the past but I promise you that my future holds no one's death at my hands unless it is someone trying to hurt you."

"I don't know what to think. I know the man that sits in front of me now is far from the monster that you speak of that existed all those years ago. However, that doesn't explain the monster you became not more than two years ago, preying on the people of the Paris Opera House. How do I know that the monster won't return again when it suits you?" she asked with concern.

Erik took her hands in his and knelt in front of her.

"I can promise this because of you. Just as you say you know that I'd help you in your time of need because of what I did for your father, I know that I won't return to the evils of that monster because of what you've done for me. Your friendship, care, and worry over me have chained that monster up with locks that don't have keys. He'll never again harm anyone." His voice cracked as tears ran down his face pleading for her understanding.

He realized in that moment that he needed her to forgive him. He was having feelings for her that he couldn't identify. All he knew was that her opinion of him mattered more than anything else.

She too, began to cry and wiped his tears from his face with her fingers. "I believe you Erik. My father believed *in* you." She smiled and quickly tried to regain her composure. "Now tell me more about you and my father." He continued his story. He told her how he had Gaston pen three letters; one to his employer, one to her mother and one to the hotel where he was staying.

"Yes, I remember how disappointed I was that Father didn't want us to come to Paris," she interrupted.

"I regret that you had to miss your trip to Paris and someday I'll make it up to you," he said with genuine remorse.

He continued to explain that he'd helped her father continue doing his mapping and inspections in the bakery storage cellars. He had written to his employer explaining to him that his work would continue at night when the bakery was closed and he'd sleep during the day in order to get his rest. The baker had no suspicions that anything was amiss and the work continued at night as Gaston had promised except it was he who had done the work and not her father. Her father stayed with him for almost eight weeks while his injuries healed. When he was well enough, Erik released him so that he could return home. He confessed that during the time of Gaston's stay they'd shared many secrets and stories of their pasts which included regrets. He had many more to confess than Gaston but her father was very understanding and forgiving. Two weeks before he had returned her father to his hotel, Gaston proposed a solution to the open passageway that lead to the bakery. He would place a drainage grate across it and fill it with water to disguise it's entry from the origin of Erik's escape route. Gaston would brick up the wall that he had entered through and Erik would be safe.

She could not resist interrupting him at this point in the story. "Erik, you know that Father never bricked up the wall, don't you?"

"Yes, I figured that out while we were in the coach on the way to your house. Your father always desired to fix everything for me….a lot like you." He laughed. "His idea of the retracting grate was quite clever and the secret door was impressive. He never told me when he was going to fix it but I assume that the baker had him there longer than even I knew."

"Erik, if you know that he didn't brick it up, it should be obvious to you how I was able to get into the cellars without your knowing."

"How clever of you to spy on me using what your father had meant to help me." Erik glared at her with disapproval in his eyes.

"I'm sorry. I thought I was doing what my father had asked of me. How was I to know that what I'd find wasn't what my father had left?" Amalie rhetorically asked.

He knew that he couldn't change what she'd seen and getting angry with her now wouldn't change that. "You're right. You had no idea what you'd find. I'm sure your actions had the best of intentions." He paused for a moment. "I'd like to know however, how you figured out how to get through my secret door into the lake house." He sat staring at her waiting for an answer.

"My father and I built a secret door to the cave; it wasn't that much different from your secret door. Besides, my father told me how you entered in and out to get to the bakery passageway when you'd go do his work for him." She smiled at him and straightened her skirt. "And after all, I *am* my father's daughter."

He sat quietly, not sure how to proceed after finding out that she'd been able to get in and out of his lake house without him knowing.

The silence continued until she asked in a very soft voice, "After Father left and returned home, is that where your friendship ended?

His mind was brought back from the past and into the present with her question and he replied, "No. We continued to write each other several times a month. He would send me his ideas for projects he was working on and I'd give him advice about it."

"Did he ever talk about Mother and me?" she asked.

"Only a few times. He spoke more about you while he was living with me for that brief time. He loved you and your mother very much. He described you perfectly to me and I wish I had gotten a chance to meet your mother. She sounded like a wonderful person."

"I wish you could've met her too but only before….." and she stopped herself from finishing her words.

"Before her accident, Amalie?" he asked with a gentle voice.

"How did you know about her accident?" She was confused. Had she given too much away? Was he just guessing?

"Your father wrote me about her terrible accident in the coach. He told me that she was alive but she would never be the same. It did something to her state of mind was the only detail he ever revealed to me." He looked closely at her face and noticed a tear coming from one of her eyes. "We don't have to talk about it if it upsets you."

"Thank you Erik. Maybe someday I'll be able to tell you about my mother's life after the accident but right now I'm not able to do that." She sighed, wiped the tear from her eye and walked over to the piano. "Mother would've loved to hear you play. She had always wished that I had learned but I spent my time painting and reading."

"You paint? Will your talents never end Mademoiselle?" He teased her.

"Yes, the painting of Father and Mother is one of my originals…… and my favorite."

"Where is your easel, your paints and your canvasses?" He walked around the room pretending to look for them.

"You won't find them in here. They are in my studio."

"And where may I ask is that? I thought I'd seen all of the rooms in this house." He was puzzled and then it came to him. "The room that is locked upstairs between our rooms: *that* is your studio."

She nodded to affirm his clever guess.

"May I see it?" he asked her.

"Maybe someday but not now. I'm working on something for Father's new room and I would like it to be a surprise."

"So many secrets for one so young, Amalie." He rubbed his chin and circled around the sofa. "I'll have much to look forward to *someday*." He teased. "I won't worry over your studio, I know your word is good and your works are even better. You really captured your father's spirit in that portrait and your mother is as stunning as you."

She felt her face get warm and immediately knew she was blushing. He was chipping away at the stone wall around her heart without knowing he was doing it. When she'd first met him she had no intentions of letting him into her world. She was just letting him stay because of a promise she'd made to her father. But now when she was with him she felt like a flower blooming in the sunlight and he was her sun. She was beginning to realize that they weren't as different as she once believed they were.

"Thank you for your kind words but I've seen much better paintings from the street vendors in Paris."

"Ah, perhaps you have but I bet none of them have ever been critiqued by the renowned Opera Ghost." He bowed to her in jest and they both began to laugh until neither could catch their breath.

After their laughter subsided they sat down on the sofa. She was ready to tell him about her comings and goings from the cellars.

"Erik, I believe it is my turn to answer your question about how I was able to be taught by you."

"Yes, Amalie, I'd love to hear how you managed to out ghost a ghost." He crossed his arms and sat back on the sofa.

She adjusted her position on the sofa, leaned toward him and whispered, "I would listen to your lessons from your lake house." He was baffled by her admission.

"How is that possible?"

"After observing your habits for many months I learned the secrets to many of your tricks and vocal illusions. I used the hollowed walls that you used to sneak in and out of the main rooms of the Opera House to hear your instructions. I'd hide myself in the walls and listen to you teach when you would go to Mademoiselle Daaé's room and then when you started bringing her to your house, I'd listen behind the secret door that led to your escape route." He had a look of disbelief on his face. "You don't believe me, do you?" she asked.

"As good as you are at sneaking up on me, I believe you Amalie. What I can't believe is that I didn't know that you had gained entry into my lake house. I've always thought of myself as a very observant person."

"You were also very smitten with Mademoiselle Daaé and that was probably why you didn't notice that I was or had been there," she snapped with a hint of jealousy in her voice. "I was always careful not to disturb anything in your house. And I'd always depart before the lesson was over."

"Smitten or not, I should've known that you were there," he insisted. "How often did you come to my lake house? You live so far away; it couldn't have been that often."

"After Father died my uncle wanted me to stay with him for a while in Paris. He thought it would be good for me to get away from the house for a while. He had never married and had always thought of me as a daughter. He was a wonderful man. He died seven months ago leaving his flat in Paris to me." Amalie began pacing around the room. "While I was living with my uncle I'd think about the stories that Father had told me about you and wondered if you were still living there. Then the stories about the Opera Ghost began to be more frequently circulated and I was certain that it had to be you." She looked at him, giving him a sweet smile. "I remembered the key my father had given me to the bakery and the door I was to use in case you needed help. I used it to find out who the Opera Ghost was. At first, I found your tricks rather childish and funny but as things progressed with Mademoiselle Daaé I started to see you do things in which nightmares are made." She sat back onto the sofa next to him.

"Please don't tell me anymore Amalie. I don't wish to relive the past nor do I want you to have to think about it either." He grabbed her hands and looked at her. "I want to tell you something else about my friendship with your father," he said in a very serious tone.

"What is that?" she asked not really caring what else there was to be said.

"Your father was my only true friend and I loved him. He was like a father to me. His friendship meant the world to me and when....' his eyes began to tear up and his voice began to quiver.... 'When his letters stopped coming three years ago, I thought that...that he had abandoned me just like my own mother had done all those years ago." The tears began to come much quicker now. "I had no idea that he'd died and if I had known, I would've never begun again what I had ended all those years before I met him." He took a deep breath and took her hands, pressing them to his chest as he knelt down in front of her. "All of the horrible things that you witnessed were because I was angry and I felt betrayed. I thought that Gaston had turned me away just like everyone else but he didn't, did he? I should've realized that he never did. When the letters stopped coming from your father it wounded not just my heart but my soul. It was those letters that proved to me that I could be a civilized human being and not the monster of my past. It was those letters and our friendship that showed me that I could be loved; maybe not by everyone but by someone; a man who I saw as my father, my friend." His grief began to consume him and he dropped his face in her lap and sobbed.

She ran her hand down his silky brown hair.

"I forgive you Erik. My father would've forgiven you too. He loved you like a son. He told me that many times before he died." She gently raised his head up with her hands and looked into his blue eyes that were now swollen and red. "You don't have to be sorry anymore. Those may have been your actions but those actions don't have to define who you are Erik. Everyone deserves forgiveness, absolution; even you." She continued to stroke his hair. He wanted to stay there with his head laid upon her lap. Her soft hands combed through his hair careful not to disturb his bandages. She never shuddered at his appearance. Since that first night they met she had always been able to look him in the eyes without fear and without disgust. She had never pulled away from his touch or the one kiss he had placed on her tender hand. She cared about him before he ever cared about her. She *was* his angel of mercy.

"Erik, are you all right?" she asked while bringing his face up off of her lap to look in his eyes.

"Yes, I'm fine. I'm sorry that you had to see me like this." He took his handkerchief and wiped his face of the tears.

"You're entitled to your grief. It warms my heart that my father's friendship meant so much to you. I want you to know that your friendship means a lot to me also." She took him by the shoulders and brought him to his feet as she also rose to her feet. "I've been alone in this house for a very long time, with only Chester and Meg coming to visit me. Only occasionally would I venture into the village but I just never felt a connection to anyone I met. I felt more of a connection to you even before I met you." She walked over to the piano bench and sat down. "My father's stories about you made me want to know you. It was only two days before he died that he had told me about your sordid past. I was shocked that he could be friends with you after what he told me, but he assured me that you weren't that person anymore. That is the reason I went into the cellars, Erik. I wanted to watch over you but I also wanted to get to know the person that my father knew."

He sat down beside her on the bench.

"You already knew about my past?" he asked with surprise in his voice.

"Yes. Father told me all about your life before the Opera House and how your life had been determined for you by the way those that you loved did not return those feelings. He said that you were a product of your environment and that you weren't to be held solely responsible for your actions." He looked at her with his eyes begging her to continue. He had always loved to hear her father's observations about people; he just never thought that he'd ever be the subject of his observation. Amalie continued. "It's not that he didn't hold you responsible at all, he did. However, since you were remorseful and were willing to accept your part in all of it, he was able to grant you understanding, compassion and forgiveness." She turned to him and smiled.

"You knew all of the time and you made me tell you anyway." He said shaking his head. "Why?" He was not angry but he didn't understand why she had made him believe she knew nothing of his past.

"I had to know if you'd tell me yourself. I know it seems a bit extreme but I had to know that I could trust you and that you could trust me." She played with the sleeve of her dress.

He stood up and walked over to the bookshelf. "I should be angry with you for playing games with me but oddly enough, I understand." He paused for a minute. "I know it wasn't your intention to deceive me." He walked over to her and took her hands in his. "Your father always said that trust was to be earned and not given." She smiled and squeezed his hands.

"Yes, Erik and you have earned my trust and I give it to you freely. I hope that you will trust me someday."

"I do trust you. I hope you know that."

"Yes, just not enough to let me see what is behind your mask."

"I'm afraid that my trusting you doesn't keep me from my vanity. My secret causes me pain much like the secret you keep about your mother's life after the accident. When we both find the courage to finally face those secrets instead of hiding them, then I guess we'll both be free." His words were full of wisdom. If she wasn't looking at him she would've believed that her father was the one speaking to her.

"I suppose you're right. Some secrets aren't meant to be told or shown." She walked to the doors of the drawing room and motioned for him to follow.

"I'm tired and it's late. I'd like to retire to my room now, will you walk me up?" She put her arm out waiting for him to wrap his around hers.

"It would be my pleasure." He yawned. "I'm tired too."

They talked a little more on their way up the stairs, said their goodnights and went to their separate rooms. He waited for her to close her door before he shut his. He knew he was falling in love with her but didn't dare tell her. His feelings for her even surprised him. He never thought that he'd feel like that about anyone again. He wasn't sure he really ever had; not even for Christine. His infatuation and lust for Christine, which turned to obsession, wouldn't be considered love by anyone; not even him now. His definition of love had changed with every moment he spent with Amalie. He realized that the kind of love he longed for couldn't be forced upon someone. Love wasn't control or manipulation of someone; love was to be freely given. Love was trust and friendship. He now knew the reason Gaston had brought him here.

Admissions of ......

*A*nother month passed and his cut had healed and her wrists showed no trace of anything ever having been wrong with them. He continued his work down in the cave. She spent more time in her studio painting. She didn't have to take him his meals anymore; he'd come up to the house for them except on Mondays when he knew Meg would be there. On occasion she'd venture down into the cave to check on the progress of the rooms. However, he'd become very secretive about his work and preferred her not to come unless he had invited her.

One afternoon he was going through the contents of his satchel hunting for a pencil and came upon one of the two letters that Gaston had left instructions for him to open at a later date. It had now been six months since he'd begun his stay at the Girault home. He opened the envelope and inside was a letter and another envelope that had Amalie's name written on the front. He set it aside and then pulled the letter out to read it.

> *Dear Erik,*
>
> *If you are reading this then I know that you accepted my arrangements and are working on finishing what I had hoped to complete myself. I hope that you are happy in your room at the house and that you and Amalie have become friends. I know that she can be stubborn at times but I also know that she has a heart as big as yours.*
>
> *I would have never wanted you to stay with her if I thought that it would make either of you unhappy. You were the son I never had and I loved you very much. I loved my daughter also. However, I feared that she would always remain alone and someday suffer the same fate as her mother. I ask that you would watch over her for me always. Keep her safe and make her days as happy as possible. Do not be afraid to show her your heart and your trust. If you show her the man that I knew and respected, she will*

give you hers. Please do not tell Amalie that I have asked you to do me this favor. She is very independent; as I am sure you have already learned.

Thank you Erik and I hope that you liked the new mask I made for you. I thought it would show more of who you truly are.
Your Truest Friend,
Gaston

He was overwhelmed by Gaston's words. The tenderness in which he spoke of him touched his heart and made him miss his old friend. It was hard not to wonder what had happened to Amalie's mother after reading the letter. His mind raced with curiosity but he knew that it was best not to unveil something that needed to be masked. He too was apprehensive about letting something as horrific as his face be seen because the possibility of it changing the way she saw him. It was even possible that it could end or change their friendship. However, his past should've changed it already and it hadn't; at least he'd seen no evidence of it.

He folded the letter, placed it back into the envelope and put it in the satchel. He'd almost forgotten about the envelope with Amalie's name written on it. He picked it up and examined it. He wondered what her father had written to her but didn't dare let his curiosity lead him to do something he would regret. He folded it in half and put it in his pocket so that he wouldn't forget it.

Evening came and he joined her for supper. The atmosphere was very casual with no candles upon the table. They finished dining and retired once again to the drawing room. He took his usual place at the piano and she sat in the high backed chair ready to listen to the music that was to be created. He put his fingers on the keys ready to play and suddenly remembered the letter that Gaston had left for her. He rose from the piano.

"Amalie, if you will excuse me I need to go to my room for a moment."

"Don't be gone too long. I'm looking forward to hearing you play this evening," she said with a smile.

He left the room and returned with the letter. He walked over and handed it to her.

"Remember the envelopes that your father left? This was in the one that I was to open in six months."

She slowly took it from his hand.

"Has it been six months? I hardly noticed the months changing and you're telling me it has been six months since we met?" she said with playfulness in her voice. She examined the envelope and then placed it unopened in her lap.

"I'm ready to hear you play. You may start when you're ready."

"Aren't you going to read it?" he asked in disbelief.

"I don't know if I want to read it," she replied softly.

"Why? Are you afraid that your father's words will upset you?"

She smoothed the lap of her dress.

"I'm not sure if my father's words will comfort me or make me miss him more," she said with sadness in her voice.

He started to play an arrangement composed by Mozart. It was beautiful. He became immersed in his music, not noticing that she had opened the letter and began reading.

> *My Dearest Daughter,*
>
> *I hope this letter finds you well and that the situation I have put you in has not been a burden but a blessing. I was certain that when I asked you to help Erik that you had the strength and the resolve to see it through. You are a very intelligent, strong willed and beautiful woman; just like your mother. I know that Erik is different, not just in appearance but in the way he has conducted himself in the past. I hope that after meeting him you have been able to see the well-intentioned, loving, compassionate man that I saw all those years ago.*
>
> *I have faith that you will always do the right thing concerning Erik. I don't wish for you to ever be alone in this world and I hope his companionship has helped fill the void that our absence has created in your life. I pray that his companionship is as comforting to you as it was for me when I was injured and he took me in and nursed me back to health.*
>
> *I had hoped that you would marry and have many children before I died but I know that after all of the betrayal you have witnessed, it would be difficult for you to love and trust again. Don't be afraid to love, Amalie. If you only look for love with your eyes you will only see the outside of the heart but if you look for love with your heart you will see the inside of the soul and everything that makes the heart beat. You will know love from the inside and out and that is complete and total love without restrictions or boundaries. Your mother would have wanted you to find a way to forgive those that have hurt you so that you could be happy. She*

couldn't help what happened to her, but you can choose a future for yourself that brings you happiness. We can't always plan who we will love or when love will find us. However, when love comes you must hold on to it and never let it go. Choosing to love someone is the most rewarding decision you will ever make in your life. Remember that loving someone doesn't just change your life, it changes theirs too.

I love you Amalie. No matter the choices you make in your life, you will always be my proudest and best accomplishment.
Love,
Father

Tears began to stream down her face as she folded the letter up and put it back into the envelope. She was very confused at what her father had written. Why was her loving someone so important to him? She wasn't going to end up like her mother. She was stronger than that. She couldn't stop crying and she really didn't know why. Erik finally heard her sniffles and moans and stopped playing. He was concerned so he rose from the bench, walked over and knelt beside her.

"What's wrong? Did my music make you unhappy?" he asked in a low whisper. He handed her his handkerchief.

"No, it was my father's letter," she replied while wiping the tears from her cheeks.

"I'm sorry, Amalie. Was he cruel?" he asked.

"Of course not! He was sweet and concerned for me."

"Then why are you so unhappy?"

"I don't wish to discuss it with you. It's a private matter between me and my father." She wiped a few more tears from her eyes.

"It was about your mother, wasn't it?" He knew the moment he asked that he should've resisted posing this particular question.

"Why do you say that?" she snapped.

"Because there are very few things that make you unhappy and the subject of your mother seems to be one of them." He blasted back with very little concern for her feelings.

"You are a cruel man to speak to me in such a way. You have no compassion for what I've been through or for what my mother went through." She shot back at him with words thrown like spears; sharp and piercing.

He had forgotten about her feelings for the moment, letting his frustration overcome him. "How can I have compassion for events that I have no knowledge about? Enlighten me. Share your pain with me and I'll show you compassion if there is compassion to be given." He was on his feet now pacing the floor, waving his arms as if he were giving a soliloquy in a theatrical play.

She rose from her chair and confronted him, stopping him in mid-stride.

"You are the one that is cruel. How dare you mock me?" She glared deep into his eyes. "I can't believe that I was letting myself fall in love with you. You are so arrogant and unkind. How could I even think that I could love you?" She soon realized that she had made her thoughts public and Erik was visibly shocked by her admission. Her face began to turn red, not from anger but from embarrassment that she'd made known her most private thoughts. She started to walk away, even though her instincts were to run. He gently grabbed her by the arm and pulled her to him. He then put his right hand on her cheek and his left arm around her waist, pulling her closer to him. He looked into her eyes trying to decide if her words were truth or just passionate anger.

"You don't have to run away from me, Amalie. I'm not going to hurt you," he whispered in her ear.

"I didn't mean to say what I said Erik. You weren't supposed to know...." He stopped her words, pressing his finger against her soft lips.

"It's all right Amalie. You don't have to say anything." He pulled her even closer so his cheek could press against hers. "I'm sorry for my words. You're right; I'm an arrogant, unkind man, and you're a stubborn, self-righteous woman.....and I've fallen in love with you anyway."

She felt the tears from his eye caress her cheek as he pressed against her. She was confused by her feelings at this moment. Part of her was still very angry with him for pushing her to reveal what she wasn't ready to reveal. The other part of her wanted him to continue holding her in his arms, pressing the smooth side of his face against hers. His touch rendered her defenseless and she was frightened by this. She pulled away from him.

"What do you know about love Erik? I've seen how you treat the women you love. You trick them by using their dead father's love to seduce them. All the while you plan only to take them from those that truly love them only to satisfy your own fleshly urges!" She speared her words at him once again.

Her words wounded him but they had a lot of truth to them. She was right, he had used a dead father's love to entice and seduce a young woman. His motives had been selfish at that time but he promised himself he'd never return to those practices. No, if she loved him it was because he'd earned her love. He had not stooped to trickery or deception this time.

His instinct was to rage back at her but his heart was telling him that she'd been hurt enough. He walked up to her, looked deep into her eyes and said, "I ask that you forgive me for my lack of compassion toward your mother's situation but I will not apologize for loving you."

His hands reached for hers and he pressed his lips against them gently.

"What I once thought was love was not love at all. It was lust perceived to be love because of its strong intoxication over my urges to fulfill the needs of my flesh. I know now that I did not truly love Christine, I was as you said before, infatuated with her."

She pulled her hands away from his grasp and walked past him to the door. Her heart was beating faster than it had ever beaten. She felt that if she looked at him she'd dash into his arms. She couldn't look at him or he'd win, he would have her heart and she wasn't ready to give it yet.

"Why are you saying these things to me? I didn't ask you to love me. I didn't ask you to do anything for me. I wish I would've never brought you here." She slammed the door behind her as she walked out.

He raced after her but he was too late. She was already in her room. He could hear her sobbing through the door. He never intended to hurt her and that is exactly what he did. Knowing that she could love him gave him hope but how could he convince her that his love for her was not the kind of love she'd seen him so desperately try to coax from Christine.

He went to her door and knocked.

"Amalie, are you all right?" She did not answer. "Please open the door. You must let me talk to you."

She stood beside the door so he could hear her.

"I just need some time. Please leave me alone," she begged.

"I don't want us to end the day like this Amalie. Will you please open the door?"

She hesitated. She wanted to see him. She wanted to tell him that she was sorry too. What was keeping her from letting herself feel any kind of emotion that gave her pleasure? Maybe Erik was right. Maybe her father was right. She had to find a way to come to terms with the past so she could have a future, but how? She wanted to be able to trust Erik with this hurt and this pain but the last time she trusted someone it led to rejection, ridicule and isolation. No, she couldn't go through that again.

The door opened and she slowly appeared in the hall. Erik had begun to walk to his room, giving up all hope that she would open the door.

"Erik, please don't go."

He turned around to see her standing in her doorway.

"Come sit with me on the stairs?"

They met at the stairs and sat down. The silence between them seemed to last for an eternity. She was the first to break the silence.

"I don't know what it is you want me to say. I believe that my words about love may have been premature and I don't want to hurt you. I do love you, Erik. As much as a friend can love another friend that is how I love you but as far as being in love with you, I don't know that I will ever cross that threshold. Only time will tell." She paused and then put her hand on his. "Do you understand what I'm telling you?"

He pulled her hand to his lips and kissed it. He then gently rubbed her hand across his unmasked portion of his face; feeling her soft skin against his. He cupped her hand in his and placed it on his knee. He looked directly at her, ready to make his proclamation.

"Your feelings for me whether love or otherwise will not discourage me from loving you, Amalie. I won't force my love upon you but know that it is yours whenever you decide to receive it." He looked into her dark brown eyes searching for hope that she'd change her mind and return his affections. "I didn't intend to find love here, only freedom and safety. Sometimes it is best not to search for love but rather have it find you. It is true that I possess in me the power to dismiss my feelings and begin my life again as it once was before I met you. But I'd rather live my life loving you, even if it is only as a friend, than to live without you at all. I'll take your scraps of love like a dog under the dinner table waiting for a few morsels of food to satisfy his hunger. A little bit of love is better than no love at all. I have lived my entire life without it, until now." He smiled at her and kissed her hand again. "I shall wait for you as long as it takes."

She could hardly keep from blushing. She'd never had anyone speak to her with such passion and certainty about their feelings. She was smiling from the inside out but didn't dare show her emotions to him.

"Thank you. I'm sorry for my behavior in the drawing room earlier. I told you that I wasn't sure if reading my father's letter was such a good idea. It's not your fault that I can't control my emotions sometimes. Do you forgive me?"

"Always, Amalie, always," he replied as he squeezed her hand.

The Secret Door

*F*or the first two to three weeks after Erik's proclamation of love, things between the two of them were awkward. Neither knew what to say or how to act. It would've continued on this way if it weren't for unexpected conversations that Amalie had with Chester and Meg one morning.

It was a Monday, much like many Mondays before. Chester had dropped Meg off at the house with food and other household items. Meg began her cleaning duties in the study as she had always done. On this particular day Erik decided to return to the house to retrieve a drawing from Gaston's desk that he had been studying the night before when he couldn't sleep. Reading always helped him gather his thoughts and analyzing drawings could almost always cure his insomnia.

It happened that Meg was bent over collecting the dirt in her dust pan and Erik, who had forgotten that it was Monday, opened the secret door without any caution. The door collided with Meg's backside and tossed her, head first onto the floor, knocking her unconscious. He quickly shut the secret door and checked to see if she was breathing. She was. He tried to wake her but she wouldn't open her eyes. He ran through the house searching for Amalie. She was nowhere to be found. He looked outside and then he ran down to the stable. When he found her, he was out of breath and panic stricken. Amalie was talking with Chester.

"Amalie…..you… must come ….to…. the house…quickly. It's Meg."

Chester and Amalie rose to their feet. She didn't ask questions and neither did Chester which she thought was rather strange, since he had no idea who Erik was. However, she didn't have time to analyze his reasons for not asking questions, she had to get to the house to tend to Meg. They all ran as fast as they could. They reached the house, entered through the back door and followed Erik into the study where Meg was lying on the floor, but not unconscious.

Chester knelt down beside her and said, "Meg, dear, are you alright? What happened?"

She was now sitting up with Chester's help. Erik had slipped out of the room and into the kitchen to get a towel with some ice for her head.

"I was bending over to sweep the dust into my pan and then something hit me from behind and flung me into the floor head first."

"Was it a chair or a stick? Did someone attack you?" Chester asked in his best investigative voice.

"No, it wasn't either of those. It was that silly secret door that M. Girault built many years ago. That young man, what is his name again Chester?" They consulted with each other for a brief moment.

"Erik! Yes that's his name Erik." Meg exclaimed and then grabbed her head. "He came through that door without any consideration that I might be standing behind it. He must have forgotten that it was Monday."

Amalie couldn't believe what she was hearing. Erik had now returned with the ice and handed it to Chester.

"Thank you, Erik." Chester replied as he took it from his hands.

Amalie and Erik glanced at one another. Erik didn't seem worried about them seeing him and Amalie's mind was filled with questions.

"How do you know his name? How do you know about the secret door?" Amalie demanded.

Chester motioned for her to settle down.

"Erik, could you help me get my wife up off the floor?" Erik walked over and helped him lift her onto her feet and into one of the chairs.

"I'm very sorry Madame. I should have used more caution when I was opening the door. I completely forgot that today was Monday," Erik apologized.

"Meg, do you think you'll be all right?" Amalie asked with concern in her voice. She wanted to make sure that Meg would be fine and then she had every intention of getting to the bottom of all of this.

"Now who wants to tell me what is going on here? How is it that the two of you know so much about Erik *and* the secret door?"

Chester put his arm around her shoulders and gave her a squeeze.

"My dear Amalie, if you think about it for a moment you'll answer your own questions." She looked at Chester with a look that let him know that she wasn't in the mood for games. He quickly told her, "We know about Erik because your father told us about him."

She would have laughed if she wasn't so angry at that very moment. However, it did answer a lot of questions. It was now obvious that they must have known or they would've asked questions about what had ever happened to her father's friend that night that the mob went down into the cellars. And the day that Erik let Meg into the house, she never questioned it at all, which was truly not like Meg.

"How long have you been going out to the stable to talk to Chester?" she asked Erik.

"Why do you accuse me of such a thing?" He grinned.

"Because I thought I had seen you several times at the stable talking to Chester from the window of my studio. I told myself I was mistaken but now I *know* that it *was* you." She pointed her finger in his direction. She turned to Meg and demanded. "Why was I not told about your knowledge of him being here?"

"Because my dear, your father didn't want us to interfere, he only wanted us to watch over both of you." Meg slowly rose to her feet, walked over to her and gave her a hug.

"You've been like a daughter to us and ever since you were born we have taken great pride in watching you grow to be such a caring and kind woman. When your father told us about his plans for his friend and how you were to help him, we were a bit shocked at his request. But Chester, having known your father for all these many years, as I have, knew that he'd never do anything to put you in harm's way." Meg returned to the chair where she was sitting earlier and motioned to Amalie to sit in the chair next to her.

"Your father asked us to help and watch over you without letting you know because he knew, as we all do, that you're a very independent woman and rarely will take help even when offered. You're a woman that possesses great intelligence and capabilities; that is why your father asked you to be the one to help Erik. We are merely here to support you if you need us."

Erik walked over and stood next to Amalie's chair.

"I've known since the first month I was here. I'd gone down into the cave to start my work and found a curious note lying on the top of the lumber. It was a letter from your father which really baffled me since I knew he couldn't have left it there. The letter simply stated that if I were ever in need of a gentleman's help inside the cave that I was to go to Chester and ask. The letter explained that Chester and Meg were informed of my situation and that if anything ever happened to not be afraid to ask for their help. However, I was instructed not to let you know that they were privy to my existence. I can't tell you why, but I assume that your father had his reasons although they aren't clear to any of us." He laughed and they all laughed with him.

Amalie's anger had subsided and she was now smiling.

"I'm relieved that you both know about Erik. I thought I was going to go mad if I had to try to keep it from you one more month, especially since Christmas is so close to being here. You know how I like to have everyone together for Christmas." Her eyes sparkled at the mention of Christmas. It was her favorite holiday and she and her parents had always invited Chester, Meg and their son Frederic and his wife Anna and their daughter Isabel and her husband Peter along with their two children, Nicole, who was four years old and Bella, who was six years old. Yes, the house was always full of life.

Chester interrupted Amalie's thoughts of a grand party at Christmas.

"Amalie, the children aren't coming for Christmas this year."

"Do they know about Erik staying here?" she asked.

"No, they don't and that is why we think it is best that they didn't come," he said firmly.

She was disappointed but understood.

"Do you think they'd have a problem with his.....well.... you know?" She didn't want to speak so frankly in front of Erik in fear that it would hurt his feelings.

Erik leaned over the back of the chair and to Amalie's right so that he could see her face. "You can say it Amalie. It's not as if I haven't lived my whole life with my appearance being the subject of other people's insecurities and fears. It is quite all right to say it out loud. I know that your inquiry is legitimate in order to get the answers to your questions."

Chester replied, "I don't know what they'd think about his appearance but Meg and I think it is best not to bring any outside attention to him being here; at least not now. The Opera House incident is still fresh on everyone's minds and hopefully when a year or two has passed no will ever try to connect the two."

Amalie knew they were right, especially after M. Ferrot and M. Chantel had already found at least one thing to connect her to the Opera House. She, being the only one that knew that there was still a possibility that something could lead them to Erik being at the house, continued her questioning as if she didn't know at all.

"Do you really think that anyone would suspect that he was the one in the Opera House?" she questioned Chester.

"I don't know but it is best not to find out." Chester turned to Erik. "Don't you agree?"

"Yes, I agree. It is best not to tempt fate."

Amalie, still fixated on the possibility of a Christmas celebration, continued to ask about everyone's plans.

"Where will they be going this year? It has been almost six years since Frederic has come to the house for Christmas."

Meg answered, "They will be going to their relatives houses this year. Anna's mother lives in London so they'll be taking holiday there for at least a month until New Year's. Peter's family lives in Paris and they'll be staying there for Christmas until New Year's. Isabel has promised to come by after the beginning of the year with the children. I'll gladly bring her by to visit."

"Will you? I should make a fuss over them when they come. Please let me know when you expect them," Amalie said happily.

"Now, will the two of you be joining us for Christmas dinner?

"Christmas is three months away." Meg laughed. "When it comes to Christmas you are very much like a child. The thought of it makes you glow and puts that sparkle in your eye." Meg pushed herself out of the chair and picked up her broom from the floor. "I suppose you can count on us to be here. I wouldn't want to disappoint you. Now, I must get back to my work or we won't be home until dark." Meg began sweeping again and Erik bent down to help her put the dirt in the dust pan. It was the least he could do.

After making sure that Meg was feeling well enough to continue her work, he grabbed his drawing from the desk and headed back into the secret passageway down into the cave. Chester had made it to the back of the house where he was soon to exit to return to his work in the stable when Amalie stopped him.

"Chester, may I have a word with you?" she asked in a very serious tone.

"What is it that you'd like to have a word with me about, Amalie?"

"Has Erik ever inquired about Mother's accident?"

"Yes, he has and I told him that he would have to wait for you to tell him the details." Chester grabbed her by the shoulders and looked her in the eyes. "You shouldn't worry about what he will think concerning your mother's accident. If anyone would understand, I should think he would."

"What is your opinion of him Chester? Do you think that he is truly capable of changing? Do you think that he can be trusted?" she asked with skepticism in her voice.

"That is a question that only you can answer." He picked her chin up with his hand, looking again into her brown eyes. "What does your heart tell you?"

"That's the problem Chester, my heart truly wants to believe that it's possible that he has changed but the logical part of me says that it's impossible."

"Why do you think it's impossible? You must back up your reasoning with fact if you wish to make a good case against someone." His voice changed from friendly to fatherly.

"I really don't have any evidence to support my logic. However, I have no prior experience or knowledge of anyone ever changing who or what they were in such a case as this. My heart wants to believe that it is possible but ....."

He interrupted her, finishing her thought, "but you are scared of getting hurt." She looked at him with surprise. How did he know? Was it that obvious that she had feelings for Erik?

"Why do you say that Chester?" she asked.

"I've talked to Erik many times since he has come to stay here. He is quite an interesting character. He told me about the argument that the two of you had and he didn't just tell me about what happened to him; he told me what he did to you." He put his arm around her. "He didn't have to tell me Amalie. I wouldn't have ever known."

"Why did he then?" she asked with a pensive look on her face.

"You are a very bright woman; do I honestly have to tell you why?" He smiled at her and squeezed her arm. "The man is in love with you. It has been obvious to me since the week after he told me of your argument. How come you don't see it?"

"I didn't have to see it; he told me."

He gave her a puzzled look. "And how do you feel about him?"

She became very defensive and turned her back on him. "I really don't wish to discuss it with you."

"Ah, so you love him too." Before Chester could say another word she interrupted him.

"Maybe I do and maybe I don't, that is none of your affair."

"Ah, yes, you love him Amalie but you are too afraid to take a chance; too afraid of what the world would think about you falling in love with a man who doesn't follow the mores of society." He paused and then turned her to face him. "You are your father's daughter and I know that you'll make the right decision for you and for Erik. Just remember you are never alone in times of trial or joy when you let love find its way to you." He kissed her on the forehead and walked to the door.

"Chester. If I told you that I was in love with him would *you* think that my senses had left me?"

"Amalie, you can't always choose the package that love comes in, but it is up to you to decide whether to open it or not. If you choose to judge the gift by its package and throw it away without ever opening it, then I believe you may be throwing away one of the most precious gifts that God has bestowed upon you."

She sighed and crossed her arms.

"Would you please answer my question?" she asked in an irritated tone.

"No, Amalie, I wouldn't think that your senses had left you. I think he has changed and learned a lot since he has come to be with us. I also think that a lot of that has to do with you." Chester opened the door and as he walked out he said, "Everyone knows that a woman's love can change the heart of any man." He winked at her and then closed the door behind him.

Her uncertainty should have subsided but she felt more anxious now than ever. Chester's words kept replaying in her head over and over again. Was she throwing her chance for happiness away because she was afraid that the outside world would not approve? No, that wasn't it. She didn't care about Erik's disfigurement. She wasn't that shallow. It was deeper than that. After all, no one else knew other than she and Erik what had happened in the cellars after her father had died. She wouldn't ever divulge those horrible tales to anyone. That was the reason she couldn't let herself love him. She had told Erik she forgave him but did she really? Her thoughts were consuming her. She sat down and began to cry.

Meg came into the kitchen and found her in a terrible state of distress.

"Amalie, what is the matter dear?" Meg asked in her warm motherly voice.

"I'm such a hypocrite….a liar….a fraud," she sniffled as she tried to choke back the tears.

"Why do you say such things about yourself? I know none of these things to be true."

"But I'm all of those things. I go around saying things that I want to believe that I can believe about myself and then I fail to believe them when it really matters." She was clearly beside herself, rambling on, not making any sense.

"Slow down Amalie. I don't understand what you're talking about." Meg pulled up a stool next to the chair where Amalie was sitting. "Tell me from the beginning what it is that makes you a hypocrite, liar and a fraud."

"Well, I told Erik that his past didn't matter to me and that I forgave him but I'm not really sure that it doesn't and that I did. Then we were having a disagreement and he frustrated me so and I let it slip that I couldn't believe that I was actually falling in love with him, but then when he told me that he loved me too, I told him that I only loved him as my friend." She took a deep breath and began again. "Which I don't know is the truth either. Then I told him that my beliefs were as my father's but I don't even know if that is true. Erik has made me question everything that I thought I was certain about, mainly those things I thought about myself."

Meg rubbed her hand on her chin. She sat quietly gathering her thoughts. She wanted to make sure she said the right things to Amalie since her world seemed to be unraveling at this moment.

"I see. You do have a lot to think about." Meg patted Amalie on the knee and then stood up. She began walking around the kitchen. "Amalie, do you have things in your past that aren't so easy to share with other people?"

"Well, yes, but my past is nothing like Erik's," she stated firmly.

"Yes, but his life was nothing like yours either. He didn't have a mother and a father that loved him and cared for him his entire life. He also didn't have a typical home, encouragement from family and friends in his life like you did."

"But that is no excuse for what he's done." Amalie was very stern and self-righteous in her response.

"Do you hear him making excuses for his behavior? He has only had remorse, never an excuse. I believe that he *is* truly sorry for all that he's done and I do mean everything." She winked at Amalie as if she was trying to let her know that she knew more. "You're right. The absence of loving and caring people in your life is no excuse to do horrible things. However, the absence of love can influence people to do horrible things." Meg continued to pace around the kitchen, occasionally rubbing her chin with her hand. "Of course many people do horrible things in the name of love which proves that love itself cannot cause someone to do good or bad things. However, it is the examples of love and how and when love is given that may cause a person to do harm and not good." Meg paused to gather her thoughts, choosing her words carefully in order to help Amalie understand. "Sometimes our environment can create the people that we become. For example, if a child grows up believing that their only worth is in what they do and not who they are, that child will do whatever it takes whether it is good or bad to earn the attention or the approval of the person they hold in the highest regard. If the person they seek love from relishes in the evil deeds that the child does then the child will continue to do those things in order to gain their approval. In a sense isn't that what Erik did? He just wanted or needed to be accepted or loved so he did whatever he had to do to gain that acceptance."

Amalie sat listening; trying to dissect the reasoning of her sweet friend as she continued her observation and analysis of Erik's behavior.

"Of course, there are always consequences that come with the actions of someone who tries to gain approval from others. Most of the time the approval is only short lived and then the person is forced to commit another act in order to keep the approval. It is a vicious cycle that keeps its victim from ever finding real happiness or true companionship. Their relationships are based on what they can do or give someone rather than who they are. Do you understand what I am saying to you Amalie?"

She nodded in agreement. "Please continue Meg, I find your analysis of the situation most intriguing. It sounds like something Father would have concluded."

Meg stopped walking and sat back down on the stool that was next to her. She took Amalie's chin in her hands and said very softly, "It is exactly what your father concluded."

"What are you saying?" she asked.

"When your father approached Chester and I about helping or watching over you and Erik, I was not so agreeable at first. I had my reservations about Erik, the arrangement, your involvement; the whole thing. What I just told you was what your father told us. It made me realize that this could have happened to any one of us. I'm not saying that what Erik has done in his past was justifiable, it wasn't, but it was understandable considering his circumstances." Meg took Amalie's hands and held them inside hers. "Sometimes we have to take a leap of faith. Your father was willing to do that and I believe he made the right choice."

"But Meg," Amalie interrupted, "I know about things he has done *after* Father died." She realized that in her search for an answer she exposed Erik's secret or did she?

"We know about all of that too."

Her heart felt like it had dropped into her stomach. She was without a response for a few minutes and then she spoke.

"How do you know about his latest indiscretions?"

Meg looked her in the eyes and said, "He told us."

"Why would he do that? Why would he risk making himself look like a monster?"

"He is finally free to trust and to be accepted for who he is and not what he does. He has learned to trust us because we showed him that we could trust him. That trust has given him the freedom to not be afraid to admit his mistakes or his wrongdoings. He feels safe here, just as you did with your parents. You never kept things from them. Even the most despicable things you may have done didn't keep your parents from loving you and if it would've then you wouldn't be the woman you are today."

"I still don't understand why he told you."

"When he came to us he said something that your father had told him many years ago. He told us that trust was to be earned, not given and a lie separates friends but a truth bonds them forever. He didn't want anything to separate us as friends and that is why he told us. I think it was a courageous gesture on his part; one that wasn't easy for him to make." Meg got up from her stool and stretched.

"After he told you about everything, didn't you think you should call the authorities?

"Why? You didn't. Besides he has been a prisoner most of his life; a prisoner that will never escape the bondage of his own appearance and the prejudices against him. Sometimes justice is blind and sometimes it is hard to separate the sin from the sinner. Evil men prosper as do good men and good men are labeled evil because of a few mistakes they have made. I think he deserves a chance to prove that he is not as evil as his sin." She looked at Amalie and smiled. "No Amalie, Erik is a fine man. Not perfect but none of us are. We all have flaws, some worse than others but they're still ours and we have to live with them. Remember, forgiveness is for everyone not only who we think deserves it." Meg began to gather up her cleaning supplies. She had the upstairs to clean before she left for the day. "If you continue to keep looking backward you'll not see what is in front of you."

Amalie stood up, walked over to Meg and gave her a hug.

"Thank you, Meg. I'm not sure I know what I'm going to do but what you said makes a lot of sense. I guess I should stop dwelling on the past and start living in the present. If I don't, I may not ever have a future."

"You're welcome dear. If you ever need me I'll always be here for you." Meg left the room and continued to go about her duties.

Amalie was feeling better now. Knowing that Chester and Meg were there for her to talk to made it easier for her to process what she was feeling. She decided that she'd give herself time. Erik said that he would wait as long as it took. She hoped that he meant it.

Pain and Suffering

*E*rik continued to work every day on the rooms in the cave. His project was near completion but he still wasn't quite sure what Gaston's vision was for the cave. To Erik, it looked like three rooms; two smaller rooms that were side by side and one large room that resembled the drawing room in the house. He had completed all of the walls and was now ready to put the paneling and trim work into the rooms. As he looked over the drawings he noticed that the only lighting that Gaston had provided would come from kerosene lamps and candles. The smallest of the three rooms was designed to be a washroom with a small table, a wash basin and pitcher accompanied by a chair which was placed by two barrels. He assumed these would hold water for the basin; one for the clean water and one for the water that was to be discarded. The other small room was to have a bed, nightstand, chair and dresser in it. It also had a closet built into its walls. Gaston had not left a drawing of the contents of the largest room and he had been unable to find it within the papers that his friend had left him. However, the room had what resembled a rectangular platform centered in the middle of it. He assumed that this was a stage but for what purpose he didn't have the slightest idea. Gaston had always found a way to put the most unexpected elements in his designs and most of the time they were functional but also unique.

It was the month of December and the relationship between he and Amalie was growing. Even though they rarely saw each other during the day, they would always retire to the drawing room in the evenings. She looked forward to the time that they would spend together each night. Although they didn't talk much just being in the same room with him made her happy. He would play the piano and she'd listen while she sat in her chair crocheting scarves that she was making for Christmas presents.

It was late one evening and he had finished playing a beautiful lullaby; she was crocheting. When the room became silent she looked up at him and asked, "Why did you stop?"

"Generally, when you come to the end of the music, you stop," he answered with a grin on his face.

"Oh, I guess I was so wrapped up in my work, I didn't notice."

"You've been preoccupied a lot lately," he said as he rose from the piano bench and walked over to the fireplace to place another log on the fire.

"Yes, I suppose I have. With Christmas only two weeks away I have so much to do to prepare for our guests. I'm sorry if I have neglected our friendship. I'll try not to be so preoccupied when we are together," she replied apologetically.

"Why don't you let me help you? I've never really celebrated Christmas and I'd like to see how you prepare for such a celebration." The thought of Christmas used to be a reminder of loneliness and disappointment but this year he wouldn't be alone. He was almost certain that it would not carry any disappointment either.

"Would you Erik?" She jumped out of her chair and hugged him. "That would make it easier and more enjoyable to have you helping."

He put his arms around her and returned the hug. He didn't want to let her go. Surprisingly she wasn't letting go either. He felt her warm tears on his chest as he continued to hold her tightly in his arms. He stroked her hair and asked, "Why are you crying?"

"It's happiness, Erik. I'm so glad that Christmas will be a celebration to look forward to instead of dreading. I know that Christmas is a holy day that we celebrate to mark the birth of our Lord and Savior but it has always been more than that to me. Ever since I was a little girl Christmas has been about celebrating family and friendships." She lifted her head off of his chest and glanced up at him. "This year I have a very special friendship to celebrate."

He offered her his handkerchief and she wiped her eyes. She still didn't want to let go of him. She knew it was wrong to keep pretending that she felt nothing for him but she could never find the right moment to tell him how she really felt. He continued holding her in his arms as he gently ran his hand up and down her arm.

"Why don't you ever go out to see your friends in the village? I imagine a woman such as you would have a lot of friends," he inquired not knowing the emotion that his question would evoke from her. "You must grow tired of only having me to talk to every day."

She removed herself from his arms and continued to wipe the tears from her eyes. She began to pace around the room debating on how she'd respond to his question. Her mind told her that it was risky to divulge her deepest secret but her heart was ready to relieve itself of the burden. She walked over to him, took his hand and led him to the sofa. They sat down and she continued to hold onto his hand as if her life depended on it.

"Erik, you're right. I did have a lot of friends. I was even engaged to be married." He was about to make a comment and she put her finger on his lips. "Please, let me finish." He took her hand from his lips and kissed it to reassure her that he would do as she asked.

"After Mother had her accident our lives changed. I'll tell you the events of her misfortune so that you'll have a better understanding of what happened to her." She wiped a few more tears from her eyes and took a deep breath.

"It was late in the afternoon on a summer day in July. Mother was coming back from the village after visiting her friend Millie. Chester was driving the coach and they met another coach on the road. When the coaches passed each other one of the horses from the other coach became spooked; charging their coach. Chester tried to get them out of the way but in his attempt the coach fell on its side. The horses continued to run while they drug Chester behind them along with the toppled coach. My mother's body was thrown to the side that was on the ground and the window broke; exposing the right side of her face to the ground beneath her. When the horses finally stopped, Chester was badly injured. His fingers were mangled from the reins being pulled so violently by the horses while he tried to regain control, his right leg was broken and his right shoulder was dislocated. The doctor had to amputate three of his fingers."

She had to stop. She was reliving the whole thing in her mind as she told the story. The emotions were as raw and painful as they were that day. He could see that she was suffering and wanted to do something, anything to take the pain away but he knew that there weren't any words that could keep the pain from coming. He moved a little closer to her and squeezed her hand once again. She looked at him and could see in his eyes that he understood.

"Mother was not so lucky. Her face was drug across the dirt road leaving it bloody and almost unrecognizable. She had a broken arm, her right rib cage was bruised but the worst part of her injury was her mind. After she was cleaned up by the doctor she was terrified to see what had happened to her face. When she finally got the courage to look in a mirror, it was as if the mirror took her soul into it; leaving her hollow and empty. She was terribly scarred and in some places on her face the skin had been peeled away leaving the muscles exposed. She wore bandages for over six months and even after she healed she still didn't look the same." Amalie began to cry again. "I think she would've been able to recover from it all except that her friends couldn't bear to look at her. They slowly distanced themselves and eventually stopped coming to see her. Mother was still the same person they had known for years, she only looked different but I guess they couldn't see past her appearance."

He put his arm around her and drew her to him. He kissed her on the forehead and whispered, "I'm sorry Amalie. I wish I would've been here to help you and your mother."

She buried her head in his chest beneath his chin. "I don't think that anyone could've helped her. She was a proud woman and wouldn't even let my father help her cope with her condition." He continued to run his hand up and down her arm, comforting her.

"I assume your fiancée was not very understanding about your mother?" he asked.

"He was for a while but then two months before we were to be married, my mother's mental state began to deteriorate. She had confined herself to the drawing room; only coming out to go to the stable to visit the horses. She rarely took meals with us at the dining table. In fact, she almost always ate by herself. She had withdrawn so far into herself that even my presence was no comfort to her."

She sat nestled in Erik's arms. She knew that the next part of the story of her mother's life was going to be the hardest to tell. She wanted to forget it, put it back inside the box in which she kept it, deep inside her mind; never to recall it again. Maybe this time she could let the words free her of the bad memory. Releasing it into the air would let it float away, never to return.

"Are you all right?" he whispered to her. She squeezed his arm and replied, "I will be when I have told you everything." She closed her eyes, took a deep breath once again to try to contain her tears and began again.

"One day Father and I were in the kitchen preparing supper for Mother. When we went to take supper to her, she was nowhere to be found. We concluded that Mother had left the house. Father ran to the stable to see if she had gone there. She wasn't but neither was one of our horses. We scanned the wooded area behind the house in hopes that any trace of her was to be found. When Father had just about given up, the horse that was missing came out of the wooded area without Mother. He saddled up Shadow and raced into the woods. When he came back he had Mother across his lap, holding her lifeless body in his arms as he rode up to the house." She began to cry even more now. The vision of her mother was so vivid in her mind.

"My mother had hung herself on one of the trees. Father had found her but it was too late. He cut her down and brought her back to the house. After my fiancée found out about how she died he called the wedding off. He feared that the actions of my mother would cast a dark light on our future. What he feared is that I'd do the same someday and it would embarrass him," she said angrily. "I was heartbroken but later I realized that it was better that I didn't marry him. He was too driven by his ambitions and let societal rules dictate what he did *and* how he felt about me and my family. It wasn't only my mother's friends that turned their backs on us, it was mine, my father's and even Chester and Meg had become outcast among those that would socialize with them. All we had left was each other."

He kissed her forehead again and pulled her even closer. Her body relaxed in his arms as she closed her eyes. She could hear his heart beating and the rhythm was soothing. She would have been content to stay there for the rest of the night.

"I understand why you didn't want to tell me about your mother. It brings back too much pain, too much betrayal. We shall never have need to speak of it again Amalie."

He adjusted his position on the sofa, still holding her in his arms. He began to softly sing to her. He understood why it was so important for him not to wear his mask in front of her. She didn't want to be considered to be like those who had shunned her mother because of her appearance. She was a person of actions and not words. She wanted to prove to him that she cared about him no matter what he looked like. Yes, he understood her very well now.

When he finished singing he realized that she had fallen asleep in his arms. He hated to wake her so he sat for another hour watching her sleep while he sang softly to her. After realizing that the hour was late, he picked her up and carried her upstairs to her room. He removed only her shoes and covered her up. Before he left the room he kissed her on the forehead one more time and whispered, "I love you."

A Small Gesture

She woke the next morning rested. She saw that she was in her dress from the night before and smiled at the thought of him carrying her to her room. He had been a complete gentleman. She knew that she could trust him now; even with her heart. She went to her armoire and pulled out a beautiful dress made of a brocade navy blue fabric. She changed into it and then sat down in front of her dressing table to brush her hair. She finished brushing her hair and put a little bit of rouge on her cheeks. She was on her way out and noticed a package sitting beside her bed on the bedside table. The package was small and neatly wrapped in paper. It had a red ribbon tied around it and on the top it was tied into a bow. A note was placed beside it with her name written on it.

She picked it up and read:

> *My dearest Amalie,*
> *I hope you will cherish the gift I have left you. Join me in the drawing room for breakfast. I love you.*
> *Erik*

She folded the note and placed it on the table next to the gift. She sat on the edge of her bed and pulled the ribbon until it came loose. She removed the paper and pulled out what was inside; his mask. Tears filled her eyes; knowing how hard it must have been for him to make the decision to give her such a personal gift. She held the mask tightly in her hand and wiped the tears from her eyes. She put the mask back on the bedside table. She checked her face in the mirror to make sure she looked presentable and then walked down the stairs.

He was seated at the piano. He was playing one of his original pieces. Breakfast was presented beautifully on the oval coffee table. There was a bowl of fruit, some muffins that were left over from the day before and a pitcher of freshly squeezed orange juice. He had set out two plates, silverware, linens and crystal glasses and centered on the table was a single candlestick. She entered the room without him noticing her. She walked up behind him; noticing the portion of his disfigured face that was exposed. He was immersed in his music, unaware of her presence. She leaned over and gently placed a kiss on his birthmark. His hands froze on top of the piano keys. He raised his hand up and caressed her cheek. She sat down beside him on the bench with her back to the piano. He turned so that she could see his entire face. She didn't turn away from his disfigured face, instead she began to weep. She put her hand on the side of his face that he had kept secret from her. She looked into his blue eyes. He put his hand on top of hers and tears welled up in his eyes.

"I love you," she whispered. "I'm sorry that I made you wait so long to hear it."

"I would've waited for the rest of my life," he whispered back.

He removed her hand from his face and kissed it. Then she looked into his eyes, slowly leaned forward and pressed her lips gently against his. He put his arms around her, pulling her close to him. Her body pressed against his chest so tightly that she could feel his heart beating. She slowly pulled away from his kiss and rested her face against his. She whispered almost out of breath, "I don't ever want you to leave me. Promise me that you'll never leave me. I don't think I could live without you."

He didn't know what to say. He had longed for this moment his entire life and now that it was here, he could hardly speak. His emotions overwhelmed him. She'd never looked so beautiful and he couldn't believe that she was actually touching his disfigured face with her perfectly formed fingers; kissing his face with her silky lips. She was in love with him, all of him without hesitation or any inhibitions. If she had asked him to tell her how he felt, he would not have been able to do it. The feelings he had couldn't be explained with words. No one, not even Christine, had made him feel like this. He finally knew what being loved freely and completely felt like. More importantly, he knew what it meant to truly love someone.

He kissed her on the cheek then she laid her head on his chest. He spoke to her softly, "Amalie, I won't leave you until God removes me from your side."

They sat quietly on the piano bench, wrapped in each other's arms. He'd never been so happy and yet he was anxious. How would they be able to continue living in the house together knowing how they felt about each other? He didn't want to dishonor her by taking advantage of their situation. He loved her and he wanted to be able to court her as any other man would. Their living arrangements had never posed any problems before but now that he knew that she would return his affections he feared he would be tempted to exploit them. He would have to remain strong in his convictions. After all he had made a promise to Chester and he had every intention of keeping it.

He broke the silence with a question. "May I have permission to court you?" She was surprised by his question. She pulled her head away from his chest and looked at him with a smile on her face. "Erik, there is no need to be so formal, is there?"

"I promised Chester that I would always protect your honor and I believe your father would've wanted it that way too. A man is only as good as his word and I plan to keep mine," he replied confidently.

"Oh, I see. It's a matter of *your* reputation and the protection of *my* honor that you need to be so formal." She took his hands in hers, pressed her lips on his for a brief kiss and replied, "Yes, Monsieur Geraurd, you may have my permission to court me." She laughed as she stood up, pulling him with her and guiding him to the coffee table where breakfast was laid out. "I'm not sure how you'll court me when we don't leave the confines of this house or property but I'm sure since you've suggested it that you'll find a way to be creative."

"Are you poking fun at me?" he asked.

"No. I like that you want to court me. I just assumed that the past three months you had been courting me already."

"Well, then you're in for a delightful time Amalie." He kissed her hand and then gazed into her eyes. "If I won your heart by your assumption of being courted, I shall have the rest of you to cherish forever." He laughed and she laughed with him. "I think it's time we ate our breakfast," he replied. They both sat down on the sofa. She looked at him, smiled and said, "Thank you, Erik." He looked puzzled. "For what, Amalie?" She put her hand on his birthmark. "For the mask. I think you already know how much it means to me." He smiled at her, his eyes sparkling in the morning sunlight. "You're welcome."

After breakfast they returned to their separate chores but promised to meet around one o'clock for dinner. He went back to the cave and she went about making her lists of things she needed for Christmas dinner and for decorating the house. The tree would be the most important item. They would go the week of Christmas to find the perfect tree. Her lists were complete and after looking them over she realized that she had forgotten one important thing; Erik's present. She had planned on giving him one of the scarves she had made, but now that they were courting she felt that it wasn't quite good enough. She would still give it to him but she now had to decide what would be a more fitting gift for him. Walking always helped her think. She gathered her cloak and took a walk out to the stable.

He found it hard to work after what had happened that morning. He couldn't stop thinking about her. The softness of her lips against his was hard to forget and the touch of her hand on his face was engraved on his skin. He struggled to focus on the work before him. Then in his quest for something to distract him from his distraction, he fumbled through the drawings once again to try to find the final draft of Gaston's room. His search produced nothing. He did however, come across the envelope that read "Open in One Year". He had almost forgotten about it. He couldn't believe that it had almost been a year since he had arrived at the Girault home. He looked at it, contemplating whether to open it or not since there was still four weeks until the anniversary of his arrival. He took out his knife to begin opening the letter but then thought better of it. He tucked it back into the satchel. It was only four weeks. He could wait.

He went back to the papers, still hoping he could find a clue as to what was to go into the largest of the three rooms. Gaston may have never completed it or maybe the answer was in the envelope. The envelope did look thicker than the previous one. He knew that was where it had to be but he would just have to wait to confirm his suspicions. He wouldn't worry about it any longer. After all, he had plenty of things to continue working on and if he finished before the one year anniversary he could spend more time with Amalie at the house.

Amalie, after taking a walk to the stable, had returned to the house. She went to her studio and went straight to work on her present for him. Although she still hadn't finished the painting she had begun that was to hang in the large room of the cave, she decided to start her new project which she felt was more important. Besides, he hadn't finished the room yet and there would be plenty of time to finish it after Christmas.

She continued to work on her gift for him until she heard a knock on the door. She had locked the door just in case he tried to enter. She didn't want to risk her surprise being spoiled.

"Amalie, it's one o'clock. I thought we were going to have dinner together," he said while trying to open the door. "Why is the door locked? Are you keeping secrets from me?" he said playfully.

She finished putting her paints away, walked over to the door, unlocked it and slid out of the door, locking it behind her. She took his arm and began to walk to the staircase. "No, I'm not keeping secrets from you. I'm working on a special Christmas present and I don't want you to spoil the surprise."

"Well, in that case I'll forgive you."

"I don't know what we'll be eating for dinner. I completely lost track of the time and didn't prepare anything. I'm sorry."

"It's fine. When I saw that you weren't in the kitchen I took the liberty of preparing something. It's not much but I think it will do. I assumed that you were involved in something important or you wouldn't have forgotten." He squeezed her hand and led her into the dining room.

They ate dinner and talked about what needed to be done to prepare for Christmas. He was very excited about helping her find the perfect tree. He'd never celebrated Christmas in the traditional ways that everyone else had. Not that he didn't want to he just never had any reason to since most of his Christmas' were spent alone. His need for religious beliefs and rituals were not relevant since the only thing his mother ever said to him about God was that he was her punishment for her sins. No child should have to live with those words ringing in their ears. The times when he thought he might believe that God could love him, it was his sordid past that had always made him think that God wouldn't want anything to do with him, so he in turn had nothing to do with God. It was Gaston who had tried to change all of that. He had told him that God loved him and would forgive him for his transgressions. He also told him that no matter what his mother had said, he was never to believe he was meant to be a punishment for his mother's sins. Children, no matter how they looked, were always to be considered one of God's most precious gifts. He assured Erik that special gifts came in the most unlikely packages and that if we were afraid to open them, then we would never know what was inside. Gaston's perspective was interesting and always made him feel better about why he'd even been born. Yes, this Christmas things were going to be different; true love and God were no longer out of reach for him.

Thinking about all of this brought to Erik's mind the piece of paper that Gaston carried with him at all times that had his favorite verses from the Bible written on it. He had shared them with him a few times and had eventually sent him a hand written copy for his own use. He had put them in his pocket every day until the letters from Gaston had stopped coming. He regretted tearing them up now and wished he hadn't been so foolish.

"Do you remember the piece of paper your father carried in his pocket? You know the one with the Bible verses on it?" he asked her without noticing that it was completely off topic from what they were discussing.

"Yes, I do. What made you think of that?" she asked with a puzzled look on her face.

"Talking about Christmas made me think of your father and how much he loved to talk about his faith in God. He was quite knowledgeable about such things. I remembered the piece of paper he showed me when he was with me those few weeks. Did he leave it with you, Amalie?"

"No." She gave him a serious but solemn look. "He wanted it buried with him, in his pocket where he always kept it." She could see the disappointment in his face. She quickly rose to her feet and grabbed his hand.

"Come with me." She pulled him to his feet and led him to her room.

"What are we doing in here?" He had no idea why she would bring him to her room and it made him uncomfortable.

She went over to her Bible and opened it up. She pulled out a piece of paper and handed it to him. "Here, you can have my copy. I've memorized them, so if you want it, you may have it."

He took it from her hand and read them silently. As he read he could hear Gaston's voice reading it to him. He folded it up and placed it in his pocket. He took her in his arms and kissed her softly on the lips. "Thank you Amalie."

"You're welcome. I'm not sure why those mean so much to you but I'm glad that I was able to find them. Father always said that they helped him remember that he was only a man and always needed to trust God to solve his problems." She looked up at him, still in the hold of his embrace. "Is that why it's so important for you to have them?"

He looked into her eyes and said, "Yes, Amalie, that and many other reasons that are hard for me to explain."

She kissed him on the cheek and whispered, "Some things need no explanation."

They continued to hold each other for a few minutes and then out of the corner of his eye he noticed the mask sitting on the bedside table. "Amalie, I know that I gave you my mask as a gift…." and before he could finish she interrupted him, "but you would like it back."

"How do you do that?" he asked.

"I actually thought about it while I was painting this morning. I was going to put it back in your room but I got distracted."

He walked over to the table and picked it up. "You're an amazing woman, Amalie Girault. It's no wonder that I love you." He kissed her again on the cheek and then gave her one more embrace. He took her by the hand and they walked out of her room. He left her in the hallway and went back to his room to put away his mask. He knew he wouldn't need it this afternoon since Chester and Meg were going into the village. He returned and they walked down the stairs together.

"Why did the mask you wore at the Opera House cover your entire face?"

"Does it matter?" Erik asked.

"Not necessarily, I was just curious. Only half of your face has the birthmark, so why cover your entire face, especially when the other half is so handsome?" They came to the bottom of the stairs and she turned to face him. "Why would you want to cover it up?"

"My mother had given me a mask that covered my entire face when I was a child. I suppose I assumed that since she covered my entire face that the whole of my face wasn't presentable. I never thought that anyone would find the other half of my face pleasing to look at, so I continued to hide all of it," he replied honestly. "It also made it much easier to detach myself from others. If they didn't know my face then they couldn't identify me when I went outside the lake house in a disguise." He looked at her as he stated his case sincerely. "To tell you the truth, the mask helped create an image that my own face couldn't. I could manipulate my mask to create the Opera Ghost and all his death head features just by shading in around the nose or adding a thin piece of colored cloth over the eyes." She looked at him with disapproval at what he had admitted. He then added, "I know it was wrong but at the time it served me and I had no intentions of ever hurting anyone."

"Then why did you?" she asked very innocently.

"I thought I had no other choice. I know that may sound like an excuse but at the time I truly believed that those men would've taken my life had I not taken theirs first. You've seen firsthand how people's fears lead them to do things they wouldn't normally do. The only difference between your mother and I was that she was able to have been known for who she was before her appearance was altered and even in that circumstance people feared what they couldn't fix or explain."

"I know that you're right but I just wished that for everyone involved that there would have been another way." She was very solemn in her response and lowered her head.

"I do too." He picked up her chin and looked into her eyes. "However, I can't change the past; I can only try to do better now and in the future. The life I have with you here doesn't create situations in which I need to defend myself. I'm very thankful for that."

"I am too, and I'm happy that my father made you the new mask even though you don't have to wear it around me anymore." She took his hand and held it tightly. "Why do you think he made it for you?"

"Well, it was your father who told me how handsome my face was and he insisted that I shouldn't hide it. I thought he was only being polite, but now that you've told me the same thing, I guess it must be true." He laughed at his words.

"It's true Erik." She put her hand on his cheek. "You're quite handsome and I should be lucky to gaze upon your face, all of it, for the rest of my life."

He took her hand in his and began walking to the sofa in the great room. "You flatter me with your words but it is I who should be so lucky to look upon *your* beauty for the rest of *my* life. I don't know what I did to deserve this life that I have now but I promise you that I'll do good things with it."

She smiled at his words and knew that he was being sincere with what he had promised her. Apparently God's purpose for his life was becoming more evident to him. Although she had never heard him refer to God as someone he believed in, his words led her to assume that he had possibly began to believe that God could use him for something other than what his past had tried to condemn him to; a life of hate, bitterness and vengeance. Her father would've been pleased to know that his words hadn't fallen onto deaf ears. It was obvious to her that her father had hoped that they hadn't but had not lived long enough to see proof of it. It appeared that her father's promise to him didn't only change his life, it had changed hers too.

"I have no doubts about that and I'm hoping that the next good thing you'll do is get some firewood for the fire. It has gotten quite chilly in here."

"I'll be happy to get some firewood." He left the room, took his cloak out of the closet and exited the back of the house to get some firewood. As he left he noticed their dishes from dinner sitting on the table. They had become so preoccupied with each other that they had forgotten to clear the dishes. He had to admit that he was very uncertain of what his life would be like living in the house with Amalie. He thought he might miss the sometimes dangerous and always unpredictable life that he had led but to his surprise he found life with her was as exciting and sometimes even more unpredictable. After all when dealing with a woman of her aptitude life was bound to be a little unpredictable. Even getting firewood was not as mundane as he thought it might be. Life above ground did take some adjusting to but he was finding out that it suited him.

He returned with the firewood and began placing it into the fireplace. After finishing he walked toward the door that led into the foyer. She didn't ask him where he was going, instead she followed him. He had gone into the dining room to clear the table. She watched for a few seconds and then entered the room.

"Erik, let me do that. You've done enough for me this afternoon." He looked up at her as he finished stacking the dishes. "I don't mind Amalie. It was my question about your father's Bible verses that took us away from the table."

"If you insist....but I'll wash and dry them." She walked into the kitchen and put on her apron. "You may return to your work in the cave now if you wish."

"Are you trying to get rid of me?" he asked jokingly.

"No, but most of the afternoon is gone now. If you want to get some of your work done before dark I assume that you should go now," she said while washing a plate.

"Well, actually I've decided to take the afternoon off to help you with your Christmas preparations, if that is fine with you?" He grabbed a towel and started drying the plate she had washed.

"If that is what you want to do then I'll be glad to have your assistance. I need to get the Christmas tree decorations out of the closet in the sitting room. Do you think you can handle that for me?" she asked while she took the towel and the plate out of his hand.

"Yes, I'm sure I can." He kissed her on the cheek and proceeded to the sitting room.

He opened the closet door and did a quick assessment of the items that it held. There were a few small coats that looked to be for a child, possibly Amalie's from when she was younger. Then there were croquet mallets and the other accessories that went with them, two small boxes marked Christmas and a third larger box also marked with the word Christmas. As he began removing the two smaller boxes from the top of the larger one, he bumped the shelf above his head sending a shawl that had been folded up onto his head along with another object that was much heavier. It made a crashing sound as it hit the floor. He put the two boxes back on top of the larger then looked to see what had quickly come crashing down. It was a black leather physician's bag and most of its contents had spilled out onto the floor. He quickly began to pick up all of the items and put them back into the bag. As he did, he noticed a fine piece of parchment paper rolled up and tied with a ribbon. It looked as if it had never been disturbed. Without hesitation he slid the ribbon off of it and opened it up. He couldn't believe what he was reading. It was a diploma from the University of Paris and it had Amalie Louise Girault, M.D. listed as the recipient. She was a doctor? Why didn't she tell him?

She had heard the crash. As he was rolling the diploma up and sliding the ribbon onto it, she entered the room. She had forgotten that her medical bag was in the closet; easily forgotten since she hadn't had use for it in years. She'd never formally practiced medicine anywhere but did tend to the people in the village if they asked her to do so. She looked at him with disappointment but was not angry.

"Amalie, I'm sorry. I didn't mean to pry…..it fell on my head….and well…." He stumbled on his words hoping he could deflect her obvious disappointment.

She took it out of his hands, opened it up and looked at it. "Well, go ahead. Ask me why I didn't tell you that I'm a doctor."

He just looked at her. He'd never heard her speak with such a tone as this. He did as she asked. "Why didn't you tell me that you were a doctor? Why keep it from me? I don't think it's something worth keeping secret but it explains why you did such a great job of bandaging my head wound." He wanted to continue on with his accolades but she put her hand up, which meant that he needed to say no more.

"I suppose you think it's wonderful that I'm a doctor. I used to think that too until my mother's accident and my father's illness. What good does it do to be a doctor and not be able to help the one's you care about the most? Tell me, Erik, what good does it do?" Her words were full of anger. "I did what I could for both of them but I couldn't keep them from dying." Her eyes began to fill with tears.

He stood up, walked over to her and embraced her. "A doctor can do many things that are good but a doctor is not God. Only God can keep people from dying. Sometimes he may use a doctor to save someone but ultimately life and death are to be left in His hands." He picked her chin up and kissed her on the cheek. "You saved me, didn't you and not only from bleeding to death on the drawing room floor."

She looked up at him and smiled. "Are you making fun of *me* now?"

"I'm merely pointing out that your life saving capability goes beyond your medical training." He walked back to the closet, picked up her medical bag and handed it to her. "I think you may want to keep this where you can use it. A good doctor is very hard to find these days."

He laughed. She took the bag from his hand and returned it to the shelf in the closet.

"I promise if we ever need it, I won't hesitate to retrieve it. As for my diploma, maybe you can find a nice box in which to put it." She handed him her diploma. He took it and said, "I will find a safe place for this. Maybe someday you'll want to display it as your father has done all of his diplomas." He turned and walked out of the room. She didn't know where he was going but she thought it best to let him go. She went to the closet and began removing the small boxes from the closet.

Mistletoe

Christmas Day was almost over and Amalie and Erik had entertained their first guests in the house since he had come to live there. Meg and Chester were a delight to be around and they enjoyed their company all afternoon and early evening. After dining on a wonderful feast that Amalie had prepared they retired to the drawing room where they listened to Erik play the piano. Erik managed to persuade Amalie to sing a few songs for their guests. Never having heard her sing, they were quite surprised at her vocal talent. She, as usual, was modest and gave all the credit to God first and her excellent teacher second.

Chester and Meg had opened their gifts from Amalie and were both very pleased with their scarves. The handmade accessory was just what each of them would need as the days grew colder during the winter months. She also gave Erik a scarf which he immediately wrapped around his neck. Erik gave her a kiss on the cheek as a gesture of thanks and then handed her a gift that was the size of a ring box. She untied the ribbon around the box and opened it slowly. She was very surprised at what she saw. It was a small key that he had carved out of wood which was tied to a ribbon. Inside the box there was a note.

> Amalie,
> This key represents how you unlocked my past and freed me from my past. You not only freed me but you have taught me to love with all of my heart. Wear it and think of me. I will always love you.
> Love,
> Erik

She took the necklace in her hands and pulled it over her head. It fell nicely onto her skin just below the base of her neck. She gave him a hug and kissed him on the cheek. She then whispered in his ear, "I'll give you a proper thank you later." They exchanged wanton glances then remembered that they weren't alone. Meg walked over to Amalie to have a better look at the gift she had been given.

"It's beautiful," she said as she dropped it from her hand. "Erik you're a gifted craftsman." She patted him on the shoulder. "It's absolutely breath taking."

Erik walked over to the tree and pulled two small boxes out from the branches. He handed one to Meg and one to Chester.

"What is this?" they said simultaneously.

"They are Christmas presents, of course. It would be a crime not to give my two favorite people presents."

Meg's eyes began to tear up before she even opened the gift. "You really shouldn't have. We didn't get you anything."

Erik put his arm around Meg gently squeezing her and said, "You have both given me your friendship and your trust which is a gift that I'll treasure always."

Chester opened his first. It was a wooden cross that was attached to a long purple ribbon. "Thank you Erik, it's very nice. I'll put it in my Bible to remind me of our friendship."

Meg opened hers next. He had carved a small heart out of wood that was tied to a ribbon that would fit around her neck. "It's beautiful. I don't wear a lot of jewelry but I'll definitely wear this." She slipped it over her head and around her neck. "Thank you Erik."

Amalie examined each of their gifts and agreed that they were of fine quality. They gathered around the fireplace and Amalie handed out hot cider that she had brought out earlier to cool on the coffee table. Chester was about to give a toast when there was a knock on the door. Panic immediately crossed Amalie's face. "I'm not expecting anyone else this evening. I wonder who that could be."

Erik looked at her and knew that their evening of merriment was to be cut short. "I'll go into the study and stay there until you come get me," he offered. He started to walk out of the great room and Amalie stopped him. "No, this is your home too. I don't like it that you think you must hide."

"It's quite all right; I know it's only for a short time." He went to the study, shutting the doors behind him and locking them.

Amalie, Chester and Meg all went to the front door. Amalie took a deep breath, slowly opening the door. Chester and Meg let out a sigh of relief which accompanied their cheerful greeting when they saw their son Frederic and his wife Anna standing on the front stoop. "Merry Christmas," Frederic and Anna proclaimed together.

Meg and Chester hugged both of them. Amalie welcomed them into the house while taking their coats and hats, hanging them in the closet. "Please come inside and have some hot cider with us." Amalie led them into the great room and then excused herself to retrieve a few more cups for her guests. Before she went to the kitchen she took a detour to the study. She found the key that was in the foyer table, unlocked the door and entered. He was sitting at her father's desk reading her father's Bible.

"How are you doing in here?" she asked with genuine concern.

"I'm fine. Who was at the door?"

"Frederic and Anna and I'm afraid they may be here a while." She went over and sat on the edge of the desk which was facing Erik. He grabbed her hand. "Don't worry about it. I knew this day would come. I've lived in hiding all of my life and now will be no different."

She took his other hand and pulled him from the chair. "Yes, it will. You're coming with me. I need help getting more cups for our guests." He thought about resisting but deep down inside he wanted to go with her. He also knew that if he tried to argue with her, he'd lose.

"All right, I'll come with you but what are you going to tell them about me?"

"You leave that to me. I'm sure once I start you'll be able to improvise the rest. After all we make a pretty good team when it comes to weaving fiction."

They left the study and went to the kitchen to retrieve more cups and cider.

In the great room, the others were catching up on recent events and things that were going on in their lives. Frederic was a prestigious lawyer in Paris and Anna was a woman of many talents, one of which was spending Frederic's money on any and everything she desired. They were both very spoiled and rarely came to see Chester and Meg because they were too busy climbing the social ladder in Paris. Even though he loved his parents he made it very clear many years ago that what his parents did for a living was quite beneath him and wanted them to live a life that he could be proud of telling all of his friends about. As it was, he didn't tell his friends much about his family and Amalie had always suspected that he probably fabricated some kind of story about his parents to present them in a more glamorous light to his friends. He was about appearances and the life that his parents lived didn't fit in with his ambitions and his ideas of how happiness was to be measured. He'd offered to buy them a home in the city but they declined his offer. They had no desire to leave the life they'd worked so hard to make with their own skills and know-how. They were simple country people who were very happy where they were and with what they had. Frederic couldn't understand his parents or the relationship they had with the Girault's, especially with Amalie. After Louise's accident they became even more adamant about staying put and he finally gave up trying to get them to move. Amalie knew that they wouldn't abandon her after the accident. They loved her like their own child and the tragedy bound them together which was something he had grown to resent. He was jealous of their relationship but he could never resist an opportunity to come brag about his life and his accomplishments.

"I wonder what is taking Amalie so long." Meg pondered aloud. "I'll go check on her to see if she needs some help."

Meg had only taken three steps when Amalie and Erik walked into the room. Amalie was carrying the tray of cups full of cider and Erik had a tray of Christmas cookies. Meg and Chester exchanged a surprised glance and then Meg walked over to the coffee table to clear a space for the two trays. Frederic and Anna were both curious about the man who'd entered the room, especially because he was hiding part of his face with a mask.

"Thank you for helping get everything from the kitchen," Meg sweetly told Erik as she took the tray from him to set on the coffee table.

"Yes, thank you Erik. It's so nice to always have your help when I need it." Amalie smiled.

"I didn't know it was a masquerade Christmas party or I would've brought my mask too." Frederic snidely commented.

"Mind your manners," Meg snapped at him.

Amalie quickly jumped into the conversation.

"I would think that someone of your intelligence and social status would be less rude when meeting someone for the first time. However, because it is Christmas I'll forgive you for your lack of sensitivity to my gentleman friend," Amalie smugly replied. "Frederic and Anna I'd like to introduce Erik Geraurd, my friend and suitor. Erik, this is Frederic and Anna Rousseau, Meg's and Chester's son and daughter-in-law."

Erik put his hand out to shake Frederic's but the gesture was not returned. "It's a pleasure to finally meet both of you. Chester didn't tell me how lovely you were Anna nor did he tell me how much you looked like him, Frederic. The resemblance is uncanny."

Anna blushed at the compliment. She was quite taken with his manners and charm. Erik turned to Amalie and said, "You didn't tell me that they'd be joining us this evening."

She walked over to him and entwined her arm with his and replied, "I wasn't expecting them. Remember, they were supposed to be taking holiday in London with Anna's family."

"We're still planning on going but we were unable to leave when we originally planned because of an important social obligation we had to attend. We'll be leaving late the day after tomorrow so we decided to come see Mother and Father before we left since we had time," Frederic stated arrogantly.

"Well, we're glad to have your company this evening as I'm certain your parents are too. After all, Christmas is best celebrated with family and friends," said Erik as he looked lovingly at Amalie and put his hand over her hand.

"We won't be staying long. We have to travel back to Paris as soon as the sun comes up in the morning. We still have to pack for our trip but we thought it would be nice to see everyone since we haven't been here for such a long time," Anna said. "I like coming to the country. It reminds me how wonderful the city is. I don't know how you live without anywhere to shop or dine. It is always so dark here with no street lights to guide you. It's just dreadful."

"Some of us prefer the stars and moon lighting up the darkness. It is a celestial masterpiece on a clear night," Erik eloquently stated.

"Yes, well I suppose someone who hides their face behind a mask would prefer to live in the darkness of the night. It keeps them from being noticed," Frederic rudely commented.

Chester was embarrassed by his son's rudeness and spoke firmly. "You have insulted Erik twice this evening and I won't stand for such behavior from my son. You will apologize to him now and with great sincerity."

"Oh, Father, you are overreacting. He has taken no offense to what I've said or he would've defended himself."

"No Fredrick that is not the reason he hasn't defended himself against your words. It is because he is a gentleman and doesn't wish to spoil the mood of the evening." Chester looked at Erik and Amalie as he continued to scold his son. "You, on the other hand, have come into this house insulting Erik and embarrassing your mother and me with your lack of respect for others."

"I'm embarrassing you! That has got to be the most absurd accusation I've ever heard. If anyone in this family is an embarrassment to anyone, it is you and mother who embarrass me with your common way of life, living as servants when you could clearly be living as the master. It is obvious to me that you'd rather defend a complete stranger than to stand behind the comments of your own son."

"We won't apologize for being who God meant us to be. As far as us being an embarrassment to you, that's something that you'll have to come to terms with on your own. I never said you were an embarrassment to me. I'm proud that you're my son. However, your words and actions are embarrassing to your mother and me at this moment. I wish for you to apologize and make things right so that this evening can continue in the spirit of joy and peace." Chester put his hand on his son's shoulder and looked him in the eye. "Is that too much for me to ask of you?"

"For someone of lesser status it would seem the right thing to do but I'm not that person so I don't feel obligated to apologize or defend my words." He removed his father's hand from his shoulder. "If the truth offends people I can't control that, nonetheless, the truth is all I have spoken."

Amalie was still holding tightly to Erik when he decided that he'd better put an end to this test of wills between Chester and his son. He released her hand and walked over to Chester.

"It's quite alright Chester. He does have a valid point. I do, in fact, hide my face behind a mask and I don't like being noticed. However, it is not for the reasons that he wants so badly to be right about." Erik turned to Frederic and stared directly into his eyes. "I prefer not to be noticed for the simple reason that it protects me from the ignorance and false judgment of arrogant men that seem to believe that they're regarded more highly than someone who looks like me." Erik turned and walked back to Amalie's side. "Chester, it's alright that he says what he wishes. I've heard comments like his before and they do nothing to harm me. I've lived with my condition my entire life. I have learned to disregard the opinions of others. I know who I am. I have no need to prove I'm worthy of your son's approval. Unlike me, your son wasn't born with his condition but has merely taken it on in order to compensate for his insecurity. So, as you see, no apology is necessary."

Chester looked at him with approval. Even though he agreed with what was said about Frederic's condition he was disappointed that someone had to verbalize it, placing it on the ears of everyone in the room. Frederic was agitated and surprised that someone would speak to him, a well renowned lawyer and wealthy social figure in Paris, in a manner in which Erik had done. It was then that he realized that he was not dealing with a common man but a quick minded man with the capacity to spar with words. He had thought that Amalie was the best sparring partner he'd ever come across but it seemed now that she had taken a suitor that was just as good at using words for weapons.

"I appreciate your honesty. Pretending that we were to be friends would be a ridiculous assumption. I have no clue what insecurities you think I'm compensating for but I assure you that I have no insecurities that you need be concerned about. I'm *very* confident about who I am," Frederic retorted.

Erik took the lull in the conversation as an opportunity to speak once more. "I never said we weren't going to be friends. I'd rather hoped that we could be friends. Just because we don't necessarily see eye-to-eye on everything doesn't mean that I wouldn't want to be your friend. Even the best of friends have their disagreements and their differences of opinions."

By now the Christmas spirit was beginning to creep slowly away into the night. The women gathered around the coffee table pouring cider and placing cookies on separate plates for everyone. Meg and Anna were uncomfortable with the conversation and were trying hard to ignore what was going on around them by talking with each other while busying themselves. Amalie, however, was interested in hearing her beloved put Frederic in his place while making him also look like the pompous fool she knew him to be. She took great joy watching as Frederic struggled to better his own image in the face of a man who she knew he'd never be friends with for as long as he breathed air. Although she continued to listen to them she also busied herself with preparing cookies and cider to be served.

"Erik, I guess you're right. It doesn't matter that we don't agree on everything. I suppose we could be friends, even if it's only for this one night. After all, it *is* Christmas." Frederic decided that he would give in this one time in order to keep the peace. If he continued to argue with Erik he knew he'd end up looking like the fool. He couldn't allow that to happen. He knew that he'd have an opportunity someday to put Erik in his place.

"I agree," said Erik. "Let's have a Christmas toast." Amalie handed each of them a cup of cider. They stood in a circle and Erik raised his cup and said, "To Christmas; a celebration of the birth of our Lord and Savior and to friends and family; may we always remember that it is our friends and family that help us grow in love and maturity."

"Here, here!" exclaimed Chester. They raised their cups, bringing them together to create an ensemble of clinging and clanging that rang throughout the room. "Would anyone like a cookie to go with their cider?" Amalie asked. Everyone answered sporadically a firm yes to her question. She began handing out the small plates of cookies. The mood had definitely changed in the room but Amalie knew that given the chance, Frederic would change all of that.

Anna's curiosity had been brewing since she had met Erik. She wanted to know more about him. Even though the thought of what might be behind his mask disgusted her, she found his charm refreshing. His chivalrous disposition was something that her husband lacked. "Amalie, where did the two of you meet?"

She knew this moment would come and she'd already concocted her story in her head. Without hesitation and with a very convincing delivery she answered, "Erik was one of my father's apprentices fourteen years ago when he was working in Paris. They had kept in contact for years but had stopped corresponding after Father died. He was unaware of Father's death, so when he stopped receiving his letters he became concerned. He was in another country working, I can't remember which one. Erik, what country was it?" He joined Amalie who was now seated on the hearth of the fireplace, picked up her hand and looked into her eyes. "It was India." She smiled at him knowing that he was now a part of the game. "Yes, that's it, India. It took him almost a year to finish his work and then another to return to France. Once he had made it here he found out that Father had died. However, he remembered that Father had a daughter and came looking for me. He found me staying at my Uncle's place in Paris. Even though Father had told me about him, I never thought I'd ever meet him; much less find myself so taken with his charm and good looks." She squeezed his hand gently.

"No, it was I who was taken by your charm and beauty. You're a hard woman to forget. I'm just glad that you've given me the pleasure of your company." He smiled and then took a seat next to her on the hearth. "I guess we're both very blessed to have met each other."

Anna walked over to Frederic, rolling her eyes at Amalie's comments about his good looks. "I don't mean to pry, but what is it that you keep behind your mask; the good looks that Amalie speaks of or something else?" Anna smugly asked. Amalie was displeased by Anna's comment. She was about to reply to her smugness and then Erik replied very calmly.

"What lies behind my mask is merely a birthmark that has left my face misshapen. And yes, Amalie does find that my good looks transcend the outer appearance of my disfigured face. After all, beauty is in the eye of the beholder and is found within a person's character not in their appearance. A wise man once told me that a person that appears beautiful on the outside can have a dark and twisted soul just as a less attractive person can have the most beautiful of souls. It's up to us as individuals to seek the truth in every person and not to be fooled by what our eyes see."

Amalie beamed with pride at the words of her beloved. He truly had a way with words. He wasn't afraid to show people their ugly reflections in the mirror of the truths his words created. He released her hand, rose to his feet and then walked over to Anna and said, "I hope that my answer has satisfied your curiosity."

She found herself speechless for only a few seconds, and then she found her voice and replied, "Yes, I suppose my curiosity has been satisfied. Do you intend on keeping the mask on or will we be able to see your birthmark?"

"My birthmark is not for public viewing nor shall I put it on public display so that it will become the subject of idle gossip in social circles. My vanity precludes any obligation that anyone else may feel that they have to see what lay behind my mask," Erik replied sincerely.

"Vanity is the least of your concerns I should think," Frederic said under his breath where he thought no one could hear him. "You know Erik, your mask reminds me of a story I read recently in the paper. It was the most fascinating story I've ever read. It was about the corpse of the rumored Opera Ghost being found in the cellars of the Paris Opera House. I don't suppose any of you have read the paper lately?"

Amalie and Erik exchanged glances with Chester and Meg and then proceeded to act as if they were only slightly interested in the topic even though they wanted to know more. Amalie spoke first. "No, Frederic I haven't had a chance to pick up the paper lately. Do you mind telling us what they found?"

"It was extraordinary. In all the years I have lived in Paris I never thought the rumors were true. I thought that it was a stunt or idle stories told by the players of the theater to pass the time, but there it was in black and white, printed for all to see. They say that his body was decomposed; leaving only slight traces of flesh on the bones. I'm sure it was disgusting nonetheless. What was odd was the gold ring they found on his finger. It appeared to be a wedding band. Some Persian who claimed to have known him years before identified his remains. He said that he did wear a gold band but never knew of a wife."

"How can they be sure that it was the Opera Ghost?" Amalie inquired once again.

"They say that the strange happenings in the Opera House stopped on the night that Mademoiselle Daaé disappeared with her lover Raoul de Chagney. Neither of them has been heard from since that night and neither has the Opera Ghost."

Erik decided that he needed to act at least a little interested in the subject less someone suspect him of something. "Frederic, did they write whether the Opera Ghost had a real identity, you know, a name?"

"Yes, The Persian said his name was Erik but apparently never knew of him having a surname. I found that quite odd too but isn't it a coincidence that his name is the same as yours?" Erik was now sorry that he had asked the question.

"Not really, Erik is a common name for men, as is your name. I'm sure that you've met many men in your profession with the same name as yours, have you not?"

"That is true; I have met many men with the same name as my own. However, don't you find it strange that the Opera Ghost was told to have had a hideous face that he hid behind a mask as you do?"

Erik decided he'd ignore the comment about his face because considering that it was said by Frederic made it easier to do so. However, his urge to lash out at this man was growing inside him. If he didn't love Amalie so much he'd dispose of this man and his arrogant words with little hesitation but his conscience wouldn't let him. He would have to use his words to disarm this man's theories instead of physical violence this time.

"Did anyone ever see what was behind his mask?" Erik calmly asked. "Could he have not worn the mask to have hidden his identity so that he couldn't be found out or noticed?"

Anna felt that her husband's indirect accusation was unfair and without merit. Although she was repulsed by what may be behind his mask she was drawn to him by his charm. He may have exposed her true prejudiced nature earlier but he did it in such a way that only she knew he had done so. She felt that she owed him for his discretion, so she came to his defense. "As far as I know, no one ever saw what was behind his mask. They certainly didn't say it in the paper." Frederic gave his wife a displeasing look for coming to his adversary's defense.

"Then I guess it is possible that he was merely hiding an ordinary face. Did they write that his skull was misshapen in any way?" Erik inquired once again.

He knew that Erik's assumptions were probably the most logical and to continue to argue about it would be a practice in futility. "I concede to you, my friend. Your arguments are as good as any legal counsel I've ever come up against in court. You're probably right. This gentleman was using fear of what might be behind his mask to enslave his victims.

Anyhow, he is of no consequence to any of us now, he is dead and the Paris Opera House flourishes."

Amalie had grown tired of the conversation. It was time they moved on to an activity that had to do with celebrating Christmas. "Everyone that's enough talk of tragic things, it's time to retire to the drawing room for some Christmas music." She stood up, walked over to Erik, took his hand and began walking into the drawing room. "Erik, would you mind playing "Silent Night" for us tonight?"

He looked at her lovingly and replied, "Only if you will sing it."

"If you insist," she replied with a smile. She took her place beside the piano as he took his place on the bench; preparing to play. Their guests took their seats; awaiting the performance. Erik began playing and Amalie's voice rose above the room in a great melodic symphony. When she finished they clapped. Even Frederic and Anna couldn't help but be moved by the performance. Frederic stood and cheered, "Bravo, Bravo. You play very well. I'm surprised you're not a featured player in an orchestra somewhere." It was a compliment that came from Frederic's mouth that fell on Erik's ears. He wasn't sure he should trust it but felt compelled to give him the benefit of the doubt. "Thank you, Frederic. I play for my own pleasure, not for public displays. I guess you could say it is a hobby of mine." He turned and winked at Amalie, who in turn smiled.

"Well, it's a waste of talent I say," Anna broke in and added her opinion. "You could make a lot of money with those magical fingers."

"If Erik had to use his talent to make money he probably wouldn't enjoy playing as much," Chester chimed in on the conversation.

"Well, if Amalie sang while he played they'd be sure to make headlines wherever they went," Meg said.

Erik put his arm around Meg, squeezing her shoulder. "I agree. As long as Amalie would sing we would certainly bring rave revues around the world."

"Stop it, all of you. We enjoy entertaining our family and friends with our talents. We have no ambitions of fame and fortune." She took his hand, leading him back to the piano. "Let's sing another song, one that everyone can sing." Amalie turned to Anna. "What song would you like to sing?"

Anna thought a minute and said, "How about *Jingle Bells?*" She turned back toward Erik and said, "*Jingle Bells* Maestro." He took a moment and then placed his fingers on the keys. The joyful tune spread across them like a wave. Everyone joined in once she began singing. When they finished, they were laughing and began reminiscing about

Christmas' when they were all much younger. Erik enjoyed listening to their stories but was also saddened by the thought that he really didn't have any Christmas' to reminisce about; at least not any that he wanted to remember. He was glad that this Christmas would be one that he'd want to remember in the years to come.

The hour grew late when their guests decided that it was best that they take leave. After all, Frederic and Anna had to get up early so that they could get back to Paris. They said their good-byes and wished each other a Merry Christmas once more as they parted ways. Amalie was tired and yet she wasn't ready to retire for the evening. She still had one surprise for her Erik.

Erik took her by the hand and they walked back into the great room. He took her over by the Christmas tree and pulled something out from within the branches. He held a sprig of mistletoe above her head. As she looked up to see what he was holding in his hand, he placed his lips gently on hers, pulling her to him. Her arms wrapped around his body, returning the embrace.

"I've been waiting all night to do that," he said with a smile on his face.

"And I have been waiting for you to *do* that all night," she said with a little laugh. He gave her another kiss and then held her again, this time more tightly.

"Thank you Amalie," he whispered.

"For what?" she whispered back to him as she returned his embrace.

"Not hiding me from the world, for not being ashamed of me and for loving me as I am."

"You're welcome. I didn't see the need to hide you. You pose no threat to anyone that was here; except maybe Frederic and his ego." She began to laugh and he laughed with her.

"He does think a lot of himself, doesn't he?" He released his hold on her and walked over to take a seat on the sofa.

"Yes, he does but I think he met a worthy opponent this evening." She began picking up the cups and plates, putting them on the tray. She started to lift the tray but he rose quickly from the sofa and offered to take it from her. She handed it to him and they walked to the kitchen together. They looked at each other, then at the dishes and they knew that the look meant that the dishes could wait to be cleaned in the morning. He held her hand as they walked back into the great room.

"Do you suppose that Frederic will try to find a connection between you and the deceased Opera Ghost?" she asked.

"Why would you ask that, Amalie? I don't think that he has much evidence to prove it even if he thought he could. It's good news that they found my rotting corpse and that my friend positively identified me. That means that I no longer have to worry about anyone suspecting me to be the Opera Ghost." He looked at her and smiled.

"I wouldn't be so sure that he won't try to figure out a way to create trouble for you, even if it has nothing to do with him suspecting you to be the Opera Ghost," she quickly replied.

"Why would he do that? I barely know the man. Why would he seek to hurt me?"

"It has been my experience that he doesn't need a reason to try to hurt people. I think he does it for pleasure."

"Is there something about him that you aren't telling me? It appears to me that the two of you have a past." He looked at her with that look she knew all to well; the one that made her unable to keep a secret from him.

"I wouldn't call it a past but yes, there is some history there. He has always been jealous of me and even more so when his parents wouldn't be bought by his money. He thinks that my father and I persuaded them to stay here but we didn't. They stayed because we treated them more like family than he ever did or does."

"This jealousy began before you became an adult, I suspect." He got up to tend to the fire while she stayed seated on the sofa. "Let me guess. He was jealous that his parents spent so much time with you and your parents when he was a boy and he is about ten years older than you. Your mother needed a nanny and Meg happily took on that duty as well as housekeeper." He turned away from the fireplace to look at her. "Am I right?"

"You're close. He is actually eight years older than me and yes, he was jealous of the time his parents spent with me and my parents. However, he figured out a way to remove the obstacle that he believed kept his family from him." She paused for a response from Erik and he obliged.

"And what was his solution?"

"Please don't be angry with me when I tell you. Promise me?" He sat down beside her. She took his hands in hers, looking him straight in the eyes. "Do you promise?"

He touched her cheek with his hand and replied, "I promise."

"Frederic decided that the best way to have a relationship with his parents was to become part of *my* family. Keep in mind that by the time I was old enough to have an interest in men that he'd already gone out into the world to seek his future. I hadn't seen him in almost fifteen years since he had left to attend the university. He was only Meg and Chester's son to me when I was a young girl, nothing more." She straightened her dress, and then looked back at Erik's face to see if she could read his thoughts. She was unable to detect any emotion from him at all so she continued.

"Frederic was an up and coming lawyer when I became taken by his interest in me during one of his visits. I wasn't married and my father thought that he'd be a good husband for me. I agreed to let him court me and a year later we became engaged to be married. After he moved to Paris for his new job he became more interested in making money and going to social gatherings than spending time with me. I thought that it was something that would change once we were married but as the time passed I noticed that he was more distant and more driven. I suspected that there might be someone else but didn't dare tell anyone my thoughts. When my mother's accident happened the true Frederic made himself known. I was heartbroken at first when he broke off the engagement, as were his parents, but months later I found out that he was seeing someone else in Paris and that is when I realized that he was only using me to get the attentions and affections of his parents. Meg and Chester felt horrible about what he'd done. That is the reason they stayed here with me. I hated him for years but my father convinced me that hating him only hurt me. Frederic would continue on with his life not worrying about what I thought of him." Her voice grew softer. "Father was right, as usual, so I gave up my hate and forgave him. I did it for myself...... and for Meg and Chester. I couldn't hate their son when I loved them so much. They were embarrassed enough by his actions and my hating him wasn't going to heal me or them." She stood up and walked over to the fireplace. "I was actually relieved when I heard that he was marrying Anna. She was more suited for him. I actually like Anna. I know she appears to be like him but she isn't. She has a big heart and is quite the philanthropist. I don't think she knew that he was engaged to me when she met him. Forgiving her really wasn't hard to do. My knowing that he'd met someone more suited for him made me realize that God had someone else for me. I just hadn't met him yet." She walked back over to the sofa and sat down.

Erik kissed her hand and then chose his words and tone carefully. "Why didn't you tell me all of this?"

"I didn't think I'd ever have a need to tell you. It has been years since he's come for Christmas at the house. He has come to see his parents only once during that time. I had spoken with his wife at numerous social gatherings in Paris when I was living there for a time but I never dreamed he'd ever show his face here. I didn't tell you because he means nothing to me. He's an arrogant man that likes to think that everyone wants to be him." She gripped his hand tightly. "Please forgive me."

He looked into her beautiful brown eyes and saw that she was truly sincere. He loved her so much that even this small infraction couldn't make him angry with her. "I forgive you Amalie. Is there anything else that you've neglected to tell me about your past?"

She looked at him with her big brown eyes, leaned over and whispered in his ear, "No, I think that is all." As she began to lean back she placed a kiss on his cheek.

He smiled at her sweetly and with forgiveness in his eyes he spoke. "Remember Amalie, we have to trust each other if we're going to make this relationship work. I understand why you didn't tell me but had I known he was the one who had broken your heart so long ago, I would have thanked him."

"Thanked him for what Erik?" she asked with a surprised tone in her voice.

"For letting you go so that I might have you to love for the rest of my life." He caressed her cheek with his hand and she blushed at his touch.

"You're impossible. Does your romantic side have an end?"

"I certainly hope not or our courtship will turn out to be a terrible bore," he said with a laugh.

"I doubt that anything in your life was or ever will be boring." She rose from the sofa, took him by the hand; pulling him up off of the sofa. "I have one more gift for you but you'll have to come to my studio to see it."

He walked with her up the stairs to the door of her studio. She unlocked the door and led him over to a large painting that was covered with a heavy sheet. "Close your eyes," she told him. He did as he was told. She pulled the sheet off of the painting. "You may open them now."

He opened his eyes. He was overwhelmed at what was before him. She had painted a portrait of him that reflected his likeness but showed no signs of his disfigurement. Somehow she had managed to create his face as if he'd been born without his birthmark. "Amalie.....I don't know what to say. It is absolutely astounding."

"Does that mean you like it?" she timidly asked.

"I think it's...... wonderful." His emotions overcame him and tears began to stream down his face.

"I wanted to paint a portrait of you that reflected how *my* heart sees you. When I look at you, this is the man I see. This is the man I love." She stood next to him holding his hand.

"This is how you believe I'd look if I didn't have the birthmark?" he asked her.

"Yes. You're quite handsome even with your birthmark but without it I think you'd have many women swooning at the sight of you." She looked at his face for an expression of any kind but he stood stoically staring at the portrait.

"Would you rather I not have my birthmark?" he asked with no change in his mood.

"No! I love you no matter whether you have the birthmark or not." She turned to face him; wiping the tears from his cheek with her finger. "It is *you* I love not your appearance. I painted this so that you could see that God gave me eyes to see you as He does. Your birthmark is a part of you and I'll always be glad that you have it. Without it I may have never met you. I fell in love with who you are. I love you because of who I know you to be on the inside."

He put his hand over her hand as she wiped the tears from his cheek, brought it to his lips and kissed the palm of her hand. "Your heart sees me in a better light than I've ever seen myself. I often wondered what my face would have looked like without my disfigurement. Now I don't have to wonder any longer." He kissed her cheek and then embraced her. "This is the best Christmas present I have ever received. Thank you. I will cherish it always."

She started to pull the drape over it and he stopped her. "Why are you covering it up?"

She stopped and replied, "I don't want anything to get on it. Sometimes when I'm painting I trip or some paint may splatter from my brush. I don't want to take any chances. When we decide what room we want it in then I'll uncover it and move it to the room where it is to be hung." He was satisfied with her explanation, so he grabbed the drape and helped her place it over the painting.

They exited the studio. This time she didn't lock it. She gave him the key. "This is yours now. I won't need it anymore. The last secret I kept from you has now been given to you. All the rooms in the house are unlocked, like my heart. You're free to roam wherever you may choose just as you do in my heart."

"Now who's the romantic?" he teased.

"You're not the only one that has romance in their blood. Besides, I have had a good teacher these past few months."

They walked back downstairs and into the great room. It was nearing midnight and Christmas Day was almost over. She sat quietly next to him on the sofa with her head against his shoulder, staring into the fireplace at the flames which were almost reduced to burning embers. He held her hand and quietly hummed *Silent Night*. The large grandfather clock that stood near the wall of the staircase rang out twelve chimes notifying all that could hear that it was midnight. A few minutes passed and then without any apparent reason he stopped humming, stood up and knelt on one knee in front of her. She was confused by his sudden departure from her side.

"Amalie, I have courted you now for three months. I know that most courtships are at least six months to a year in length but I find myself unable to continue on in this manner." She was taken off guard by what he said. Although she wondered why he didn't want to continue courting her anymore but she couldn't bring herself to ask him. He continued to explain his position on the matter. "I love you and I know that things won't always be easy for us, for obvious reasons, but I love you. I believe that we can have a life together that neither of us will ever regret." His heart beat quickly and it felt like his words were sticking to the inside of his mouth as he spoke. Then the words that he had longed to say flowed smoothly from his lips, "Amalie, will you marry me? Will you be my wife until I breathe my last breath?" He was nervous about what her answer would be but was glad to have finally said what had been in his heart since the day he realized he truly loved her and that she loved him.

Her eyes began to fill with tears and her cheeks blushed with the color of a pink rose. She could hardly believe the words that she was hearing. Her heart pounded and her mind raced with thoughts of joy, excitement and then doubt and fear. She wanted to marry him but she feared for what their lives would be like. However, she knew they couldn't continue on the way they were. It would be better if she were his wife and he, her husband. This wasn't the time for her to be logical, this was a time for thinking with her heart and her heart wanted to be his wife. Together they could face anything and he wouldn't have to continue to hide and she would no longer be alone. She deserved some happiness after all of the tragedy she had suffered in her young life and he loved her like no man had ever loved her. More importantly, she loved him with all of her heart and soul. She believed in her heart that it had been God that had brought them together with the help of her father. Who was she to argue with what God had planned for her life?

"Erik, I love you very much. Yes......I'll marry you. I'll be your wife until I draw my last breath." She placed her hand on his face and kissed him gently on the lips. He put his arms around her and stood up, bringing her with him. He spun her around as he continued to kiss her. "You've made me the happiest man in the world." He gazed into her eyes that were full of tears. He felt so much love for her that he wanted to take her upstairs and show her how much but he knew that it wasn't the right time. Those thoughts would have to be put to the back of his mind.

"I know that traditionally the man gives his future bride an engagement ring but honestly Amalie, I hadn't planned on asking you to marry me tonight so I'm completely unprepared."

"Why did you ask me if you hadn't intended to do so?" she asked with a confused look on her face.

"As I was sitting beside you in the warmth of the fireplace, I knew at that moment that I never wanted to be anywhere but here with you. I couldn't wait another three to six months to ask you to be my wife. I love you and I want you with me always."

She hugged him tightly. "Your explanation is better than having a ring." She kissed him on the cheek and then she laid her head against his chest while he stood holding her in his arms. "You've given me the best Christmas present *I* have ever been given," she whispered.

The love she felt for him was overwhelming. She took him by the hand and led him to the stairs. He followed her until they reached the top of the staircase and found themselves outside of her room. She opened the door and led him into her room closing the door behind her. He opened his mouth to speak and she silenced him with a passionate kiss. His arms drew her tightly to him. He knew that he should be the strong one and resist the urges of passion that he was having but his flesh had longed for her touch for so long that he was finding it hard not to succumb to her advances. She removed his jacket, then began to unbutton his shirt and then he took her by the arms and said, "Amalie, we can't do this; not now....not this way." She stopped to look at his face. She knew that by the look in his eyes he was serious. She noticed that his eyes were different and that his voice was humbled. "I want to honor you and your parents. I made a promise to Chester....... remember? More importantly I made a promise to God that if you said yes, that I'd do this His way, not mine." He buttoned up his shirt, put his jacket back on and kissed her on the cheek. "We'll become one on our wedding day as God intended. I love you Amalie." He kissed her again on the other cheek.

"I love you too, Erik. You're right. I'm sorry. I only wanted to show you how much I love you." She put her head down, ashamed of her own actions. He lifted her head up with his hand, looked into her eyes and replied, "You've no need to apologize to me. I had the same thoughts you did. I know that you wouldn't have gone through with it either. You would've come to the same conclusion inside your head that I did before it went too far."

"What conclusion is that?" she inquired.

"That anything worth having is worth waiting for. Although God would have forgiven us, you wouldn't have been able to forgive yourself. After all, you made your promises to your father before he died and I'm sure that one of them was to keep your virtue intact until your wedding day. I couldn't bear the thought of doing anything that he'd disapprove of, especially bringing dishonor upon his daughter and his house."

She walked him to the door of her room, kissed him good night and said, "I love you." He replied, "I love you, too." He walked to his room and closed the door behind him. She was exhausted but also excited about planning a wedding; her wedding. She wondered if her mother's wedding dress would fit her. Her mind raced with all of the details of the wedding, and then her thoughts were interrupted by a knock at her door. She went to the door, opened it and found Erik staring at her.

"Erik, what is it?" she asked not noticing that she sounded fearful.

"Did you lock the front door to the house?" he asked.

"I think so. Why do you ask?"

"I thought I heard someone downstairs. I'd like to go down to investigate but I'm without my sword and in need of a weapon to protect myself. Do you have anything?"

She walked over to her armoire, opened the top drawer and pulled out a revolver and some bullets. She loaded it then handed it to him.

"Here, it was my father's. He gave it to me so that I could defend myself if I ever found the need to do so." He took it from her and kissed her on the cheek. "Thank you. I'll be back in a minute."

"Please be careful." She watched out her bedroom door as he walked down the stairs into the great room.

He checked the front door and found it locked. Then he went into the sitting room, the study and then into the kitchen. A loud clatter alerted Amalie, then a crash and then silence. She was relieved that she didn't hear a gun shot but Erik had not emerged from the kitchen. She waited for what seemed like an hour but was only a few minutes. He entered the great room carrying something black. As he got closer she recognized the small black object. It was Sampson.

"Here is our burglar," he laughed. "He was helping himself to some Christmas cookies."

She laughed as she took Sampson out of his arms.

"You've been a very naughty cat Sampson. How did you get into the house?" Sampson purred and rubbed his head against her hand as she pet him.

"He must have come in when we were saying good-bye to our guests earlier this evening," he concluded. "Would you like me to put him out?"

"It's freezing outside," she scolded. "I think we should let him stay in for this one night. After all, it is Christmas." She continued to stroke his fur.

"It *was* Christmas, Amalie and he has caused enough trouble for one night but he is your cat. If you want him to stay, then he stays." He pet Sampson on the head and kissed her on the cheek. "I'm going to bed now. I'll put this back into your armoire."

"No, Erik, you keep it. I'll feel better if you're the one protecting us."

He nodded in agreement, kissed her on the cheek again and retired to his room. She went into her room where she placed Sampson on the foot of her bed. He curled up in the warm blankets, closed his eyes and went to sleep. She went to her dresser and began brushing her hair. When she was done she changed into her nightgown, crawled into bed and fell asleep.

Premonition

She woke the next morning to the sound of Sampson pawing at her door to be let out. She pulled on her robe, picked him up and walked downstairs to the kitchen. She gave him a saucer of milk and while he drank she started cleaning the dishes. Sampson finished his milk and then rubbed his body on her leg, purring loudly with delight.

"Yes, Sampson, I love you too." She picked him up, took him to the door, opened it and put him outside. "Have a good day Sampson." She closed the door behind him and when she turned around Erik was standing by the small table fully dressed, looking very handsome. She was not expecting him and so she let out a gasp. Realizing that she hadn't brushed her hair and was not dressed, she pulled her robe tightly up around her neck with one hand and attempted to smooth her hair with the other.

"I wasn't expecting you to be up for at least another hour. Forgive my appearance, I'll go make myself more presentable," she said with embarrassment in her voice.

He stopped her as she tried to move past him. "You look beautiful this morning. In fact, I've never seen a woman look more beautiful than you do now." He kissed her on the cheek. "Remember that once we're married, I'll get the privilege of seeing you look so lovely every morning."

"Thank you for your kind words and I know that you mean them but if it is all the same to you, I'll feel better if I'm dressed and groomed properly until that day comes." She smiled at him as she exited the room.

He watched her as she disappeared into the foyer. He was so happy that they would be married soon but he worried that she would want a big formal wedding, which he had also thought would be nice but had later concluded that a small private ceremony would be best. Then there was the problem of the ring. How would he ever get her a ring? Maybe Chester would be able to help him. He thought that perhaps

Chester was already at the stable so he retrieved his cloak from the closet in the foyer and went out to find him.

When he arrived at the stable, Chester was busy grooming Shadow. "Good morning, Chester."

"Good morning, Erik. What brings you out to see me on this cold morning?" Chester asked.

"I need your help. I need to get an engagement ring and wedding band for Amalie."

Chester suddenly stopped what he was doing and walked around Shadow so he could look Erik in the eye. "Are you going to ask her to marry you?"

"I asked her last night and she said yes." His happiness could be heard in his words. "I hadn't intended on asking her until much later in our courtship but there was something about the way she looked last night that made me realize that I couldn't wait that long to make her my wife."

"She was fine with you not having a ring to give her?" Chester asked.

"Yes, she was fine but *I* don't want her to go another day without one. She deserves a ring."

"I agree. She is a wonderful woman. I couldn't be happier for the two of you. Meg will be so pleased to hear of your plans."

"Can you help me Chester? Can you help me get her a ring?" he asked almost to the point of pleading.

"I can do better than that."

Erik gave him a puzzled look. "What do you mean?"

"Remember the last envelope that Gaston left you?"

"Yes, but how is that going to help me get a ring for Amalie?"

"It has been more than a year so it's alright if you open it now. If you still need my help after that I'll be here." Chester went back to brushing the horse.

"You're a mysterious man but that is part of your charm. Thanks for your help…..I think." He walked out of the stable and headed back to the house.

Amalie had finished dressing and made her way back to the kitchen. When she arrived he was entering the back door. He removed his cloak and laid it across his arm. He kissed her on the cheek as he passed her to return his cloak to the closet. She followed him.

"Where have you been this morning?"

"I decided to go see Chester this morning. I wanted to make sure that everything was all right between him and Frederic."

"So, what did you find out?"

"Everything is fine. Frederic and Anna are on their way back to Paris now." He knew he shouldn't lie to her but he wanted the ring to be a surprise. He took her by the arm, walked back into the kitchen and asked her a question she was not expecting. "Have you thought about when you'd like to get married?"

"Erik, we just got engaged last night. I haven't had much time to think about it but apparently you have. What are your thoughts?" She was very curious to know what he was thinking. She was guessing that he'd want to get married as soon as he could. However, she didn't know what would be soon to him. She wanted to get married soon too but she didn't want to seem too eager.

"I think that we should get married as soon as possible. Next month would be good. What do you think about January twenty-fourth or twenty-fifth?" He looked at her with his big blue eyes that were begging for her to agree with him.

"I think that it doesn't give me much time to plan the wedding, but I wasn't going to plan anything big or elaborate anyway. I can wear my mother's wedding dress, you can wear that wonderful black suit you wore the first time we had a formal supper together. You know the one with the white ascot and gold accented vest? And then I can ask Chester to give me away and Meg can come too. I'll invite Isabel, Peter and their girls and if it's alright with you I'd like to invite Frederic and Anna too. I wouldn't want to hurt their feelings. I doubt they will attend anyway."

Erik was now seated on the kitchen stool. He was listening very intently to the plans of his bride-to-be. "For someone who hasn't had much time to think about it, you've done a good job of planning the wedding very quickly and quite nicely I must add." She detected the sarcasm in his voice and ignored him as she continued.

"The only problem I can foresee will be finding a reverend to marry us. I haven't been to church in a month and I don't know if Reverend Troudeaux will perform the ceremony. I can't imagine he wouldn't. He was always so fond of Mother and Father and he did the services for both of their funerals. I'll get Chester to deliver a message to him immediately so that we may speak to him." Her mind raced with ideas, messages and plans for the wedding. She wandered around the kitchen like a lost sheep, not knowing what to do first. "I have so much to do now."

He enjoyed listening to her plan the wedding that she hadn't had time to think about. He could tell that she was about to plan herself right into a panic so he needed to put an end to it and quickly. He walked up behind her, put his arms around her and kissed her on the neck. "Amalie, why don't we eat some breakfast first? It doesn't have to all be done today. We'll have a couple of days to figure out all of the details. I want our wedding day to be a day to look forward to, not a day that you will be glad to have come and go because you wore yourself out planning it."

"You're right. Let's eat something first. Then we can make a list of all the things that need to be done." She took his hands, turned to face him and hugged him. "We'll be happy forever, won't we Erik? Promise me that we'll always be happy even if bad things happen? Promise me we'll find the good in them and that we'll be happy because we're facing them together."

His chin was gently placed on her head as he embraced her. He held her a little tighter as she spoke to him. "I promise Amalie. I'll do everything I can to make sure that we're happy, even when troubles come."

They ate breakfast and then she went to her father's study to start making her list. He told her that he would join her later because he needed to check on some things in the cave. He hadn't worked on the room since before Christmas and wanted to refresh his memory on what he would need to do next. He opened the secret door, closed it behind him and walked down the tunnel to the cave. The air was frigid in the cave which made him glad that he had put on his topcoat. He found the satchel that held the last envelope that Gaston had left him. He pulled out the envelope, took a deep breath and opened it. There were many things in this envelope: a letter addressed to both of them, the final sketches of the room, a small key and a letter addressed only to him. He glanced over the drawings for the room and mentally gave himself a pat on the back for guessing correctly where Gaston had put the final drawings. Then he tore open the letter addressed to him.

Dear Erik,

I hope this letter finds you doing well. I hope that you have either figured out what God's purpose is for you or you are at least closer to realizing what His purpose is for your life. I will explain each item that I have left in this envelope in great detail so that there is no error in its interpretation. The letter I have left for you and Amalie must not be opened until you have used the key to open the box that I have left for you in the bottom drawer of the armoire in your room. If you have discovered it, I am sure you have wondered where the key has been hidden. Now you know. Once you have opened the box, everything will become clearer to you and no explanation will be needed. The drawings are the final sketches of the room you are constructing. If you are think-

ing that it resembles a church sanctuary, you would be correct. I always felt as if God was with me, talking to me when I was in the cave and so I promised Him that I would give this cave back to Him since He was the one that showed it to me. I don't wish for any formal services to be held in the cave. I only wish for you and Amalie to use the room as a place to worship and honor God, to collect your thoughts and regain focus on what is important in your lives. I know that you will make it as beautiful as your talents will allow. You have great vision and I know that no matter how it looks when it is complete, God will be pleased because you are His creation.

Thank you for honoring a dying man's wishes. You were and continue to be a true friend.

Many Blessings be Upon You,
Gaston Girault

He folded the letter, placed it in the envelope and then back into the satchel. He took the key, the other letter and put them inside his topcoat pocket. He was curious about what Gaston had left him in the box in the armoire. Surprisingly, he had never opened the bottom drawer of the armoire. He never felt comfortable going through the drawers of the furniture in the house. He didn't know why he didn't since he never found it to be an issue when he'd go through the belongings of the managers of the Opera House but it was probably because this was his friend's house and to do so would be breaking the trust that they had worked so hard to gain from each other.

He reached the secret door and opened it very quietly. Amalie was not in the study anymore. He was relieved. He didn't want to have to lie to her about why he couldn't stay to go over the list with her. However, he did wonder where she had gone. He quietly made his way up the stairs and into his room. He opened the doors to the armoire and then pulled open the bottom drawer. The box was there exactly like Gaston said it would be. The box was slightly deeper than a cigar box but as long and wide as the drawer in which it was placed. It was almost undetectable because of its color and size matching the drawer it had been cleverly designed to look like. He took it out, placed it on the bed, put the key in the lock and turned it. He heard the click and the lock released. He opened the box and couldn't believe what he saw. There was a letter folded on the top of several stacks of francs. There must have been at least 200,000 francs in the box. Tucked tightly into the right top corner of the box was a small black pouch. He pulled it out, opened it and poured the contents into his hand. In his hand appeared three rings; a single, pear-shaped diamond that was set onto a gold ring and two gold bands. One band was larger than the other but they were identical in appearance. They were simple but beautiful.

He took the letter that had been placed on top of the money and read it.

Dear Erik,

I'm sure you have many questions about what I have placed in the box for you and Amalie. Make no mistake, but this box was and is meant for the two of you. Chester and Meg have been instrumental in helping to arrange everything being that my health is declining quickly. Please tell them how much I appreciated their friendship and loyalty.

I had hoped to introduce you to Amalie myself before I became ill but the opportunity never presented itself, so I began planning all the arrangements and letters during the last days of my life. I'm not certain that you will ever read this but I wouldn't be the friend I had claimed to be if I didn't at least try to figure out a way to help you even if I couldn't do it myself. I had hoped that after I had introduced you to each other that the two of you would become friends.

After her mother's death and her broken engagement Amalie withdrew from people and it was as if she had died with her mother. I had hoped that you would be a good friend to her knowing that you too had suffered great losses in your life much like she has. I also had hoped that possibly Amalie could grow to love you and you, her. I had thought many times that the two of you would suit each other in that manner but I didn't dare intervene for I know that each person must choose who they love and not have love thrust upon them.

If you have fallen in love with my daughter and you want to marry her, I give you my blessing to do so. The rings were her mother's and mine. Use them for the wedding ceremony. My only regret will be that I won't be able to share in the happy moment. I know you will be a good husband and father. No matter what your past has been Erik, I know that God has changed you if my daughter has accepted your proposal. If you love Amalie but don't wish to marry her, please give her the rings and tell her that I love her and that I only wanted what I believed was the best for her.

Yes, Erik, I believed that you would be the best man for her. I have no way of knowing that I was right about God's purpose for you but I hope that you have figured it out by now and if you haven't I pray that you will soon.

The money is yours to keep. You are probably wondering where it came from and if you thought about your past you would figure it out. However, I know that riddles try your patience so I'll elaborate on how I came to have all of the funds you now see before you. You need only look into the mirror to see where the money came from Erik. Yes, you're the one that gave it to me. After you heard of Louise's accident and that I had stopped working in order to help take care of her you began sending me 10,000 francs each month. You did this for almost two years and although I appreciated it, it was not necessary. I had plenty of funds to support my family. Your gesture was so grand that I didn't want to belittle it by asking you not to send it. Instead, I kept it and had planned to return it to you after I had introduced you to my daughter. That day never came so I had to come up with another way to get it to you. It is your money to keep. If you marry my daughter you may need it someday to take care of your family. If you don't, then you can use it to start the life that you have always dreamed of having.

The letter that I addressed to the two of you is only to be opened if you have asked her to marry you and she has agreed to become your wife. My prayer and hope for you and Amalie is that you will both live your lives doing what you know to be right and not worrying about what the world would have you to do. I love you both. Thank you for taking care of Amalie this past year. If you are reading this, then I know that something is keeping you there with her and although it may only be your loyalty to me, I am indebted to you always for looking after her for me.

Your Most Trusted Friend,
Gaston

The letter brought tears to his eyes. He was flattered that he had chosen him to be his daughter's spouse long before he had ever met her. The trust that Gaston placed in Erik's ability to love his only child was beyond comprehension. Why, after all he knew about him, would he ever want him to marry his daughter? It didn't make sense at all. Gaston must have seen something in him that even he hadn't seen in himself. It was as if Gaston had received a premonition about his life. He took the letter and placed it in the top drawer of the armoire underneath the scarf that Amalie had made for him.

He took the pouch with the rings in it, put it in his pocket and then closed the box and locked it, returning it to the drawer from which he had retrieved it. He put the key with the letter in the top drawer of the armoire. He was about to walk out of his room and Amalie appeared in the doorway.

"I thought you were down in the cave? I walked all the way down the tunnel to find you missing from your work. What do you have to say for yourself?" she asked with humor in her voice.

"Well, I would have to say that I've been busy hunting down the rabbit trails that your father left me inside the last envelope." He took her in his arms and kissed her firmly on the lips. "I have something to give you and something to tell you but not here. Let's go to the drawing room."

They walked down the hall, then down the stairs and into the drawing room. She was curious and suspicious of his odd behavior. She didn't know whether to be concerned or not. They took a seat on the sofa.

"You're being awfully mysterious Erik and I don't mind telling you that it is making me uncomfortable."

"You've no need to worry. You'll understand why I'm not myself after I give you this." He picked up her right hand and slipped the diamond engagement ring onto her finger. She looked at it, not recognizing it to be her mother's ring at first but with further examination she gasped at the sight of it and began to cry. "Where did you get this Erik? This is the ring my father gave to my mother when he asked her to marry him all those years ago." Her face was pale and her heart was racing.

"It was a gift from your father. In the last envelope I was to open, he left the final plans to the room, a letter to you and me, another letter only to me and a small key. In the letter to me he told of a box in the armoire in my room. He said the key would open it. Inside the box there was another letter, a large amount of money and your mother's and father's wedding rings. He told me that I was to use them if I loved you and wanted to marry you. He gave us his blessing." She put her hand on his lips stopping his speech. She was more confused now that he began telling her this unbelievable tale.

"What do you mean he gave us his blessing? How is that possible? How could he have known that we would fall in love and want to get married? Please don't lie to me Erik, this isn't funny?"

"I'm not lying to you Amalie. If you want to see the letter it is upstairs in the top drawer of my armoire. You may read it anytime you wish," he offered. She quickly stood up, walked out of the room and returned after a few minutes with the letter. She sat on the sofa and read it not once but twice. She was surprised at what she read. How did her father know that she would fall in love with him? Why did he pick him for her? Why did he think Erik would fall in love with her? None of it made any sense but somehow her father felt strongly enough about his feelings to put it on paper and to arrange the series of events that had led them to this moment.

She sat in a state of shock and he sat with her, holding her hand to comfort her and assure her that everything would be fine. "Did you know that my father wanted me to meet you?" He shook his head and then said, "When I read the letter, it was the first time I had any knowledge of his plans. I'm as shocked as you are. However his plans may have turned out, we came to our destination of our own accord Amalie."

"I know Erik, I know. But to think that my father somehow knew years ago that if we had only been introduced we'd have fallen in love and married; well, it's unbelievable."

"Amalie, he didn't know. Your father *hoped* and *prayed* for us to fall in love and marry but he didn't *know* it would happen. He said as much in the letter. I'm just happy to know that he gives us his blessing, aren't you?" He could tell that her mind was trying to logically sort out all of the details of her father's letter. It pained him to see her so tormented by something she would never be able to explain.

"I know it shouldn't matter, but why didn't he tell me that he thought you'd be the perfect companion for me? I had thought we were able to talk about everything and now I find out that he was keeping secrets from me." She began to pace around the room. Walking usually helped her to think but at this moment even pacing didn't help clear her mind.

"Amalie, when it comes to matters of the heart no one can tell someone that they're perfect for each other. I think your father was wise not to tell you. It has been my experience that when someone tells us something is good for us we usually choose the opposite because we want to be able to make our own choices. I think that is why your father didn't tell you or me for that matter. He wanted it to be your choice to love me as well as my choice to love you. Your father was always sensible and fair when it came to matters of the heart. That is how he and I became friends, remember?"

His words were full of truth. She knew that her father was not the kind to force her into something she didn't want to do and he also knew how independent she was. He was right to assume that her father wouldn't tell her for fear that his prayers and hopes wouldn't come true if he did.

"I'm so glad I have you to unravel my confused thoughts. My father was right; you are the perfect companion for me." Her eyes began to tear up as she hugged him. She knew in her heart that no matter when they would have met they would have always fallen in love with each other. She wished her mother and father would've been there to see how happy she was. "I love you and I want us to be married as soon as possible."

"What are you saying, Amalie?" He pulled back from her embrace to look at her.

"I'm saying that as soon as we can get Reverend Troudeaux to come to the house and agree to perform the ceremony, we should get married. No guests other than Chester and Meg, no reception and a honeymoon here at the house."

He held her chin in his hand and gazed into her eyes that were full of tears. "Are you sure, Amalie? I want you to have the wedding you've always dreamed of having and if it takes time to plan it, then we can wait."

"I'm going to have the wedding of my dreams. You are all that was missing and now that I have you, any wedding I plan will be the one I've always dreamed of having." She smiled and then kissed him.

"You are full of surprises, Amalie. Then I guess it is settled. We'll marry as soon as the Reverend is available."

"I'll ask Chester to take us into the village tomorrow morning to see him."

"You want me to go into the village with you?" he inquired.

"Of course, the Reverend will want to meet the man I'm going to marry. He won't marry us unless he does. I think it's time for you to stop hiding. After all, with the mask my father made you, your differences are hardly noticeable."

"If you think it will be fine, then I'll go with you. Remember, not everyone thinks like you do. You may hear some things when we're out together that may be hurtful. Don't let it bother you. My ears have grown accustomed to such language. Unfortunately, ignorant people tend to say unspeakable things about things they have no knowledge about."

"I too have heard unspeakable things. Remember my mother's accident let me experience all of that."

"Then I guess we'll be quite a sight when we go into the village tomorrow."

"I have one more request Erik. I want to be married in the church. Father and Mother would have wanted it that way and...." He interrupted her, "I want it that way too. After all, I believe it is God who has brought us together. We *should* marry in the church."

"Thank you Erik. I know in my heart that this was all God's plan too." She kissed him on the cheek and walked toward the doors of the drawing room.

"Amalie, aren't you forgetting something?"

"Not anything I can remember. Why do you ask?"

"Don't you want to read the letter your father left us? I have it here in my coat pocket." He produced the letter and handed it to her. She looked at the handwriting, recognizing it to be her father's. She took Erik's hand and placed the letter into it. "Will you read it to me? I don't think my nerves can take reading it right now."

"Of course I'll read it to you." He opened it up, pulled the letter out and began to read.

> *Dear Amalie and Erik,*
>
> *I will assume that the two of you are engaged to be married and if I were there I would hug both of you. It was always my hope that the two of you would find love in this world, but it was only during my last years of life that I prayed that you would find love with each other. I have no real reasons or explanations as to why I prayed for it other than that I loved you both so much that I wanted the best for each of you. Erik, in my years of writing to you, I learned many things about your character. Naturally I knew your character, Amalie. As the years went by I realized that the best in one of you was what was lacking in the other, therefore together you would complete each other, as Louise and I did all those years ago.*
>
> *I have no further instructions for either of you except to love each other as if every day could be your last, honor God, do His work and He will bless you as He always blessed me and Louise. And the most important thing to remember is to fill your lives with laughter, joy, music and children. You will both make wonderful parents.*
>
> *Amalie, you were the best part of your mother and me. Erik, you were one of my best and truest friends. Remember, love is the only gift that no one minds having returned. So give it freely and hope that it is always returned to you.*
>
> *Congratulations on your impending wedding. I love you both.*
> *Your Loving Father,*
> *Gaston*

He attempted to hand the letter to her but she shook her head waving him off. She had a few tears streaming down her cheeks. She could hardly look at him. He took the letter, folded it up and returned it to its envelope.

"Is there something wrong Amalie?" He waited for her to answer.

"No, it's just that those are the last words my father ever wrote to me; to us. I suppose he is truly gone now." Another tear streamed down her face.

"He will always be here, as your mother will always be here as long as we remember them." He pulled her head to his chest and put his arms around her. They stood there entwined in each others arms for a few minutes. He kissed her on the forehead and looked into her beautiful brown eyes. "Are you going to be all right?"

"Yes, I'll be fine." She wiped the tears from her face and walked toward the drawing room doors once more. "I'd better catch Chester before he leaves. I want to make sure he hitches the horses to the coach first thing in the morning."

He thought about offering to go to the stable for her but he decided that she probably needed to walk and get some fresh air. The events of the past few hours were a lot to process and just as he needed some time to realize what had transpired, he knew she would need time alone to do the same.

The Reverend's Instructions

Chester and Meg waited at the nearby bakery as Amalie and Erik spoke with Reverend Troudeaux inside the church. Reverend Troudeaux was an older man in his sixties and had been the Girault's spiritual leader for eleven years. He knew the family well and wanted what was best for Amalie. It was expected that the Reverend wanted to know more about Erik and about what kind of man he was. She told him the same story she had told Frederic and Anna on Christmas Day. She felt horrible not telling the truth to the Reverend about who Erik had been in the past but she figured that God already knew who he was and He was the only one that really needed to know. Erik spoke openly about his newfound faith in God and his honesty about it appeared to win the Reverend over. Erik's manners and humility were noted by the Reverend as well as his eagerness to listen to everything he was saying to them. They spoke to the Reverend for over an hour and when they were finished the Reverend couldn't find any reason that they shouldn't be married.

"Erik and Amalie, I'd like to see the two of you in services regularly once you're married. It is important that God is always kept in your marriage." Erik nodded in agreement as he shook the Reverend's hand.

"Yes, Reverend, I'll make sure that we're both here every Sunday."

"Then I'll see you both in six days. I'm so happy for you, Amalie. Your parents were wonderful people. I'm so sorry that things turned out the way they did. I continue to pray that people will look past the outer appearances of others but it seems that the world is full of prejudices that even my prayers can't erase."

"Thank you for your empathy Reverend. The world is not all lost; there are people that *do* look past the appearances of others. I believe God has heard your prayers and is answering them. You may not be able to see the results of them immediately or directly but I know in my heart that He *is* answering them." She smiled at the Reverend, reassuring him that she hadn't given up hope.

"Your faith is strong Amalie. I know that God will certainly bless this marriage." His eyes darted from Erik to Amalie and then back to Erik. "And you, young man are going to marry one of the best doctors that I know. She was the only doctor I would trust when I broke my arm two years ago. I'd fallen down the church steps after services one morning and she was behind me. She rushed to my aid like a good doctor should. Yes, she cared for me like no other doctor ever has. Even came to my house to check up on me." The Reverend patted Erik on the shoulder. "She is a wonderful woman. I can tell by the way you look at her that you love her very much but remember, sometimes love isn't always enough. Loving someone is more than just having feelings of love. Loving someone is the decision to do so even when there are times you may be disappointed, angered or frustrated with that person. Love is action!" The Reverend raised his arm, pointing his finger toward the ceiling. "Remember that Erik and you too Amalie. Love is not a feeling; it is a call for actions that transcend the feelings we have for someone. If you remember that, then you should always be able to love each other, no matter the circumstances."

The Reverend walked them to the door of the church and watched as they boarded the coach. They were glad that he'd be able to perform the ceremony soon. However, Erik was very perplexed by the Reverend's last instructions. He'd never heard anyone speak about love in such a manner. He agreed with what the Reverend had said but he could never imagine Amalie not being loveable. She was so perfect to him even with all of her obvious flaws he couldn't imagine not ever being able to feel love for her. His curiosity as to why the Reverend would make such a point prompted him to ask, "Why do you think the Reverend made such an effort to tell us that love isn't just a feeling but an action?"

"I'm not sure. My explanation for his words would only be a guess and it's probably not even close to what he wanted us to learn from it."

"That's quite all right. I'll take your guess over my assumption."

"I suppose that he wants us to remember that life is not always easy and that we, as people, are not perfect. This can make it hard for us to show our love sometimes. So, we must always try to show our love even when we don't feel like it." She smiled and then took his hand in hers, holding it gently. "I remember my mother telling me that she and Father made it a habit to always spend the last hour of every day talking to each other. She said that sometimes married couples take each other for granted and forget to talk to each other about even the simplest of things. Their talks reminded her of the reasons she married my father."

She looked at him as the coach turned down the country road that led to the house. "I guess he was trying to make sure we knew that feeling love is different than the action of loving someone. When we choose to do so in the absence of those feelings it will help remind us of why we loved each other in the first place. Does that make sense?"

"It makes perfect sense, Amalie. Right now, I'm going to make love an action." He leaned over and kissed her passionately. She fell limp in his embrace but then realizing that Meg could be watching, she gently pushed him away.

"Erik, you must control yourself." She tried to scold him but laughed instead.

"It's hard to control my love for you when you show your analytical capabilities as you have just done." He liked to tease her about her aptitude for abstract thought because she rarely showed this side of herself to him. She was very modest when it came to any of the talents she possessed and didn't like to flaunt them only to prove that she had them. Most men would've been threatened by her intelligence but he welcomed it from the day he met her. He had no need for mindless women who could only hold a conversation about fashion or social engagements. He needed someone who could provoke thought and give her opinion without any inhibitions or fears. She was definitely capable of doing all of these things and it was almost an aphrodisiac for him when she did.

"You're impossible Erik Geraurd. I know that life with you will never be boring. Everything you say and do is a surprise; a welcomed surprise but all the same a surprise." She held his hand and laughed as she laid her head on his shoulder.

"Did you realize that we'll be getting married on New Year's Day?" he asked.

"I hadn't thought about it but I guess you're right and I think it is only right that we do. A new year to start our new life together, it's perfect." She glanced up at him and smiled.

"Yes it is, just like you," he said as he kissed her on the forehead.

The rest of the ride home they sat quietly holding each other. They sat together watching the scenery of the countryside bounce by through the windows of the coach. The motion was relaxing and Amalie fell asleep with her head on his shoulder. They reached the house and Chester opened the coach door. As he did he noticed that they were both asleep. He tapped Erik on the arm, waking him gently. Erik, not wanting to wake Amalie, gently picked her up, carried her out of the coach and into the house. Meg and Chester followed. He took her upstairs and placed her in her bed. Meg waved Erik out of the room and she took over, removing her shoes and covering her up.

Chester was waiting for Erik downstairs. "Is she ill?" he asked with concern in his voice.

"She is very tired Chester. She has had a lot happen in the past few days."

Meg had joined them in the great room and had taken a seat on the sofa. "Erik, when is the wedding going to take place?"

"We'll be getting married on New Year's Day at four o'clock in the church. Will you both be able to be there?" He inquired not knowing what the answer would be.

"Of course, we will. After all, I'm giving the bride away. Didn't she tell you?" Chester asked.

"No she didn't but we really haven't had time to discuss the details. That is wonderful Chester. Meg, I assume that means you'll be there as well?"

"I wouldn't miss it, Erik. She's been like a daughter to me and you have been like a son. Do you need my help with any of the preparations for the wedding?"

"I believe you will have to discuss that with Amalie. I know that she isn't planning anything extravagant but I would assume she'll still need some help." He walked over to Meg and took her hands in his. "I'm glad that she has you to help her. She's been missing her mother a lot lately and I know having you here to help will make it easier for her."

"I'm glad that I can help. Do you think she'd mind if I sent word to Isabel and Peter about the wedding? I know Isabel considers Amalie to be her sister in many ways and would want to be here for her. They are in Paris visiting Peter's family and they could possibly make it to the wedding. What do you think?"

"I think that it is a wonderful idea Meg. I know she would love that. It will be our surprise." Erik's eyes sparkled and Meg could tell that he wanted what was best for Amalie. "I would invite Frederic and Anna but I don't think word would get to them in time." She looked at Erik's face, noticing he wasn't as thrilled at this particular suggestion she had made. "I know that she told you about their past together and although I love my son very much, I wouldn't want to ruin your wedding day only to save Frederic's feelings from harm. He and Anna are best left in London for this blessed event. I'll send word after you're married, and then there will be nothing he can do to stop it."

Erik was confused by her last comment. "Why would Frederic want to keep us from getting married? What consequence is it to him?"

"Oh Erik, there are many things you don't know about our son." She quickly glanced at Chester. "He may have convinced himself that he didn't love Amalie, but a mother knows things about her children. I know that even though he married another he still has feelings for your Amalie. I saw the way he looked at the two of you when he was here. He isn't usually so rude to strangers but when Amalie introduced you as her suitor that was when I saw the jealousy come out." Meg led Erik to the sofa and they sat down. "He loves Anna but sometimes loving someone isn't enough, especially when you feel like you made the wrong choice about who you chose to love."

Chester walked over to the fireplace, sat on the hearth and joined the conversation. "You see Erik, it isn't that Frederic wants her for himself, he just doesn't want you to have her. He doesn't think you're good enough for her and said as much on Christmas Day after we left the house. His life is all about appearances and somehow feels slighted that she would choose someone who looks like you to court her. If he found out that you were to be married, there is no telling what he might do. He is not a rational person and tends to act without considering the consequences of his actions or his words for that matter."

Erik wasn't sure whether he should thank them for sharing this information or to wish that he didn't know any of it at all. "Does Amalie know these things about Frederic?" Erik asked.

Meg looked at Chester not knowing whether he would answer the question or if she should. Meg nodded to Chester for him to do the honors and Chester obliged. "She knows that he is not a rational person and that he acts out of impulse but as far as him not wanting you two to be married or his opinion that you aren't good enough for her; no, she doesn't know anything about that."

"How does she know about his irrational actions? Did he do something to her?"

"He didn't do anything to *her* but she witnessed him slapping Anna one night at a social gathering in Paris. He didn't think that anyone was around to see it but you know how Amalie is so very good at being undetected in a room. He apparently had noticed Anna speaking to another man. She was laughing and it looked to Frederic that she was having a wonderful time; too much of a wonderful time according to him. He didn't like it and so he pulled her into one of the rooms off of the main ball room. Amalie followed them and she witnessed his tongue lashing and his abuse. Amalie found out later that the man she was speaking with was a well-known attorney in London and she was trying to get him to donate money to one of the many charities for which Anna helps with raising funds. She was also putting in a good word for her husband." Chester paused to catch his breath and then continued. "She checked on Anna to make sure she wasn't hurt. She wanted to confront Frederic but Anna wouldn't let her. She said that it was the only time he'd ever done something like that. I only wished that I believed it. Frederic has quite a temper, especially when he doesn't get his way or he feels threatened."

Erik couldn't believe what he was hearing but he almost felt sorry for him. He too, had once been where Frederic had been. It amazed Erik that someone who he perceived to have everything could act in such a manner. He had lashed out to preserve his own life; Frederic lashed out because of fear of losing control or because of his fear of what other people thought. They were the same in many ways but their motives were very different. Erik wished only to control what he had to in order to survive and to be able to do the things he loved to do. Yes, there were times when his motives weren't so honorable. He regretted that very much. He just hoped that he wouldn't ever do anything like he had done ever again. It was clear now that even people that had good lives could do bad things and even Erik wasn't immune to it *not* happening again.

"I can't judge your son's actions after the life that I've lived. He and I are a lot alike in many ways."

Meg put her hand on his shoulder, looking him in the eye. "Yes, you are but *you* have confessed your wrong doings and have expressed sincere remorse for them. You also told us about them even when you didn't have to do so. Our son unfortunately sees himself as being above all of that and takes no responsibility for anything that he does wrong, only right." Erik could see the disappointment in Meg's face at her son's choices. He wished that he could take away her sorrow but knew that only Frederic could do that. "Should I be worried after we're married?" His concern for their safety grew and could be detected in his voice.

"No, No, Erik. Frederic hasn't done anything like that for years; at least we don't believe he has. Besides he wouldn't do anything to jeopardize his career and status in Paris. If he comes to Trie-Chateau, his mother and I will deal with him. We are, after all, still his parents and have some, although it be very little, influence over him." Chester laughed a little at his own words. "We didn't mean to scare you. We just wanted you to be aware of certain things. Please don't tell Amalie any of this, she'll worry and it will ruin her wedding day. I wouldn't want anything to spoil it for her. Don't you agree?"

"Yes, I agree. There's no need to upset here when there's no real threat of anything happening." Erik rose from the sofa, as did Meg. Chester took his wife's hand and Erik walked them to the front door.

"Tell Amalie that I'll be by in the morning to find out what she needs my help with for the wedding," Meg reminded Erik.

They said good-bye and Erik closed the door. The conversation about Frederic made him uneasy and he needed something to calm him. He walked into the study, sat at Gaston's desk and reached for the Bible that was in front of him. He began reading in the book of Psalms which was one of Gaston's favorites and had become Erik's. He read from Chapter thirty-seven verse one. "*Fret not thyself because of evildoers, neither be thou envious against the workers of iniquity. For they shall soon be cut down like the grass, and wither as the green herb. Trust in the Lord, and do good; so shalt thou dwell in the land, and verily thou shalt be fed. Delight thyself also in the Lord; and he shall give thee the desires of thine heart.*" He continued to read the entire passage until he reached Psalms thirty-eight. His heart and his mind were cleared and his worry had subsided. He was reassured by the words of David that God would take care of him against evil people and even thoughts of doing evil things. He would continue to seek God's guidance and not act alone as he had done so frequently in his past.

No Longer Two

New Year's Day had come and it was to be one of the most memorable days of Amalie's life. She and Erik had stayed up until midnight to welcome the New Year so they didn't wake on New Year's Day until mid-morning. She was trying her best not to overwhelm herself with all of the tasks she hadn't completed for the wedding. She knew that Meg would soon be there to help her. Erik had told her that he'd be in the study reading and may go down to the cave to work for a short time. He was just as nervous about getting married as she was but he didn't want her to see it.

It was noon and she was upstairs going through her armoire looking for her stockings. She had already laid out the items that she would wear underneath her wedding gown. Her mother's wedding dress was beautiful. It was made from white crepe backed silk satin charmeuse which would drape nicely revealing her figure. There were forty-four buttons that went up the back and eight buttons on each sleeve. The gown had no train but fell all the way to the floor. It had beautiful lace that created the puff sleeves, neckline and back which would cover her and leave Erik wanting more. Her mother's dress was indeed a work of art and she couldn't wait to put it on and walk down the aisle to be with her future husband. As she continued to look for her stockings she heard a voice from downstairs calling to her. It was Erik. She walked out of her room and stood at the top of the stairs noticing that Meg was not alone. Chester, Peter, Isabel and the girls were with her. She ran down the stairs. Isabel met her at the last step and hugged her.

"I'm so glad that you're all here. How did you know?" She could hardly catch her breath.

"Mother sent word to us since we were in Paris visiting with Peter's family. I couldn't let my little sister get married without me." She laughed and then hugged Amalie again.

"I can't take all of the credit for this happy reunion," Meg interrupted, "Erik is as guilty as I am."

Erik took great joy in seeing his bride-to-be so happy. "I'm guilty as charged." He walked over to her and kissed her on the cheek. "I'm so glad that you approve."

"Has everyone been introduced to you yet?" she asked him.

"Yes, they have and I'm very glad to meet my new family, especially these two beautiful little girls." Erik smiled at them as he gave his compliment and they hid themselves behind their mother's skirt.

Amalie agreed. "They *are* beautiful Isabel and they have grown so much since the last time you visited."

"Peter has offered to help me get ready for the wedding while Meg and Isabel help you." he explained to her.

"I think that's a wonderful idea." Amalie walked over to Peter and hugged him. "Thank you. I knew the day that Isabel married you she had picked a man of good character."

"I'll do my best to make sure that he is there on time."

"We aren't riding to the church together?" Amalie asked with surprise in her voice.

Isabel took Amalie by the hand. "Of course not Amalie, it is bad luck for the groom to see the bride in her dress before she walks down the aisle. You'll go to the church in our coach and Erik, Father and Peter will come in your coach. Our driver will get us there on time."

Amalie was being scurried up the stairs by Meg and Isabel while the girls followed behind them. "It's almost time for us to go and you're still not dressed Amalie. We have your hair to do and where did you put the bouquet?"

Peter slapped Erik on the back and laughed. "Aren't you glad that I'm the one helping you and not them?"

Erik smiled and knew immediately that he liked Peter even though he knew very little about him. The fact that he hadn't commented on his mask made him more likeable than his brother-in-law, Frederic.

"Yes, I am. I would think that it will take me less time to dress for this occasion so what would you gentlemen say about having a drink while we get better acquainted?" Erik led them into the study where Gaston had been known to keep several bottles of brandy. He poured three glasses and handed them out. Peter raised his glass and said, "A toast: To Erik and Amalie; may their love never waiver and their troubles be few."

"Here, Here," shouted Chester. Erik was delighted at how easily Peter had transitioned from stranger to friend.

"Thank you, Peter," Erik said expressing his thoughts with great sincerity.

"You're welcome. I feel that I owe you a great deal of gratitude today."

"Why is that?" Erik asked.

"You're not only marrying someone I have grown to love as a sister but in doing so you have managed to do the one thing that I've never been able to do." He paused, took a drink of his brandy and then continued. "You have single handedly wounded, if not destroyed Frederic's ego."

"And how might I have done that?" Erik inquired. Chester glanced at Peter and then at Erik.

"You and Amalie getting married will prove to Frederic that she hasn't been pining away for him all of these years. He really thought that she would wait for him forever and that *that* was why she hadn't married. I can't wait to see the look on his face when he gets the news." Peter laughed almost uncontrollably. "You did invite the poor man didn't you?" Erik was surprised that he would say such things in front of Chester about his only son. However, Chester didn't defend him either so it must not have upset him.

"No we didn't. Meg and Chester thought it best not to have them attend and I agreed. Amalie doesn't need any distractions today. Besides, I don't harbor any ill wishes toward Frederic. What good would it do to provoke him? "

"Oh you'll learn that it doesn't matter whether you provoke him or not. When he feels like he has lost the battle, the war will begin. However, there is nothing he can do to win the battle or the war where Amalie is concerned. You'll have cleared the battlefield and declared victory the moment you kiss the bride." Peter continued to drink his brandy and laugh heartily at Frederic's expense.

"I guess I must be missing something. Amalie told me that you and Frederic got along well with one another." He took a drink from his glass. "Is that not so?"

"Erik, Peter and Frederic are family so they put their differences aside for the family's sake but if they weren't family, I doubt that they'd even look at each other while crossing the street." Chester took the decanter and poured more brandy into his glass. "Of course, Peter didn't always feel that way about Frederic but as Meg and I have informed you, he has changed and not for the better. Believe me, none of us wishes anything bad to happen to him, we only wish for him to share that same sentiment when it comes to all of us."

"So what you are saying is that he has brought this upon himself." Erik took the decanter from Chester, pouring more into his glass and Peter's.

Chester nodded and raised his glass. "Yes Erik. *That* is what I'm saying."

"Peter, if you would've met me on the street before meeting me today, would *you* have looked at *me*?" Erik's question caught Peter and Chester off guard.

"Erik, it would be hard *not* to look at you. Your mask tends to draw a person's eyes to you. Now whether or not I would speak to you, now that is the real question for which you seek an answer." He continued to drink his brandy and then took a seat in one of the chairs. "Honestly, I don't know that I have one. Being that I've never met anyone who wore a mask, I believe that I'd simply tip my hat to be polite and continue on my way. However, if you spoke to me first, I wouldn't hesitate to carry on a conversation with you. Your mask doesn't strike fear into me nor does what may be behind it. I believe curiosity is what your mask evokes from most people." He raised his glass, drank the last of it and put his glass on the table.

"Thank you for your honesty. I'm sure that whether we are to be considered family or not, you and I are destined to be good friends. We men of good character must stick together after all." Erik finished his drink and then put his glass on the table too.

"We should probably get you ready for your plunge into matrimony. We have only an hour and a half before the ceremony and my wife has committed me to getting you there on time," Peter said as he rose from his chair. As he walked Erik to the door he put his hand on his shoulder and said, "Your life is about to change my friend, I hope you are prepared." He said with seriousness in his voice that quickly turned to laughter.

Peter's friendliness toward him wasn't expected but welcomed. He had imagined that this is how Gaston would have spoken to him had he been around to see this day come. He didn't want to think about the possibility of Peter's actions and words not being genuine so he would enjoy it until he was proven otherwise.

In the room down the hall Isabel was helping Amalie with her hair. After they finished, it was time to put on her wedding dress. When they were finished buttoning all of the buttons they took a step back and marveled at how beautiful she looked. The time was nearing for them to make their departure from the house so Isabel went down the hall to see if the men had left. She found Erik's room empty and the house was quiet except for the girls playing in Amalie's room. They packed up everything they'd need and escorted Amalie to the coach. She was excited but nervous. She never dreamed she'd be getting married a year ago when she met Erik. And yet, here she was about to marry the man she swore she was only helping because of a promise she had made to her dying father. She knew now that there were no guarantees in life especially when it came to matters of the heart. Her father had been right; choosing someone to love was best left to the heart and not to the eyes.

They arrived at the church with only minutes to spare. The girls, Isabel and Meg took their places next to Peter in the pews of the church and Chester stayed with Amalie in the foyer awaiting the cue from the pianist. Erik and the Reverend Troudeaux stood at the front of the church waiting for her entrance. The music began and Amalie with Chester escorting her appeared. His heart began to race at the sight of his bride. She was a vision of grace and beauty. He'd never seen her look more beautiful. Her bouquet was one white rose surrounded by four red roses tied with pink ribbons. Her face was shielded by a veil but he could see her smile which let him know that there was no need to be nervous.

The ceremony began as most wedding ceremonies did. Chester gave Amalie to Erik and took a seat next to Meg who was already crying. They faced each other as they repeated their vows. She placed her father's ring on Erik's finger and then he placed Amalie's mother's ring on her finger. The Reverend Troudeaux pronounced them man and wife. Then he lifted her veil and after searching her brown eyes for any signs of regret, pulled her to him and kissed her passionately. The Reverend then presented them to their friends that had come to witness the event. As they walked to the back of the church, Amalie and Erik stopped to say good-bye and thank each of them for making their day so special. Peter shook Erik's hand very firmly and then gave him a brotherly hug.

"Welcome to the family. My driver will take you and Amalie back to the house. I'll take your coach to Chester's house and return it in the morning," Peter told him. Peter kissed Amalie on the cheek and whispered in her ear, "You are a beautiful bride."

They all watched as they boarded the coach. Amalie threw her bouquet out of the coach window and little Bella caught it. Everyone began to laugh. "It will be a while before you have any need for that young lady," Peter told his daughter as he took it from her and handed it to Isabel. He leaned over and kissed his wife. "You're as beautiful as the day I married you."

"Thank you. Now I think that we need to get the girls to the house for something to eat." She took his hand and held it tightly as they walked to the coach. "I'm so happy for Amalie... and Erik too. He seems to be a good man."

"Yes he does. I could only find one thing I didn't like about him today," Peter stated.

"And what was that," Isabel asked.

"That he didn't hold any ill will toward your brother."

"Now Peter, let's not spoil the day with talk of Frederic. Maybe Erik wanted to give you a good first impression. After everything that Mother told me Frederic said to him, I can't imagine him not holding any ill will toward him. Frederic has been acting more spoiled than usual lately. I hope that when he finds out that Amalie is a married woman that his ego survives the blow."

"I doubt you'll have to worry about that. If anyone can survive a blow to his ego, it is your brother," Peter said as he rolled his eyes.

The ride back to the house felt like it would go on forever. Erik couldn't wait to get his bride home and start their new lives together as man and wife. She couldn't take his eyes off of him and he couldn't keep himself from kissing her over and over again. She knew that tonight would be the first time she would ever give herself to any man but wondered if Erik had ever been with a woman. She was nervous about her wedding night and hoped that he was too, at least then she wouldn't be alone in her insecurity.

The coach reached the house and Charles, the driver, opened the door to let them out. He smiled at them as he caught them in a tender embrace inside the coach. "I'm sorry, Monsieur, I didn't know...." Charles' words stumbled out of his mouth as he tried to hide his embarrassment of catching them in such an intimate moment.

"It's quite all right Charles. Thank you for bringing us home." Erik shook his hand and Amalie thanked him too.

Erik took the key to the house and unlocked it, pushing the door open. Then he picked her up and carried her over the threshold. She shut the door with her hand as he passed through the doorway. He set her down gently and then kissed her on her forehead. "Welcome home Madame Geraurd. I love you Amalie. Today a dream that I never saw coming true has been granted to me because of your love."

"I love you too." She threw her arms around him and kissed him passionately on his lips. They became entwined in each others arms and the passion that they felt for each other the night he proposed once again surfaced but this time there was no reason to dismiss their urges. He picked her up, carried her up the stairs and into her room which was now to be their room. After he set her down, she looked in his eyes and saw that they were full of lust and passion meant only for her. She began unbuttoning the buttons on the sleeves of her wedding gown and Erik began unbuttoning the buttons that ran down the back of her gown. His hands were big and were awkward with the buttons. He was becoming frustrated with them as he got half of them unbuttoned. She could hear the frustration in the groans as he tried to get them unfastened.

"Erik, you can stop now. I only need it to be unbuttoned partially to step out of it."

"Thank goodness, I thought that our wedding night would be spent trying to get you out of this dress." He laughed in spite of the nervousness he was feeling on top of the excitement. This was the first time he was to ever be with a woman and was not sure that he'd live up to her expectations.

She shimmied out of the dress which she let fall to the floor leaving her standing only in her corset and stockings. Erik couldn't take his eyes off her as he took off his coat, then his vest and ascot. She approached him and put her hands on his mask, removing it from his face. She let it drop onto her wedding dress while she continued to caress his entire face with her hands, tracing every part of his flawed flesh with her fingers and then with her lips. He never dreamed that anyone could make him glad to have the displeasing mark upon his face but she made him feel like it wasn't something to loath but cherish for it was her touch that made it disappear leaving only the scar of her soft touch in its place. She unbuttoned his shirt and removed it from him leaving him bare-chested. She slid her hands down his sinewy chest and she could feel his heart beating quickly. He loosened her corset from her curvaceous body, watching it fall to the floor while he kissed her neck and worked his way down. He laid her on the bed as his hands glided across her bare back and then over her thighs as he unhooked her stockings from the garter that held them in place. He pressed his chest against her breast as he kissed her lips and his hands traced every inch of her body as if he were memorizing every part. He stopped to look into her eyes for a moment to assure himself that he was not dreaming. He whispered softly to her as he lay there looking at her, "Tonight we are no longer two; we are one for eternity, until death separates us. I love you and I'll never leave you." He kissed her so passionately that the force of his lips on hers caused her to swoon. He took her into his arms and made love to her for the first time. It was a night of passion and love; a night that the two of them would never forget.

You Don't Think.....

S ix months had passed since they had married and Erik had all but completed the sanctuary in the cave. Amalie had finished the painting that she had started and was now readying it to be hung in the cave. It was a marvelous room and the painting was just as extraordinary. She had painted a picture of a cross that had sunlight streaming down upon it from a break in the clouds that were above it. At the base of the cross she had written the word "Sins". Her father had always told her that Jesus had laid their sins at the foot of the cross and that is where they would stay for eternity. She had begun painting it for her father before he died but since his death she couldn't bring herself to finish it. After she brought Erik to live at the house and he revealed her father's plans for the cave, she decided it was time to finish it, if not for herself then in memory of her father.

Erik enjoyed working down in the cave but his work was near completion. He wondered what he'd do to keep busy after it was done. He thought maybe he would try to return to his earlier profession of being a building contractor but he didn't know how he'd be able to do that living so far from Paris. It had crossed his mind that perhaps it was time for them to move somewhere that things weren't so familiar and where they could both create a life together that they could call their own. He feared, however, that she wouldn't want to leave her childhood home. Peter had extended them an offer to come visit in London but he hadn't told her because he knew he couldn't leave until the room was finished. He loved living at the Girault family home but not having anything to occupy his time would soon create a boredom that even he did not want to face.

One afternoon she had gone to the cave to see the progress that he was making and to take him something to eat. He had been working before sunrise until sunset the last few days. She was becoming lonely at the house and needed to see him even though he was not particularly happy when she came down to the cave uninvited. It wasn't that he didn't want to see her it was just that he wanted the room to be a surprise. This day would turn out to be quite different from others when she came to visit. She was almost to the entrance to the cave from the tunnel and she became dizzy, her head began to swoon and her stomach churned. She set the basket of food on the ground and leaned up against the wall. She had been having spells like this one off and on for over three weeks but this time her stomach was more upset than usual. She left the basket and made her way into the cave while she called to him.

"Erik, where are you? I need you to…," and her voice faded. Erik found her next to a barrel regurgitating her breakfast. Her face was pale and he was concerned after seeing her appearance. "What's wrong? Tell me what you need me to do." He turned a bucket over for her to sit on and helped her take a seat.

"I need some water. Can you get me some water?" He went to his water barrel, filled his tin cup and brought it to her.

"Do I need to go get a doctor, Amalie?" He asked in his panicked voice forgetting that she *was* a doctor.

"No, I don't need a doctor at least not today."

"What do you mean? You're obviously not well?" He held her hand and then kissed her forehead. "Do I need to carry you back to the house?

"My condition isn't fatal. I can walk back to the house but I'd love it if you would accompany me." She kissed him on the cheek as she smiled at him. "I've been feeling like this for some time now but I wanted to be sure before I told you."

"Told me what Amalie?" He inquired not understanding.

"I'll have to have it confirmed by another doctor, of course, but I believe the illness I have is called morning sickness and the only thing that causes it is being pregnant." She smiled at him and watched his face for his reaction. His eyes sparkled and the expression on his face changed from worry to elation. He pulled her face to his and kissed her.

"You're with child; our child? Do you know what this means?" He put his hand on her neck and kissed her again. "It means I'm going to be a father."

"Yes, and it means I'm going to be a mother." She smiled at him and then hugged him tightly.

"How long until he or she is born, Amalie?"

"I would say that I'm only a month or two into my pregnancy, so next spring would probably be my guess. I'll need to go see the doctor so that he can verify it though."

He began pacing around the area where she sat. She could see that he had questions or concerns about what she had just told him. His face was easily read when he had doubts in his mind. She rose from where she had been seated on the bucket and walked over to him, placing her hand on his arm and turning him to face her.

"Are you happy about having a baby?"

"Yes, but do you think…" He couldn't finish his words before he was overcome with emotion. His eyes filled with tears and she knew what he was concerned about.

"Do I think that the baby will be born with a birthmark like yours?" She looked in his blue eyes as she completed his question.

"Yes, Amalie….do you?"

"Anything is possible Erik. It is possible that this child won't have a birthmark like yours and then again this child *could* have a birthmark like yours. It doesn't matter what this child looks like I'll love it and so will you." She put her hand on his disfigured cheek. "A birthmark can't keep someone from being happy or loved. You are proof of that."

"No my love, you're the one that has made my being loved possible, not me. I don't know if there will ever be anyone in this world with a heart as big as yours to love a child that looks like me other than you."

"I'm not going to worry about things that haven't happened yet. I'm going to find the joy in our happy news and be glad that God is blessing us with a child. I was beginning to think I'd never get pregnant." She laughed at her own words and then kissed him on the cheek.

"It wasn't for lack of trying, that is for certain," he said as a smile returned to his face and they both laughed.

"I'm glad that you're feeling better. I'll walk you back to the house and tomorrow we'll go into the village to see the doctor." His hand met hers and they walked down the tunnel back to the house.

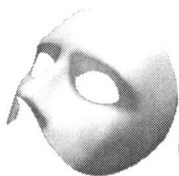

Suspect

$\mathcal{T}$he summer months came and went as the baby continued to grow inside of Amalie. He was becoming more and more protective of his wife and unborn child. He gave up the idea of the room being a surprise and insisted that she join him every afternoon while he worked. The day came that Gaston's *Room of Tranquility* was finished and he took great joy in telling her that it was complete. He had hung her painting so it was visible as you walked into the main room. It set the mood in the room as a place of reverence and worship; a holy place, a place of tranquility.

"Father would have loved it Erik. It looks exactly like his drawings. He was right when he told me that you were the only one that could bring his drawings to life." She walked around, looking at all of the furnishings and details he had added. The raised platform had two small steps that went up the front and a beautifully carved rail on either side. He had arranged the two small sofas that Gaston had drawn into his plans where they were facing each other and a nice rectangular coffee table was in the center of them. The lighting presented the biggest challenge but he had managed to find several kerosene chandeliers and light fixtures that illuminated the darkness. It was a masterpiece unlike anything she had ever seen.

"You've been quiet since we got here. Are you not pleased with your work?"

"I'm only as pleased as you are Amalie. I don't usually critique my own work but if you're happy, then I'm happy."

She put her arms around him, hugging him very gently and placing her head on his chest. "I'm very happy."

He kissed her on the forehead and hugged her tightly not wanting to let her go. With the room being completed it meant that he'd have more time to spend with her. They could finally start turning her studio into a nursery. His thoughts of moving to London had quickly disappeared after the news of the baby coming. He wasn't disappointed however;

he was actually excited about raising this child, his child, in a beautiful home in the country. Something he'd always wanted for himself but never had achieved. His child would have everything that he hadn't been afforded; especially love. After they finished turning down all of the lights they entered the tunnel with lanterns in hand and walked back up to the house.

They entered the study to find Chester and Meg waiting for them.

"What brings the two of you to the house this afternoon?" Erik asked as he closed the secret door.

"Amalie, Meg, do you mind leaving Erik and I to talk?" Amalie nodded her head in agreement and she and Meg exited the room.

"What is this all about Chester? Why can't you talk in front of Amalie?"

"I came to tell you that Frederic and Anna are coming for a visit in a week. I know that you don't hold any ill wishes toward him but in his last letter to Meg he was quite hostile about the fact that Amalie was having your child. It was bad enough to him that she married you but in his mind having your child is even a worse offense. He sees you as less than human and has assumed the worst of you. He wrote to Meg that he was close to proving that you were the man that was living beneath the Opera House. Although we know that to be true, I'd like to question him once he is here to find out what he knows and what he *thinks* he knows about the Opera Ghost. His actions as of late have been unpredictable. I only wanted to apprise you of the situation."

Erik rubbed his chin while pacing around the room. "I appreciate your letting me know that he will be visiting. I'll try to keep my wits about me and my tongue sharpened for a verbal dual if he shows up."

"I'm not worried about him hurting you with words. I fear that he may be coming to do some real physical harm this time. He is like a dog with a bone when he gets his mind set on something." Chester went to the cabinet where the brandy was stored. He pulled out two glasses, filled them and handed one to Erik.

"I don't suppose you know what evidence he thinks he has to prove that I'm the Opera Ghost?" Erik drank from his glass and then sat on the edge of the desk.

"He mentioned that he was going to visit that Persian gentleman that identified the body. However, he was having trouble locating him. This was about two weeks ago that Meg received that letter. Do you think that if he finds him he'll give him any information that will help Frederic?" Chester sat in the chair that was in front of the desk.

"It's possible that my friend, the Persian, may show him some of the papers and other items that I had sent to him but everything that Gaston ever wrote me I had burned long ago when I thought he had abandoned me. As far as being able to identify me by my face, the Persian never once laid eyes upon what I hid behind my mask. There was only one thing that Gaston had given me that I couldn't bring myself to get rid of and that was a small pick hammer. I used it for many things while living at the Opera House and don't recall the last time I held it in my hands or where I may have laid it." Erik took a drink of his brandy and then walked to the window behind the desk and looked at the picturesque view of trees and rolling hills.

"I'm probably wrong but I think that if there was any evidence connecting you to the Opera Ghost, the Inspector Magistrate's Office would have paid a visit already." Chester got up from his chair and retrieved the decanter from the cabinet. He filled his glass with more brandy and then returned to his seat.

Chester's assumption was not only correct but it also brought to mind that they'd already had a visit from the Inspector Magistrate's Office and Amalie was the one who had spoken to them. She assured him that they were only doing follow up interviews with the people that had been at the opera that night but Erik had sensed that evening that there was something she wasn't telling him. He barely knew her at the time so he didn't press her to tell him what they were really doing there. Chester didn't need to know what he knew so he carried on without mentioning it to him.

"You're probably right Chester. I wouldn't think that even with them having the hammer they would suspect that Amalie or I would have had anything to do with it. They would however have made an attempt to return it to its rightful owner though, wouldn't they?" Erik took another drink as he continued to look out the window.

"I'm quite certain that if the hammer is the evidence that my son thinks he has to prove you to be the Opera Ghost, we'll soon find out. He's not one for keeping quiet when he thinks he's about to prove someone wrong. I'll find out what he knows." He joined Erik in front of the window.

"I wouldn't be so sure of it Chester. He knows that you and I are friends. He can't risk letting you in on anything that might hurt me. He would be too afraid that you'd tell me." Erik finished his glass of brandy and set it on the desk. "No, I'll have to find out what he knows on my own."

"How do you intend to do that?" Chester inquired as he finished his glass of brandy.

"I haven't any idea. But if I'm going to protect my family from the likes of Frederic I'm certain that I'll figure something out." He put one hand on Chester's shoulder and shook his hand with his other. "Thank you for being such a good friend to me. I want you to know that I still don't wish any harm to come to your son but if it comes to it I may not have a choice in the matter."

"I understand Erik. You have to do what is required to protect your wife and child. I would do the same. He is my son but sometimes we have to choose between what is right and wrong no matter who is committing the offense. Just because he is my son doesn't mean that I should turn a blind eye to the pain and anguish he chooses to inflict on others." Chester put his hands on Erik's shoulders and looked him square in the eyes. "You do whatever is necessary to defend yourself and protect Amalie. If I didn't want you to be able to do that effectively I would not be standing here today."

Chester hugged Erik and his actions took Erik by surprise. He'd never witnessed this much emotion from Chester before now. He imagined that if his own father would've ever hugged him that this is what it would've felt like. It felt good to know that he now had a family that wasn't horrified at his appearance but chose to love him in spite of it. Although his past actions could be compared to those of Frederic they were willing to accept that he had changed and allowed him to continue to do so.

They opened the door to the study and exited the room. They found Meg and Amalie in the great room discussing names for the baby. Chester motioned to Meg that it was time to leave so she kissed Amalie good-bye and hugged Erik. They walked them to the door and watched the coach disappear down the country road.

"I don't suppose you are going to tell me what that was all about?" she asked him as they walked back into the great room.

"Chester doesn't think that I should but we promised we wouldn't keep secrets from each other." He stopped walking and grabbed her by the hands. "I'm going to tell you what this is all about but I don't want you to worry." She couldn't help but be concerned now that he told her not to be. He continued. "Frederic and Anna are coming for a visit soon and it seems that Frederic has been busy trying to convict me of being the Opera Ghost in his spare time. Obviously, he must be able to obtain certain information from officials due to his profession but he has written to Meg that he is close to proving it. I'm not sure what evidence he could possibly have to prove it but nonetheless, the threat is there."

"What evidence could he have?" she asked with visible concern in her eyes.

"I'm not sure but I have an idea about what he thinks he may have as evidence." He led her to the sofa and seated her. He sat next to her, taking her hands in his. "I'm going to ask you a question and I want you to tell me the truth. It doesn't matter what the answer is, I need to know the truth." His face became serious and she knew that she couldn't deny him what he wanted even if it hurt him.

"On the day that the Inspector Magistrate's Officers came to visit, were they only here to talk to you about what you saw on that night or were there other things they were inquiring about? Remember, no matter the answer I need you to tell me the truth." He looked into her eyes waiting for her answer.

"There was something else," she said with sadness in her voice. "They brought me something that they claimed to have found in one of the tunnels of the cellars."

"What was it Amalie? What did they bring you?" He was anxious to hear her answer.

"It was my father's small pick hammer. My mother had given it to him as a gift. He had told us that he lost it when he was working at the bakery. I was disappointed when they told me that you had it all along. I didn't want to tell you because I wasn't sure how you came to be in possession of it and I'm still not sure." His eyes sparkled and a smile appeared on his face. He leaned over and kissed her.

"Your father gave it to me Amalie. He wanted me to have it in exchange for my helping him complete his work in the bakery. He said that without me he wouldn't have ever been able to fulfill the obligations of his contract. I didn't want to take it but he insisted." He kissed her again. "I'm sure he didn't want to hurt your mother or you, which was why he told you that he had lost it." She smiled at his explanation. His assumption about her father telling them he had lost it to spare their feelings sounded a lot like what her father would've done. She knew that Erik hadn't taken it from him now and she could put her suspicions of such an act out of her mind.

"I'm sure you're right. I'm sorry that I didn't tell you about the gentlemen bringing it to the house but at that point in our relationship I wasn't ready to trust you."

"It's quite all right dear. I assumed as much. I'm just glad that you're in possession of the hammer now. However, I need to know why they were so willing to leave it with you?"

"What do you mean?" she asked with a confused look on her face.

"Well, it's obvious that they thought your father must have known the gentleman in the Opera House or perhaps was the man in the Opera House. Otherwise they probably would've just sent it to you. Can you recall their reason for bringing it to you?" His face returned to its serious facade.

"They wanted me to identify the hammer and to know if my father or I had ever been in the cellars. I told them that neither of us had ever been in the cellars of the Opera House and that the Opera Ghost, if there was such a person, had obviously stolen it from my father. They were easily convinced that that had been what had happened, almost too easily convinced." She walked over to the fireplace to stir the embers and then turned to him with a most serious look on her face. "I asked them if the hammer had been used on one of the victims and they said that they had no evidence of it ever being used in that manner. Can you promise me that this is true?"

He could tell by the tone of her voice that she was concerned about this particular subject. He joined her by the fireplace, put his arm around her and whispered in her ear. "I promise. I wouldn't have ever used such a special gift for such treachery."

She turned and hugged him. "I love you Erik."

"I love you too." He kissed her on the forehead and then hugged her tightly. "I hate to spoil this moment, but I have to ask; where is the hammer now?"

"It's in the drawer in my armoire underneath my scarves. Why do you need to know where it is?"

"If Frederic asks either of us about it, I want to be able to tell him everything he'll need to know, even where it is. Actually, I think we should put it back in your father's study. Hiding it will only raise his suspicions even more but if we display it, then it will shatter all of his theories."

"Won't that provoke him even more though?" she asked with concern returning to her voice.

"It might, but at least this way we'll have set his investigation back a bit. No one who is guilty would be so bold as to flaunt the only thing that could convict them in the face of their accuser, now would they?" said Erik while crossing the room to the stairs.

"You can't be certain that the hammer is the only evidence that he may have against you though? What if he has something else?"

"There isn't anything else or the Inspector would've come back already. I can't be sure but I assume that once the body was found the Inspector was probably glad to be rid of the famed Phantom of the Opera."

"What if Frederic's inquiries lead them to believe otherwise?"

"Amalie, even if his inquiries led them back here, they'll still have no reason to suspect me."

"They never questioned you and if Frederic starts telling them about the similarities between you and Opera Ghost, they may want to speak with you to verify where you were that night. How will you deter them when you have no alibi?"

Erik loved that Amalie was so intelligent but at times he wished that her inquisitive nature and analysis of situations weren't so accurate. She was right; he had no alibi for the evening in question and never thought to create one. He would definitely have to find a way to fabricate an alibi just in case the Inspector showed up to question him.

"I'll tell them that I was traveling in the Eastern countries while on holiday and that I didn't arrive in France until months after the headlines of the Opera Ghost were made. I still know plenty of names of hotels and restaurants from India and Asia to create an itinerary that could fool anyone." He laughed as he continued to walk up the stairs.

She watched him as he went upstairs and returned with the small hammer in his hands and the revolver in his other.

"Why do you have the revolver Erik? What are you going to do with it?"

"Don't worry my love. I'm just putting it in your father's desk drawer. I'll feel better knowing that it is accessible if I need it when Frederic comes to visit."

"Are you planning to kill him?" She had now risen from the sofa quickly and met him at the foot of the staircase.

"Of course I'm not. It's better to be prepared for trouble and not have any than to be unprepared and be taken by surprise. I want you to know where it is too, just in case you may need it. I've loaded it so it will be ready to use. If Frederic is as unpredictable as everyone says he is, then I don't want to leave anything to chance." He made his way to the desk, pulled the top drawer open and placed the revolver into it. He then took the small hammer and set it inside the cabinet that held the brandy decanter, which was in need of being refilled. The hammer could be seen through the glass of the cabinet doors from across the room. It was the perfect place for it.

Casting Shadows

*A*s the day came to an end the sun made its descent from the sky hiding itself among the trees and hills. They had just finished their supper and retired to the drawing room. He sat at the piano, playing as he did most nights and she sat in the chair crocheting a baby blanket. When he finished playing his first concerto he turned to her to find her rubbing her small but protruding belly.

"Erik, come quickly. Come feel the baby kick." He rose from the bench and walked over to her. She took his hand, placed it in on her belly and watched his face. His eyes danced with happiness and his lips carried a message of joy without speaking a word. She stroked the back of his hair as he knelt beside her.

"Does it hurt you when the baby kicks?"

"Sometimes, but most of the time it doesn't. The baby kicks a lot more when you play the piano than any other time. I have a feeling this child will like music as much as you and I do." She continued to stroke his hair as he laid his head on her belly. He kissed her belly after several minutes of enjoying the touch of her hands on his hair. He then returned to the piano to play once more. They were enjoying the quiet of the evening and then there was a knock at the door.

"Erik, Erik," she said loudly so that he could hear her over the melody he was playing. "Someone is knocking at the door. I wasn't expecting anyone, were you?"

He shook his head and rose from the piano bench. "You stay in here; I'll see who it is." He walked to the foyer and then to the door. He could hear several voices outside. When he opened the door he was greeted by Peter and Isabel. "Good evening Erik. We were hoping you'd be home." Peter extended his hand for a handshake and Erik returned the greeting.

"Come in and make yourselves at home. Let me take your coats and hats." Erik took their coverings from them and hung them in the closet.

He directed them to the drawing room where upon hearing their voices Amalie now stood at the door waiting to greet them.

"It's so nice to see both of you. I didn't know you were visiting Meg and Chester or I'd have made arrangements for you to join us for supper."

Isabel hugged her and replied, "That's very sweet of you but Mother and Father don't know that we're here. Peter's sister offered to take the girls for a few weeks so that Peter and I could go traveling like we used to before we had them."

"That's very generous of your sister. I hope the girls don't miss the two of you too much." Amalie returned to her chair.

"I think that I'll miss them Amalie. I didn't think I would, but not having them with us makes the world a very quiet place. You'll see. A child changes everything." Isabel took a seat on the sofa.

"If you ladies don't mind, Erik and I are going to retire to the study for a drink. May we get you anything before we do?"

Isabel spoke up before Amalie could get the words out. "No thank you. I believe we'll be fine."

Peter and Erik walked out of the drawing room and into the study. Peter made a path to the cabinet where the brandy decanter had been emptied out. "Erik, where is the brandy?"

"There's another bottle in the bottom cabinet." Peter opened the cabinet, removed the bottle and began to pour its contents into the decanter. "Have you been drinking a lot Erik?"

"No. Chester and I had a few drinks the other day. He came to fill me in on Frederic's plans to prove that I'm the Opera Ghost."

"Obviously I've missed something. What do you and the Opera Ghost have to do with each other?"

"Well, apparently your brother-in-law has decided that just because I wear a mask and my name is Erik and the Opera Ghost apparently wore a mask and his name was Erik also, we are obviously the same person." Peter took a glass from the cabinet, filled it and Erik took it from him.

"Has Frederic gone mad? He has forgotten one very important detail about the Opera Ghost hasn't he?" Peter asked.

"And what is that?"

"The Opera Ghost is dead. I believe what the paper said was that his rotting corpse had been discovered near a well lying in a coffin. I would think that you not being dead would definitely rule you out as being the Opera Ghost." Peter bellowed a laugh that made Erik smile.

"Perhaps to you that would eliminate me as a candidate but to him it makes it more of a challenge; one that he has evidently decided to take on."

"Well, if it matters at all, I don't think you're this Opera Ghost. You're not ugly enough to be him. I heard that it was the head of death that sat on his shoulders. And although you may be disfigured behind your mask, you don't fit that description at all." He raised his glass as he motioned Erik to bring him more brandy.

"I don't know whether to thank you for your words or not." Erik poured more brandy into Peter's glass and added more to his own. "I admit, my disfigurement has not brought me much in the way of friendships throughout my life but apparently I'm not so ugly that I couldn't find a wife. I find that you, Peter, are the only friend who has ever dared compliment and insult me all in the same breath." Erik smiled and then raised his glass toward Peter. "That is why I value your friendship so much."

Erik sat down in the chair behind the desk. He took another drink of his brandy and then asked, "Why was it again that you and Isabel came all of this way? Certainly it wasn't just to make small talk and drink my brandy." Erik set his glass on the desk and leaned forward to hear Peter's answer.

"You're right, I didn't come all of this way to drink your brandy. I came here to offer you a job."

"Amalie is due in three months Peter; I can't go to London for a job."

"The job that I'm offering is not in London, it's here. Isabel and I have decided to move back to the village of Trie-Chateau."

"I had no idea that you missed the country so much."

"I've never lived in the country Erik. This is where Isabel is from, not me. Evidently Amalie hasn't shared with you how I met my beloved wife while traveling through the town of Trie-Chateau. It's a wonderful story and perhaps when I have the time I'll tell it to you. But for now I must try to convince you to help restore the house I purchased that is sitting approximately one and a half kilometers southeast of your front door." Peter was beaming with pride at his acquisition of the property that lay just east of the Girault family chateau. It had been for sale for a long time and he was excited that Erik and Amalie would be their neighbors.

"You've acquired the chateau and acreage down the street? That is wonderful Peter and if I didn't say yes to your proposition I think Amalie would have my head." He rose from the chair and joined Peter as he walked to the door of the study. "We'll work out all of the details tomorrow Peter. It will be a pleasure and an honor to help you turn that dilapidated property into a grand chateau."

"I was hoping you would see it my way." Peter patted Erik on the shoulder as they entered the drawing room.

Amalie stood up, rubbing her belly as they walked into the room. "Did Peter tell you the good news?"

"Yes, and he's asked me to help renovate the place. Isn't that wonderful Amalie?"

"It is. It is very wonderful."

"I suppose the two of you will be spending a lot of time discussing the details of the house while we are here?" Isabel asked.

"Well naturally we will. In fact, I'd like to take Erik down to see it tomorrow. I'm sure it will help him get a better idea of what we'll be up against."

"It will indeed." Erik replied. "Are the two of you staying at the house with Meg and Chester?"

"Actually, Erik," Amalie interjected. "They were hoping they could stay with us for a few days since Frederic and Anna are staying there. I was just waiting to see what you thought."

Erik turned to Peter and Isabel and said, "Of course, you may stay here. You're both practically family and I wouldn't dare throw my own family out onto the street. It's a wonderful idea." He kissed Amalie on the forehead and then walked over to the piano. He sat on the bench, placed his fingers on the keys and began playing. It was as if he had fallen into his own world once again, not paying any attention that the three of them were standing there talking.

"You'll have to excuse my husband. When the mood strikes him to play, he does just that. Sometimes I'll catch him in here at two in the morning simply indulging his artistic senses until he is too tired to play anymore. It's good that you've given him something else in which to look forward. I can tell that his creativity has been silent for too long." She sighed and then rubbed her belly again.

"Let us get you settled in your room." He continued to play as Amalie gently tapped him on the shoulder. "I believe our guest may require your assistance in removing their bags from their coach."

He stopped playing and joined Peter who was unloading the coach. "Charles didn't come with you this time?"

"No, I decided that I could handle it myself. It isn't that hard to drive a coach you know?" Peter remarked as he removed a piece of luggage from the top of the coach.

"I didn't say it was. After we get the coach unloaded I'll drive it down to the stable and unhitch the horses." Erik offered as he handed Peter another suitcase.

They finished unloading the luggage which they placed inside the front door. Peter began carrying the luggage upstairs and Erik returned to the coach. He climbed into the driver's seat, grabbed the reins and vanished into the darkness which was only lit by a lantern that he carried with him. The stable was quiet other than the expected sounds of the night. He unhitched the horses from the coach and boarded them in the extra stalls. When he turned to leave he saw something or someone disappear into the darkness. He ran to investigate and noticed that Jasper's stall was unlocked as if someone had intended to release him. He grabbed the pitch fork from the bale of hay and with lantern in hand set out to investigate. It was obvious when he made it outside of the stalls that whoever had been there was gone. However, as he made his way back into the stable he noticed something red on the ground. He knelt and put his lantern closer to it to see it better. It was blood. He looked around to see if there was anymore and there was. He followed it until it disappeared into the wooded acreage that was behind the stable. It may have been a wounded animal he thought at first but when he returned to the stable he noticed a small black patch of fabric hanging from a jagged nail behind the door. He picked it up in order to get a better look at it and his suspicions were right. It was fabric from a man's topcoat or trouser leg. He put it in his pocket and locked Jasper's stall and then returned to the house.

Peter and Isabel had retired to their room for the evening and Amalie was in bed reading. He locked the house up tightly and retrieved the revolver from the study. When he walked into the bedroom she noticed that he wasn't as cheerful as he was when he had gone out to tend to the horses and coach. She put her book down in her lap.

"Erik, you look like you've seen a ghost. Is there something wrong?"

"Not a ghost but definitely something," he said as he took off his mask, placing it on the dresser.

"What do you mean? Was there someone outside?" her concern could be heard in her voice.

"I'm not sure if it was someone or some thing. But whoever or whatever it was left a trail of blood and this." He pulled out the piece of cloth and handed it to her. She looked at it and then handed it back to him.

"Blood, Erik. Why was there blood?"

"Whoever it was must have ripped their clothing on one of the old nails. It looks to have left a wound that produced quite a bit of blood. I followed the trail as far as I could until it disappeared into the wooded area behind the stable."

"Who do you think it was?"

"The obvious choice would be Frederic but I'm not sure why he'd feel the need to sneak around our stable like a fox looking for chickens. However, I won't be unprepared if the prowler tries to enter the house." He took the revolver and placed it into the drawer of the nightstand and continued to get ready for bed. He took one more look out of their bedroom window to see if there was anyone outside casting shadows in the moonlight. He could only see the shadows of the trees which were swaying in the gently blowing wind. He climbed under the covers, pulling them up to his waist as he sat up in the bed. Amalie, fearing that someone could be outside, moved closer to him. She laid her head on his chest and closed her eyes. He kissed her on the forehead then slid with her in his arms down under the covers. He knew he wouldn't sleep well but he hoped that she would.

The sun rose as Erik was leaving the house with the revolver in hand. The stable looked to be still and quiet but he knew that looks could be very deceptive. He rounded the corner of the stable that faced the house and went to the opposite end where he had found the trail of blood. The light of day was helpful in determining how much blood was lost and pinpointing the exact location of where the trail became cold. He continued to look around in hopes of finding something that would tell him who or what had been at the stable. His search and investigation continued for at least an hour and although it did not produce a clear suspect, it did produce a motive. His diligent search had unearthed two small pieces of paper; one with partial letters scribed on it and the other was printed in black ink. The first two words were legible but the third was not. It read, "Erik is …....." It was accompanied by a newspaper clipping about the Opera Ghost's body being found. He knew that if it wasn't Frederic, it was definitely someone who had thought that the two had many similarities and was destined to find out whether their suspicions were right or wrong.

Amalie had risen from her slumber, readied herself for the day and made her way to the kitchen. She assumed that he would be there or in the study reading. She searched both rooms and didn't find any trace of him. She continued to enter and exit all of the other rooms in which she thought he may be inside; he was not found. She thought that perhaps he went to the room in the cave but assumed he probably wouldn't risk it with guests in the house. Then the events of the evening came rushing over her like a wave and she hurried to the back door, opened it and began searching the landscape for him. Her eyes caught movement near the stable, not knowing whether to be scared or relieved she called for Peter and Isabel who were in the drawing room.

"Have either of you seen Erik this morning?"

"No Amalie, I can't say that we have. Where do you suppose he's gone off too?" Peter asked rubbing his chin.

"I think he may be down at the stable. Would you mind seeing if he is there? I would like him here for breakfast. Would you tell him that for me?"

Peter kissed Isabel on the forehead, slipped past Amalie and exited through the back door.

She watched as Peter made his way down to the stable. She hoped that he would find him and not encounter any trouble.

"Amalie, you seem preoccupied this morning. Is everything all right?"

"Erik said that someone was at the stable last night while he was un-hitching the horses from your coach. He didn't catch them but I'm sure that he won't give up until he does. I just hope he is careful. The baby will be here in three months and Christmas is a week away. I wish all of this nonsense about him being the Opera Ghost would disappear."

"Who is accusing him of being the Opera Ghost?" Isabel asked.

"Who else but your silly brother. He thinks that because they have the same name and that they both wear masks that Erik is the Opera Ghost. Never mind that they found the Ghost's body decomposing down in the cellars of the Paris Opera House and my husband lives." She began to cry and turned to Isabel for comfort. "I just want my life to be normal again."

"I think you gave up that chance when you married Erik. He is anything but normal and frankly, I don't think that that is a bad thing. You've lived a life full of education, charming gentlemen, wealth and status. It's about time you had some adventure to add to it." She wiped the tears from Amalie's eyes.

If only Isabel had known how much adventure Erik had already brought into her life she wouldn't have said such a thing. She would never be able to share it with anyone and promised that until the day he died she would always keep it a secret.

"Why don't we start making breakfast? It will get your mind off of everything and I'm sure that Peter will return with him shortly."

"You're right. You are always right."

Peter had entered the stable doors that faced the house and found no signs of Erik. As he walked by the stalls, he made it a point to say good morning to each horse before he exited the stable through the doors on the opposite end. That is where he found Erik leaning up against a tree waiting, as if he knew Peter would be coming.

"Good morning Peter. Let me guess, my beautiful wife has sent you to come fetch me from my morning walk."

"Actually, she has sent me to retrieve you for breakfast. By the look on her face I would say she was worried that something may have happened to you. Does she have need to be concerned for your safety?"

"It's possible that she may need to worry about all of our safety. We had a visitor last night while I was down here unhitching the horses. I didn't catch whoever it was but they were definitely wounded."

He proceeded to recant the entire account about what transpired at the stable. He showed him the blood, the nail and the blood trail. However, he didn't reveal to him the newspaper clipping and paper with the illegible lettering on it. He thought it was best to keep even that from his new friend lest he tip Frederic off, not intentionally of course, that he had lost it and it was now found; if it was indeed Frederic who had been there. Peter listened while he filled him in and then they decided to return to the house since nothing more could be gained from staying at the stable.

The day progressed as usual after the excitement of the morning. The entirety of the day she could sense that he was very uneasy about something. She excused herself from Isabel's company and entered the study where she asked Peter if she could speak privately to Erik. She closed the door behind her and took a seat in one of the chairs that sat in front of the desk. He was seated behind the desk.

"Erik, I'm not sure what is going on inside your head but I fear that you're planning to do something that will put your life in danger. I know the look you get when you are trifled with and it doesn't make me feel any better about our situation."

He rose from his chair, walked over to where she sat and knelt next to her holding her hand in his. "You worry too much. I have no plans to hunt down this person or thing that came to our property last night. I wouldn't do anything to put you and the baby in harms way."

"Then why do you have that look of dissatisfaction on your face? I know you're disappointed that it wasn't Frederic but there are other people out there that may want to do you harm other than him."

"How do you know it wasn't Frederic? I've not learned that to be true."

"Isabel went to visit them this afternoon and Frederic didn't have any wounds of any kind, nor had her father seen any evidence of it, so it couldn't have been him."

"Then we have an even bigger problem. If he isn't the only person that believes me to be the Opera Ghost, then that must mean that someone else is prying into our affairs. I know you may not like this but I have to find out who is stirring up mischief. I promise that I'll be very careful. Remember, it is I who created this game of casting shadows."

"You are who you are Erik and I won't ask you to be less than that. I know that protecting us is the most important thing to you but please be careful. I don't want to raise this child without you."

He kissed her on the forehead and then the lips. "Being careful is why I'm still alive Amalie. I promise that I'll be extra careful while I unravel this mystery. Now, let's go into the drawing room and entertain our guests. I don't want you to worry another minute about all of this."

They joined their guests in the drawing room until it was time to retire for the evening. They said goodnight and went to their rooms. The hours passed as they slept, all except Erik. He couldn't help but think that the perpetrator would come back to look for what they had lost. The hour was around two in the morning when he dressed and quietly exited the house. He was accustomed to wandering in the darkness so it was easy for him to find his way to the stable without any aid from a lantern. The moon only showed a sliver of its light; hardly enough to cast a shadow. He listened carefully for any signs of an intruder and when he heard nothing he entered cautiously checking each stall for anyone that might be hiding. He purposely opened the stable doors at the opposite end where he had found the papers, leaving them open hoping it would entice the perpetrator to enter.

He waited for at least an hour with no results coming from his surveillance. Then it happened so quickly that he almost missed it. He had dozed off and during his slumber someone had entered the stable; going through each stall trying to find what they had lost. He rose from his bed of hay, grabbed a shovel and stealthily made his way to the shadowy figure in the dark. As he approached he heard not one but two voices. Both voices did not possess a French accent and one was younger than the other. One seemed further away than the other, possibly outside the door. He decided that he'd attack the person that was outside being that the person in the stall would be easily subdued since the stall itself served as an obstacle, especially because Shadow was still in it. His ghostlike movements brought him closely to his prey and the duel began. Unfortunately for Erik the moon cast his shadow just enough to take his element of surprise and he found himself the victim of the first blow. He quickly recovered and swung his shovel, striking the figure in the back bringing him to his knees and then Erik knocked him unconscious with one more blow from the shovel to the back of the head. As he bent down to identify his opponent, the second figure charged by him riding atop of Shadow. Erik knew he couldn't let him get away so he quickly ran to Jasper's stall, put the reins on him and jumped on his bare back. Jasper took out like a bullet exiting the shaft of a gun. He thought he had lost sight of the figure but soon found him headed toward the clearing near the entrance to the cave. Jasper was fast but it didn't seem that he would ever catch up to the perpetrator. Then it happened, just as Amalie had told him it could happen; Shadow, in full stride, slowed and then came to a complete and sudden stop throwing his rider from his back. If he hadn't seen it for himself, he wouldn't have believed it. He caught up with the man that was lying on the ground. He jumped down off of Jasper and grabbed the man by his shirt, pulling him closer to him so that he could see his face. He couldn't believe his eyes.

"Darius, is that you?" he asked with complete disbelief.

The man didn't answer. The throw had knocked him unconscious.

He grabbed him, put him on his horse's back and then mounted Jasper. He took Shadow by the reins and went back to the stable where he found his other victim still lying unconscious. He took the man from the horse and set him next to the other man that was lying on the ground. He returned the horses to their stalls and then returned to the recipients of his anger to hopefully identify them. He found the lantern and lit it. His eyes couldn't believe what he was seeing. It was his old friend the Persian and his servant Darius. He was completely baffled as to the reason they would be there. Darius had begun to awaken from his state of unconsciousness as Erik examined the Persian for any signs of life. He was still breathing but there was blood coming from his head. Not from the blow of the shovel but from the rock his head had collided with when he fell to the ground. Erik immediately tore off part of his shirt, wrapping it around the wound. He knew that he would need Amalie's skills if he were going to help his friend.

"Please sir, don't hurt me. I'm merely a man's servant obeying his master's wishes."

"Darius, I don't intend to hurt you. Don't you recognize me?"

"No sir, I don't. How is it that you know my name? He shrunk into the bale of hay that Erik had laid him on; his arms wrapped around his knees as if becoming smaller in stature he would disappear from Erik's eyes.

"I'll explain everything to you later Darius but we need to get your master somewhere safe and warm. Can you walk?"

"Do you expect me to just follow you when I have no idea who you are?"

"I expect you to think of the welfare of your master and what will happen to him if you don't," Erik scolded.

His patience was wearing thin. "Now, I'll ask you again and I expect an answer this time. Can you walk?"

"Yes."

Erik saddled Jasper and Shadow while Darius tended to the Persian. He put the Persian on Shadow with him and directed Darius to ride Jasper. He knew that he was taking a chance riding Shadow but because they wouldn't be at a full gallop he was willing to take the chance. They rode to the entrance of the cave. He carried the Persian into the cave while Darius followed. As they walked in the tunnel that led to the rooms, Darius searched his memory for any clue to who this half-masked man was. The darkness of the cave and the familiarity of the stranger's voice jarred his memory. He realized that this man who bore half the mask he used to wear was indeed Erik. Erik was not dead as they had believed but very much alive.

They entered the sanctuary of the cave and Erik placed the Persian on one of the sofas. He then directed Darius to the small room with the water, pitcher and basin where he was to retrieve a towel and some water for his master. Erik headed for the other doorway that led to the house.

"Where are you going sir?"

"I'm going to get someone to help the Persian. I'll return shortly. Try to wake him if you can Darius and tell him that his friend will be back."

He exited the room and made his way down the tunnel to the house. He reached the study and then quietly walked upstairs to find his wife absent from their bed. She was staring out the window and when she heard his footsteps enter the room, she ran to him. She embraced him as if he had returned from a long journey.

"Oh, Erik I was so worried when I woke to find you missing from our bed. Are you all right?"

"I'm fine and I'll explain everything later, but now I need you to dress quickly and come with me. I'll meet you in the study."

She quickly dressed and met him in the study where he stood holding her black physician's bag in his hand.

"Why do you have my bag? It's obvious that you aren't hurt Erik, so why do you need my bag?"

"I don't need it....you do. The person or persons that were in the stable last night are now in the cave. I have wounded one to the point that I'm not sure he will ever regain consciousness. I need you to look at his injury and help him." She started to say something and he stopped her. "We've wasted enough time with explanations. We must hurry if we are to help him."

He opened the secret door closing it tightly behind him. They walked quickly through the tunnel and reached the cave. He led her to the sanctuary where she observed one man attempting to get the other man to drink some water. They approached the men. The Persian was now conscious but still bleeding.

"Persian, I'm glad to see that you are awake. Had I known it was you, I wouldn't have struck you so hard."

"Amalie, can you help him?"

Darius offered his seat on the sofa next to the Persian. She took off the piece of fabric that Erik had tied around his head so that she could look at the wound. She cleaned it up with water while telling them that it would require her to sew it up or it would never heal and it would be likely that an infection could occur. She asked Erik to move the Persian to the bed in the small room. Once she had made him comfortable, she took out her medical thread and needle and began to sew his skin together. When she was finished she put a bandage around his head and then washed the blood from her hands in the basin.

"Are there anymore injuries that you've inflicted that I'll need to address?" She asked him with disappointment in her voice.

He walked over and kissed her on the cheek. "No my love, I believe that's the only injury. Thank you for your help."

"You're welcome. I believe you owe me an explanation of just who I've helped and why."

"Yes, I do. However, I believe that my friend, the Persian and his faithful servant owe us both an explanation as to why they've been skulking around our property in the early morning hours."

The Persian looked at Erik and then at Amalie. He was confused as to who they were. The man sounded a lot like Erik but his appearance was not anything like he had remembered. And this beautiful woman who was with child, how did she fit into his life, if this was Erik? Many questions swirled in his head that was writhing in pain.

"I can see that you are confused Persian. You had hoped to find me alive but you obviously were not prepared for the moment that you did."

She sat on the chair that was in the small room waiting to hear the explanations of all the parties involved in this early morning escapade.

"It's obvious that this is your friend that you've told me about; the one that saved your life all those many years ago. However, I'm not familiar with the man that is with him."

"Where are my manners? Amalie, this is Darius. He is the Persian's servant and dare I say friend." He looked at Darius and then at the Persian. "And this beautiful woman, gentlemen, is my wife, Amalie."

The Persian, although still in pain, found his voice when the introductions were completed. "You have a wife? What horrible games did you play to receive such a gift as beautiful as she?"

"He played no games. He won my heart honestly and I his." She reached for Erik's hand as she spoke. She held it tightly. "It's you I believe who are playing games and I demand to know what it is you want from us." She turned her fear and impatience into words which struck her guests ears like daggers.

"We came here not to play games but to put an end to one." The Persian, who was now feeling only a slight throbbing in his head, sat up in the bed. "I had received several inquiries from a man by the name of Frederic Rousseau about the intimate details of the man I knew as the Opera Ghost. This man wanted to meet with me, but I refused. I had no need to bring the dead back to life but he sent letter after letter urging me to speak with him. In his quest to force a meeting with me he sent a letter which told me about a man that lived in a country chateau near Trie-Chateau who wore a mask and bore the name Erik Geraurd. He wrote that he had suspected that you were the Opera Ghost and had somehow escaped death by some miracle or trickery. Apparently he had spoken to someone in the Inspector Magistrate's Office and they mentioned that a hammer had been found in the cellars. A hammer belonging to a Gaston Girault, which along with a few other things found in the tunnels, was the only alleged evidence they possessed. Apparently, the Inspector Magistrate's Office is unwilling to re-open the case and has bid a fond farewell to the apparition. However, this Frederic Rousseau continues to claim that the Opera Ghost is still alive and wishes for me to help find him."

Erik glanced at Amalie as she sat attentively in the chair listening to the Persian. "Well, I would say that you've found him but I hope that you don't intend on divulging his whereabouts to Monsieur Rousseau."

"I've no intentions of exposing you Erik."

"Then why have you come here?" Erik asked as he stood next to Amalie.

"I came to satisfy my own curiosity. Even though I believed that you were gone forever, there was a part of me that hoped that you weren't. After receiving the letters from Monsieur Rousseau I decided to investigate the possibility myself. Last night you interrupted my attempt to get a closer look into your home, hoping to catch a glimpse of this man who used to be my friend, the Opera Ghost." He rubbed his head and stretched his back, readjusting his position on the bed. "I came back to retrieve the papers that I dropped. It is obvious now that you must have found them and that is why you were waiting for us. I should know better than to try to out-ghost a ghost." He laughed and then winced in pain.

"Why is it that you didn't recognize Erik?" she asked.

"He has never let me see what was behind his mask. Had I not recognized his voice I wouldn't even believe it was him now."

"I assure you that I'm your friend, Persian, and this isn't the first time I have saved your life."

"Yes, but it was at your hands which my life needed to be saved." The Persian smiled and let out a small chuckle.

"True, but if you hadn't been prying into matters that weren't your concern, you wouldn't have found yourself in a situation of needing to be saved," replied Erik.

"I won't argue with you about matters that have been resolved." The Persian tried to stand and Darius caught him as he began to fall.

Amalie rose from her seat to help Darius. "You must not move too quickly. You need to lie down and rest. You've had a very busy and eventful night. Erik, will you get me one of the blankets from the closet?"

"You're not only beautiful but you are kind also Madame."

"Thank you. I'm also very tired. If you no longer need me I think I'll return to the house. Remember, we have guests Erik. I assume you don't want it known that your old friends are here. Please don't stay down here too long." She kissed him softly and smiled at him. "They are welcome to stay as long as you wish them too as long as they stay out of sight. I don't want questions being raised as to who they are or how you know them."

"I agree. I won't be long." He kissed her and walked her to the entrance of the tunnel. "Thank you for helping me."

"I'll always help you Erik. I love you. However, I wish your adventures took place during a more suitable hour." She hugged him and then made her way back to the house.

Erik checked on the Persian and Darius. Darius was asleep on one of the sofas and the Persian was still awake but lying down in the bed in the small room. He took a seat in the chair next to the bed.

"She is quite breath-taking," the Persian commented. "I would say that you're living better as one of the dead than you did when you were alive. I don't know if I want to know how you came to be in such exquisite company, but I must inquire anyway."

"It is through the help of an old friend and by the hand of God that I have this life I have now. It's a long story but I don't have time to tell it to you right now. The morning hours approach and exhaustion overcomes me. I'll return to you in time but until then I want you and Darius to stay here. There is adequate water and fuel for the lights. There are more blankets in the closet and Amalie and I will design a plan to provide you with food. You may exit only from the entrance to your left if you need to make a quick escape for any reason." He pointed to the doorway that led to the clearing. "Trust me once more Persian, I'll make sure you're safe."

"You must indulge me this one question before you go Erik."

"And what is that Persian?"

"How is it that you found your face so hideous you couldn't bear for me to look at it but now you show the world half of it?"

"It was Gaston who made me see my face through different eyes.... his eyes...when he made me this mask. His daughter has helped me to see it with more than just her eyes, she showed me with her heart."

The Persian noticed how he spoke of her. Not as an object or possession but as a person that was to be honored and cherished not controlled and manipulated. This woman had done everything that he wanted her to do but without him making her at his behest. She loved him; he could see it when he watched her with him but it was also clear that he loved her too. He knew just by the way he talked about her that she was the woman that possessed the love that he had always wanted to have given to him. That was something that Christine never possessed and although he said he loved her, he always knew that she'd never return his love the way he needed her to give it; freely and honestly.

"It appears that you have everything you wanted, now doesn't it Erik?"

"Yes, it would appear that way but there is still the problem of Frederic Rousseau, isn't there? He has been a problem since the day I met him."

"You know him?"

"Yes, Persian, I know him and I can't say that it has been a pleasure. He is the son of our friend, Chester. He has had his plans of vengeance set upon me since the day I met him."

"And why is that?"

Erik proceeded to tell him the whole ugly story. The Persian listened and sometime during the story, not because of lack of interest but because of exhaustion, he fell asleep. He noticed his friend in deep slumber and pulled his blanket over his body and turned the lights down. He then exited the cave and took the horses back to the stable. He put everything back the way it was so that Chester would not question anything when he arrived. It was nearing dawn so he hurried back to the house, undressed and crawled into bed. Amalie reached for him and he pulled her close.

Uninvited Guests

$\mathcal{A}$ malie woke during the mid-morning hours. As she dressed she was careful not to disturb Erik, who was still sleeping. He looked so peaceful there as he slept and although she was angry at him for putting himself in jeopardy, she was proud that he did it to protect them. He had always spoken the words of a chivalrous knight but she'd never thought he would have a need to produce actions to those words. However, she was glad that he could.

Isabel and Peter were in the dining room finishing their breakfast when she walked into the kitchen. Isabel caught her passing by out of the corner of her eye and rose to greet her.

"Good morning Amalie. Is Erik going to be joining us?"

"No, he didn't get much sleep last night. He tossed and turned worrying about the person or thing that visited the stable the other night. I don't foresee him getting up for at least two or three more hours."

Peter stood to pull out Amalie's seat for her. Isabel brought her a plate of food and then sat with her while she ate. Peter took his seat as well and they continued their conversation.

"Everything will be all right Amalie. I'm sure after a few days he'll forget all about it." Isabel said as she touched Amalie's hand.

"I know you're right but I just wish I could do something to help him."

"Christmas Day will be here in five days and you haven't gotten a tree yet. Perhaps you and Erik should go look for a tree today," Peter suggested. "That will get his mind off of things."

"That's an excellent idea. I've been so busy preparing for the baby that I haven't readied the house for the Christmas celebration." She rose from her chair and returned her dishes to the kitchen.

"Peter, would you mind getting the boxes of Christmas decorations out of the closet in the sitting room?"

"I'd be happy too. Where would you like me to put them?"

"In the great room. That is where the tree will be once we get one."

"Shouldn't Peter help Erik with that? I don't think it's a good idea for you to be walking around the woods looking for a tree in your condition," said Isabel who was noticeably concerned.

"I'm pregnant, not dying. Besides it's a tradition that we're starting for our family. I'll be fine. I'll make sure to pack something to eat, dress warmly and bring a blanket for the ride in the wagon. We'll be back before sunset."

Erik had entered the kitchen without making the slightest sound. "We'll be back from where before sunset?"

"Looking for a Christmas tree. I can't believe that I hadn't thought to do it sooner. The days have passed so quickly that Christmas hasn't even been a twinkle in my eye but I'm about to change that," she announced with almost a tune to her words.

He took her into the kitchen while Isabel joined Peter in the great room where he was going through the boxes of decorations.

"I must get some food to the Persian and Darius," he whispered so that his guests couldn't hear him.

"I've got it all worked out Erik. When we go off to look for our tree we'll ride out to the cave and deliver the basket of food. I've told them that we'll be taking food with us for our journey so they won't suspect anything," she whispered back to him.

"What a clever idea. I'm so blessed to have you as my wife." He kissed her passionately on the lips and stopped only because Peter walked into the room.

"Good heavens Peter, can't a man have a private moment with his wife?"

"You'll soon find that the answer to that question will be 'no' more often than 'yes' when your child arrives. Amalie, where would you like me to hang this?" He dangled a dried piece of mistletoe in front of her.

"You kept it." Erik looked at her and smiled.

"Of course I kept it. You held it over my head the night that you proposed. It's something that I'll keep forever. Hang it over the entrance to the great room. That way everyone will be able to catch their sweetheart for a kiss."

He followed Peter into the great room and helped with the decorating. Amalie went to the kitchen to prepare a basket of food for their uninvited guests that were down in the cave. As she gathered their meal she said a prayer for the health of her patient. She hoped that he would not get an infection and that she would be able to get to know him better. He was the only connection to Erik's past and it made her feel better knowing that she wasn't the only one that knew about his past and still thought he was worth keeping from harm. She finished packing the basket and then took her cloak from the closet along with her gloves and bonnet. She pulled Erik's cloak, and gloves out of the closet, carrying them to him in the great room.

"I guess this means you're ready to go?"

"Yes and I want to find the tallest and the fattest tree there is."

"Then I guess we better be on our way. Isabel, Peter, when we return we'll have the best tree in France in our wagon."

"We'll make some cider and be ready for your return." Isabel promised as they walked out the door.

They went to the stable and she sat on the wooden bench inside as he hitched the horses to the wagon. She placed the basket in the bed of the wagon and he helped her climb onto the seat. He took his place next to her and they started out on their journey. However, before they went out to find a tree they stopped in the clearing. They ventured down the tunnel until they entered the cave where Darius appeared to be looking through the drawings of the room that Gaston had drafted which Erik had left in the satchel next to the sofa. He was so involved in his task that he didn't hear them come in. The Persian was in the smaller room splashing water on his face and inspecting the work that Amalie had done on his head.

"Bon Jour." Erik exclaimed happily. "How are you this afternoon? I apologize for the lateness of our arrival but it took a planned escape for us to be able to leave without arousing any suspicion of where we were going."

She handed Darius the basket and took a seat next to him. "I hope you like what I have brought you. I assumed that since you've been living in Paris you are accustomed to the cuisine."

Darius took the basket, looked in it and his mouth began to salivate. "It is fine Madame and it smells wonderful. We are so grateful for your kindness and your help."

"You're welcome Darius. Please, don't be shy.....eat." The Persian had joined them and Darius handed him a plate while she set the food out on the coffee table.

Erik walked around the room observing his wife while she interacted with his old friends. He was impressed but not surprised at how hospitable she was and how quickly she made them feel welcomed. There was something about her that drew people to her, like a moth to a flame. Her beauty was only a small part of her attractiveness; it was her genuine concern for others that seemed to be the magnet that pulled strangers to her. She was a rare find and he was glad that she was his.

After they finished eating, Erik reminded her that they still had a Christmas tree to find. She packed up the dishes, returned them to the basket and took her place next to him as he stood beside the sofa. She started to say good-bye but the Persian interrupted her.

"Madame would you take a suggestion from me?"

"It depends on what your suggestion is."

"Well, I'd like to suggest that Darius go with Erik to get the tree and you stay with me so that I may enjoy your company. I'd think that in your condition it would be best if you stayed where it is warm and safe."

"I appreciate your concern but as I have pointed out to many people before you, I'm with child not ill. I'm perfectly capable of helping him pick out a tree."

Erik looked at her, putting his arm around her. "Amalie, I think that the Persian's suggestion is a wonderful one. I'd feel better knowing that you were out of the cold and I think that you and my friend here have a lot to talk about. I'm sure you have many questions for him." She looked at him and smiling she took her cloak off and laid it on the sofa.

"It looks like I'm outnumbered that is if Darius agrees with the two of you. Do you?"

"Madame, I do and I will be glad to accompany Monsieur Geraurd to pick out a tree."

"Then it is settled. I will stay. It will give me a chance to check the stitches and redress the wound. Please be careful and don't take too long, I'd like to get the tree placed and decorated."

"We'll do our best my love. Persian, try not to be too charming." He kissed Amalie on the forehead and smiled at the Persian as he and Darius exited the cave.

She proceeded to tend to her patient; looking at the stitching and then putting a new bandage on it. She washed her hands in the basin and then returned to where the Persian was now laying across one of the sofas.

"Are you not feeling well?" she asked.

"I'm feeling fine. I'm just a little tired. Does it bother you if I lie down while we speak?"

"Not at all. If I didn't think I'd be accused of not being a lady I would lay across *this* sofa."

"You'll receive no such accusations from me," the Persian laughed.

She fluffed the pillow on the sofa and carefully leaned against it. She pulled her feet up, placing another pillow under her knees. They both lay on their prospective sofas for a few minutes without speaking a word. Then oddly they both began to speak at the same time. They laughed at the coincidence.

"Madame, please finish what you were saying. I'm sure you have many questions," the Persian said.

"I only have one and if you answer it then I'll have no need to ask anything else."

"Don't keep me in suspense Madame, please ask."

"Why did you save Erik's life all those years ago if you knew what he was capable of doing?" She rose from her laying position and sat facing him.

"You'd think that I could answer that question very simply but as you probably know, anything that involves Erik usually is a lot more complex but I'll try to do my best." He paused and then sat up on the sofa. "We only knew each other because of our professions at first. Then as time passed I had the opportunity to watch him do many things that I could not explain. His magician's skills were fantastic as well as his ability to build things. After months of watching him I finally decided that I would speak to him. He was rather timid when I first tried to speak with him. He was always so conscientious of his appearance. With a little persistence from me, we soon became friendly with one another. I believe I even earned his respect. He was very different from any other person I'd ever met. He'd do things that I could define as wrong but he seemed not to be able to recognize the good or bad in it. He had no idea if something was good or bad, he usually judged it by whether it would help him survive or not. It was then that I realized that the condition of his face or rather the way people had treated him because of it had affected his mind and his thought process. Although he was at the age of becoming a man, he was in my eyes very much a child who was in need of love and acceptance. He would do almost anything to get it." He stood up, walked over and sat next to her on the sofa where she listened attentively to his every word.

"It was the day that the orders came to have Erik's life ended that I realized that I couldn't let them take his life just because he'd done what was asked of him. Although I knew that some of the things he'd done were wrong; he didn't at the time. Killing him would've been an even bigger injustice. I knew that saving his life would put mine in jeopardy but sometimes doing what is right is more important than personal safety. After all, what kind of man would I be if I let my friend die without just cause?" The Persian extended his hand to Amalie and in his palm he held a red stone.

"What is this?" she inquired while taking it out of his hand.

"That, Madame Geraurd is what your husband gave to me for saving his life. It is a rare red diamond. He told me that I was as rare as the rarest gem he'd ever laid eyes upon and then he handed me this stone."

She held it up to the light. "It's exquisite, isn't it?" She held it out to return it to him and he put his hand on hers and closed her fingers around it and said, "I may have been the rarest of gems he'd ever laid eyes on then but you're the rarest gem of all. The stone is yours and I concede to your rare but wonderful love for Erik. It makes me happy to see that he did find love and that he is now living the life he always spoke to me of having someday."

"Thank you. Your gesture means a lot to me as I'm sure it did to you when Erik did the same. I would think that you would want to keep it for sentimental reasons."

"You'll find that I'm not one for sentiment Madame and if there ever becomes a need for you to have money to live or flee, you may need to sell it."

"I would rather die than sell such a wonderful gift. No, I shall never do it. Perhaps I will have it fashioned into a necklace or a ring; something that will remind me of your honorable act and our friendship."

The Persian was now walking around the room looking at the painting that was hanging on the wall. "I'm glad that you think of me as your friend. I hope that we'll always be friends just as Erik and I have been."

"I don't see any reason why we wouldn't be. If I didn't have guests at the house that would question who you were, I'd welcome you properly into our home. As it were, I can only offer the comforts of our cave which is unknown to many and revealed to few. Our guests will be leaving the day after tomorrow if you'd like to stay in the house until you are feeling better."

"Darius and I would like that very much."

About that time Erik and Darius came walking through the entrance looking cold and in need of warmth. "Darius would like what very much Persian?" Erik asked as he took his cloak off.

"Your beautiful wife has invited us to stay a few days after your other guests leave. I think that it is a wonderful idea."

"I suppose you would think it was a wonderful idea. It gives you the opportunity to pry into my life with full permission to do so but if that is what my wife wishes then I'll not argue with her." He smiled at Amalie and then took a seat next to her. "I think it is a wonderful idea too. It has been too long since I have visited with my friends."

Amalie noticed how late in the day it was and reminded Erik that they needed to return home before the sun went down. They bid their guests good-bye, bundled up in their cloaks, hats and gloves then exited the cave. As she marveled at the size of the tree that lay in the bed of the wagon she couldn't stop thinking about how her life had changed in such a short time. She was happy and yet she missed her mother and her father. She had only wished they would've been there to share in her happiness. Erik took her hand and helped her into the seat. He climbed in next to her and they began their trip back to the house.

Well Written

*T*he tree was in place and it was ready to be decorated. Although she had hoped to have it decorated after they placed it in the great room, the trip to and from the cave had tired her and so she left it for the next day. They rose early so that she would be able to pack some food for their guests in the cave and he would be able to take it to them before anyone else woke. Afterward she made breakfast for her other guests. As she finished setting the table, Erik came through the back entrance carrying a fairly large black ball of fur in his arms.

"I see that you've found a friend this morning," she laughed.

"Actually, he found me. I had no choice but to pick him up. He kept following me and weaving in out of my steps. I decided I'd better carry him before he tripped me." He put Sampson on the floor and she placed a bowl of milk in front of him. She kissed him on the cheek and then continued to set the table.

Their guests had risen from their slumber and joined them at the dining room table. While they ate they discussed what plans they all had made for the day. With it being the last day that Peter and Isabel would be in the house before they went back to Paris to join his parents and their daughters for Christmas, there were a lot of things that needed to be done. Christmas was only three days away so Peter and Isabel told of their plans to go shopping in the village with her parents. Amalie was intent on getting the tree decorated before the day was over and Erik planned to help her but also wanted to go to the house that Peter and Isabel had just purchased to start measuring and drawing up renovation plans.

After breakfast they all parted ways but not before Amalie made them all promise to meet back at the house around six o'clock for supper. They agreed and then Peter and Isabel went upstairs to finish getting ready for their trip into the village and Amalie and Erik went to the great room where they began placing decorations on the tree. An hour had passed before Isabel and Peter were picked up by Chester and Meg in the coach. After they left she thought how wonderful it was to have Erik to herself once more. They were walking back into the great room when she stopped him in the doorway.

"What's wrong Amalie?"

"There's not anything wrong, in fact, things are just perfect. Look where we are standing." Her eyes glanced upward and his followed.

"Oh, I see, the mistletoe is above us. I suppose you think I should kiss you now that you have managed to entrap me?" he said as he spoke his words with a light laugh.

"Well, I suppose you don't have to but if you don't kiss me, then I'll be forced to take matters into my own hands."

"You will, will you? Well, I can't have you doing that now can I?" he smiled at her as he put his arms around her, pulled her closely to him and then kissed her. He pulled his lips from hers slowly and then looked into her brown eyes.

"I love you." He kissed her again and then held her in his arms. She held tightly to him, not wanting him to release her from his tender embrace. Several days had passed without them being able to have a moment to themselves. He missed being able to hold her in his arms without worry of being interrupted or watched by one of their guests. She missed him holding her, reassuring her of her safety and of his love for her and their unborn baby. She would be glad to have their guests, all of them, out of the house and cave so that their normal routine could be resumed.

"I love you, too," she whispered as she pulled away from his embrace. "I'll be so glad when we're alone in the house again. I miss our quiet nights in front of the fireplace in the drawing room. I miss listening to you play the piano."

"I miss it too and soon we shall be back to our life the way it was before all of our guests arrived. Remember it was your idea to invite the Persian and Darius to stay after our other guests leave tomorrow."

"I'm quite aware of my ideas Erik. However, if you hadn't injured him I wouldn't have felt obligated to ask them to stay on a couple of extra days."

"You're right my love. It's my fault that you've had to extend the stay of my friends, but I promise you that I'll be here to keep him from taking advantage of your hospitality."

"I don't think that the Persian would dare exploit my kindness, you on the other hand....." her eyebrows raised and she smiled a crooked smile at him.

He put his arms around her once more pulling her close to him. He kissed her on the forehead and then on the lips. "Guilty as charged but I don't regret it at all." He laughed and then released her from his embrace.

She rolled her eyes at him and then walked back to the Christmas tree where she continued to put ornaments on it. "You're impossible but that is why I love you so much. Don't you need to get over to Peter's property to do some work on your plans today?"

"Yes I do but I wasn't planning on leaving until we finished decorating the tree. If I didn't know better I'd think you were trying to get rid of me."

"I'm always glad to have your company Erik but I also don't want you to be late for supper this evening. I know how you lose track of the time when you're working."

He hung an ornament on a branch and then kissed her on the cheek. "I'll make sure that I return in time to help with supper. Please take time to rest today. I'll take some food down to the Persian and Darius before I go to the property."

"Thank you for helping me with the decorating and be careful in that old house. I wouldn't want anything to happen to you. Give my regards to the Persian and Darius. Tell them that we'll come to get them as soon as Peter and Isabel leave."

With those final words he kissed her again on the cheek and exited the room. She continued to decorate the tree and then after she finished she sat down on the sofa to admire her work. It was the most beautiful tree she'd ever seen and the decorations made it even look more magnificent. Erik had outdone himself this time selecting the tree. It was as grand a tree as she could remember laying eyes upon. It was nearly nine feet tall and it was almost as wide as the fireplace. She noticed a few places that needed more attention but she needed to rest. She decided to go upstairs to her room to enjoy a very well deserved nap.

It was an hour before noon when she fell asleep and when she woke it was half past three. She was obviously more tired than she had first thought. After she touched up the appearance of her hair and put her dress back on, she ventured down the stairs and into the kitchen for a bite to eat. She made herself a plate of leftovers and sat at the table in the kitchen. As she finished eating she heard a knock on the front door. Leaving her plate on the table she exited the kitchen and went to the foyer to greet whoever was at the door. When she opened it she was very surprised to find Frederic standing in front of her. So much so that she could hardly find the words to greet him properly.

"Are you just going to stand there or are you going to invite me in Amalie?"

"Oh....well yes....please Frederic....come in. I'm sorry. I just woke from a nap and I'm afraid I have not awakened fully. Where is Anna? Didn't she come with you?"

"No, she said she wasn't feeling well so she was going to stay home. Besides what I need to discuss with you doesn't concern her."

"What would that be Frederic?" She closed the door behind her but purposely didn't lock it. She didn't want to be locked in the house with him since she wasn't sure why he had come. They walked into the sitting room which had two entrances; one from the foyer and one from the hall down from the dining room. She sat on the sofa facing the window where the drapes were opened and she could see the flower garden. He followed her into the room and stood in front of the window facing her.

"What I need to discuss with you is your husband. I'm going to be honest with you Amalie. It was bad enough when you decided to marry him but to have a child is a whole different matter."

"What concern is it of yours who I marry or if I have a child? Is it jealousy that drives you to concern yourself with such things?"

"Me? Jealous? Are you mad woman? It's not jealousy that drives me to my concern it is proof that your beloved Erik is the Opera Ghost that brings me here."

"What proof is it that you have Frederic?"

"I have obtained one of the letters that the Opera Ghost had written to the managers of the Paris Opera House and I have compared the handwriting to a letter that I found in your father's study that Erik had written. The handwriting was practically identical." He laid both of the letters out on the coffee table so that she could see them. She picked them up, looked at them, folded them carefully and held them in her hand.

"You aren't just someone who makes accusations but you are also a thief. You took something out of my father's study without asking. You stole a letter out of my father's desk. When did you do this Frederic? I can't remember you ever going into the study when you visited the house."

"Well, just because you didn't see me doesn't mean that I didn't." He was scrambling now to cover up his crime. "And I didn't steal it, I borrowed it."

She rose to her feet, walked over to him and proceeded with her interrogation. "You broke into the house didn't you?" She waited for his answer but received only silence from him. "You're unbelievable. It isn't enough that you insult Erik with your ludicrous accusations but then you continue to make it worse by breaking into the house to steal things that don't belong to you." Her anger at his apparent lack of respect for her and her property had come to the breaking point of her patience. The volume of her voice rose as she said, "It really doesn't matter when or how you did it. I don't care if the writing is so well written that it looks as if the letters were mirror images. I want you to leave this house now!"

"I understand that you're angry but I'm not the person upon whom you should be venting your anger. It's your husband who has duped you into believing he is someone he is not."

She glared at him with eyes that bore daggers. "Erik has never lied to me about anything, especially about who he is. Unlike you, who strolls the streets of Paris acting like you're a righteous man with no secrets to hide when you are even more despicable than a criminal." She crossed the room and stood close to the doorway that entered the foyer.

"I have no idea what you're raving about and as I've said before, it's your husband that you should worry about. After all, my evidence proves that he *is* the Opera Ghost and we all know what heinous acts *he* has committed. Your safety and the safety of your child, although it is his monstrous seed, should be more of your concern." Frederic said very arrogantly as if he knew more about Erik than she did.

"Your evidence proves nothing or you would've gone to the authorities. I know for a fact that the authorities have closed this case and want no more to do with it. This is just your way of trying to hurt me. You've always been so jealous of me, the relationship I've had with your family and what I've accomplished. I believe you thought I'd completely fall apart when you told me you didn't love me and didn't want to marry me all those years ago." As he approached her she stepped back into the room, meeting him halfway. "Well I didn't and my life is even more wonderful now than I could have ever imagined it would be with you."

"You can't be serious. You call this a life? I believe Anna would have to argue with you about how wonderful her life is with me compared to your life with that half man, half monster you call your husband."

"Oh yes, I'm sure she's happy to have a husband who likes to hit her when he throws his childish fits. Yes, that's definitely the life I would've wanted," she said sarcastically.

His anger could clearly be seen on his face as she fired her accusations at him. He didn't know how she knew about the abuse he had bestowed upon Anna but it didn't matter, she knew and that was not acceptable to him. All he could do was continue to deny it and hope that she would not press the issue.

"Once again, you don't know what you're talking about."

"Oh, but I do Frederic because I was there. I saw it with my own two eyes. The night that we all attended the ball in Paris at M. Lebeaux's chateau, you and Anna were in the library having an argument. Do you remember now?"

With those few words he knew now that she had witnessed his wrath upon his wife. If she knew of the one incident she must know about all of the others. However, she did not. She had only witnessed the one event and knew nothing of any other attack on his wife. His anger grew and his temper flared at her words. He grabbed her by the shoulders and pushed her against the wall.

"Amalie, who have you told about this?"

She was scared but wouldn't let him see it. She stood pressed against the wall willingly without a struggle and looked him in the eyes. "I've told no one," she lied. "Anna wouldn't let me. She loves you Frederic even though you chose to hurt her. I don't understand it but she has only wanted what was best for you. She knew exposing you would only keep you from becoming the prestigious lawyer you have always wanted to become."

"Of course she loves me. Look at all the things she wouldn't have if it weren't for me. Her life is good because of me."

"I'm sure it is Frederic and I'm sure that the two of you will live happily together forever. Who am I to judge what your relationship is really like? After all, looking in from the outside doesn't always present all of the facts." She was trying to pacify his anger by agreeing with him. She had hoped that he'd release her from his grasp but he didn't. Instead he took her jaw in his hand and squeezed her face. He then put his face within centimeters of hers and whispered, "We will be happy forever and neither you nor your mother will ever stop me from being happy ever again."

She was confused by his words. She didn't understand what her mother had to do with his happiness. Her mother was already dead when he broke the engagement.

"What does my mother have to do with your happiness Frederic? You were the one that broke off the engagement to me. You were the one that was seeing other women while you were engaged to me. The only person keeping you from what I thought would give you your happiness was you."

"It was your mother who made me break my engagement to you." Her face drained of color as he released his grasp on her jaw and released her from the wall.

"Don't pretend you didn't know Amalie."

"I didn't and I demand to know what you're talking about." She followed him to the window.

He turned to her and without any emotion at all on his face but with eyes full of hate and disdain for her mother *and* her, he spoke. "Your mother found out about my affairs in Paris and of my many fits of rage toward other women that I had courted before you. Some of them didn't fare well after my tirades which she found out about with the help from some of her friends in Paris. She told me before her accident that I was to break the engagement or she would turn me into the authorities and tell you about my affairs which would certainly cause you or your father to keep the wedding from happening."

"But you didn't break the engagement until after Mother died. So, then why did you decide not to marry me?"

"After I thought about it, I realized that I didn't love you and the thought of being married to a woman I didn't love would've been too much for me to live with the rest of my life. I couldn't be married to a woman whose mother everyone thought to be insane, now could I? That wouldn't have reflected well on my career or my personal choices." His arrogance seethed from his lips and dripped from his words.

The confession that he had just made churned her stomach and turned her brave face into one of fear. This man wasn't who she thought he was at all. He was a very unpredictable and violent man and she was in her home alone with him. She slowly began to back away from him toward the entrance into the hallway. He quickly grabbed her by the arm, stopping her.

"Where do you think you're going? I don't believe that I'm done with you yet."

She tried to free her arm from his grip but was unsuccessful. She looked around the room to see if she could find something to defend herself against him. As he pulled her in the direction of the sofa she grabbed the lip of a vase from the small table that stood against the wall; cracking it over his head. It didn't make him let her go, it just made him angrier.

"You aren't going to get away from me. I didn't come here to hurt you but I see now that I may not have a choice. I just wanted to save you from that despicable monster you married. Don't you see that if you have his child that it will be just as monstrous as he is and who knows what horrors it will bring upon your family. Just like your mother did."

She began to cry as she struggled to free herself. He threw her onto the sofa and then slapped her across the face. "What are you going to do? Please don't hurt my baby. Please don't......" Her sobs drowned out her words making them inaudible for anyone to hear. He put his face close to hers and whispered into her ear. "I can see that subduing you won't be as easy as it was with your mother. However you should be proud of yourself, at least you are putting up a fight which is more than your mother did before I killed her."

She felt like she had stopped breathing for a second or two after the words entered her ears. It took a moment for her to process what he had just said. "What do you mean? My mother hung herself in the wooded acreage behind the house."

"That's what I wanted everyone to think but that isn't what happened." He smiled an evil smile.

"Why are you telling me this Frederic? Why now?"

"I believe you deserve to know the truth before you greet your mother."

"If you did kill my mother, you killed her for nothing Frederic. You didn't marry me just like my mother asked you and so you killing her served absolutely no purpose at all." Her voice quivered as she spoke and her tears impaired her vision. The anger and hate she felt for him grew inside of her like a seed pushing through the soil and unfolding it's leaves. "You're worse than a monster Frederic...you are the devil himself!"

"I'm no monster Amalie. I'm merely ridding the Earth of those not fit to breathe the air that I breathe."

"How is it that my mother fell into that category?"

"She didn't. She was an obstacle that I needed to rid myself of in order to continue to live my life." He tightened his grip on her wrists as he pushed her further into the cushion of the sofa. "Your mother threatened to tell my parents about my previous dealings with women. Although her face was destroyed her mind was still capable of plotting to destroy my life. What the rest of you took as her being depressed was really just her conscience eating away at her. She didn't know how to keep me from hurting another woman without turning me over to the authorities which would have hurt my parents. Her loyalty to them was her undoing. Instead she thought by threatening to tell them I'd stop what I'd been doing. I knew she'd never tell them but I couldn't risk her telling anyone else. She, unlike me, cared more about their feelings and what they thought of me. Unfortunately for her, that was the last mistake she would ever make."

She spit in his face and tried again to free her wrists from his grip. She hated him. She wished she'd never let him in the door. He continued with his confession of his crime. "You and your father were in the kitchen when she walked out of the house. I was coming to the house to try to convince her to drop the whole thing. I watched her leave the house and then it came to me that this would be the perfect opportunity for me to be rid of her forever. I waited until she entered the stable. Then I approached her. We exchanged a few words and then I subdued her. I bound her hands with a rope and gagged her with my handkerchief. I didn't bother to saddle the horse, I put the reins on him and then I set your mother on his back with me. We rode out to the wooded area behind the stables. I tied the rope around the tree branch and then around your mother's neck. I took the rope from her wrists and the handkerchief away from her mouth and all she said was "I'll not beg you to spare me, for it is you who will have to answer for what you're about to do. I've made my peace with God and I'm not afraid to die." Your mother didn't even try to save her own life. I guess I should've been moved by her words but I had no reason to be remorseful for what I was about to do. I've never been one to let guilt control my decisions. I slapped the back of the horse with my riding crop and your mother dropped like a meteor from the sky. I heard her neck snap instantly. Then I made my way back to my parent's house. No one suspected anything."

Hearing what were the last words of her mother should've angered her more but somehow it gave her peace knowing that she was ready to die and met death with dignity. She was proud that her mother had been willing to die for her principles. However, she was not; at least not now. She managed to pull her knee up under her and then thrust it as hard as she could into his chest as he leaned over her. He flew backwards onto the coffee table breaking it. She was free. She scrambled to her feet quickly and ran toward the entrance that led into the foyer but before she got two steps away from him he grabbed her dress. She felt the tug and without thought turned and kicked him in the face. He turned her loose and she ran to the study where she had hoped she'd be able to get to the secret door to make a quick escape but just as she entered the room she felt a hand grab her by the arm, pulling her. He slapped her across the face and then threw her against the wall. She needed to get to the desk where she knew Erik had left the revolver in the top drawer. She decided that she'd pretend to be unconscious in the hopes that he would leave her there but her plan didn't work. He picked her up off the floor and laid her in the middle of the floor then stood over her limp body.

Erik had finished his work at the property and ventured back to the cave to check on his friends. He visited with them for a while and then excused himself from their company so that he could return to the house to check on Amalie. He hadn't been comfortable with the idea of leaving her there alone knowing that Frederic was still visiting his parents but he had to trust that she'd be safe in their own home. The ride back to the house gave him time to reflect on how different his life had become and how happy he was that he'd finally let himself trust others. Some days he'd wake thinking he'd only dreamt it. He never thought he'd have to defend his life again but he was about to find out that it would be necessary not to save his life but Amalie's and their unborn child's.

After taking the saddle off of Jasper and putting him back into his stall, he began his walk back to the house. He would usually go through the back entrance but today he wanted to see the full effect of the Christmas decorations as his guests would when they entered their home. He took his key out to unlock the door but when he touched the doorknob the door slowly opened. It wasn't locked. There were no signs or sounds of Amalie. Immediately he knew something wasn't right. He'd locked the door when he had left. He knew she wouldn't have left the house without locking it. Quietly he entered and as he passed the entrance to the sitting room he saw the broken coffee table. Thoughts of what had possibly happened were flooding his mind. He decided not to call for her just in case whoever or whatever had been party to the destruction was still there. He didn't want to bring attention to his presence.

In the study, Frederic had thought that Amalie was unconscious so he walked across the room to the cabinet where the brandy decanter and glasses were kept. He spied the small hammer that bore Gaston's name. He poured himself a glass of brandy. As he did, she slowly and quietly got onto her knees and began crawling toward the desk. When she had made it to the desk she opened the drawer. Her hand searched for the revolver but it was missing. Erik must have put it upstairs after he'd gone out to the stable that night. Frederic seemed to have forgotten about her and poured himself another glass. He drank it and then took the hammer from its place of honor on the shelf. He stared at it and then turned around to find her missing from where he had laid her.

"I know that you're still here." He began searching for her behind the chairs and then he noticed her skirt behind the desk. He walked toward the desk and she stood up. When she did she noticed Erik quietly coming into the room. She knew that she'd be safe now but didn't let on that he was there. She knew what she had to do. She'd pretend that she'd surrendered to provide Erik the chance to help her. "You've decided to give up. I guess you truly are your mother's daughter."

She walked toward him as he approached her. He grabbed her by the arm and then pushed her against her father's desk. As he raised his hand to strike her, this time with her father's hammer, Erik caught his hand as it came forward. He delivered a blow to Frederic's jaw with his fist that sent him flying backwards. Frederic rose quickly from the floor and jumped on Erik, pushing him into the wall. He punched Erik in the face and Erik returned the blows; one to his opponent's face and one to his ribs. Frederic stumbled backward and then pulled a knife from his boot. Frederic swung and the tip of his blade caught Erik's mask, cutting the leather, causing it to fall from his face onto the floor. Erik noticed a letter opener on the desk. He slowly slipped it into his hands concealing it from Frederic. Frederic came at him, swung and missed as Erik was able to swiftly move out of the way. Erik used one of the chairs to separate Frederic from him.

Amalie found an opportunity to leave the room and took it. She ran up the stairs and to their bedroom. She found the revolver, made sure it was loaded and hurried back down the stairs. She knew she should run to get help but she couldn't leave Erik. She had to help him. She entered the study to find that Frederic had somehow managed to overpower Erik and pin him on the floor. Both men were suffering from numerous flesh wounds made by their prospective weapons but neither had succumbed to their injuries. Frederic was about to drive his knife into Erik's chest when she screamed, "Put your knife down Frederic or I will shoot!"

She was pointing the revolver directly at his head as she walked over to him.

Frederic looked at her and laughed. "You don't have it in you but don't worry I'll kill him first and then you. You'll be together soon enough."

He raised his knife once more in preparation to drive his knife into Erik and then a single gunshot rang out, then another. The knife dropped from Frederic's hand and his body fell on top of Erik. Erik freed his arms and pushed Frederic's lifeless body off of him, then fell back to the floor.

Amalie looked at her gun, knowing that it had jammed and not fired. She looked around and in the doorway of the study stood Anna with a revolver. She dropped it and then ran to Amalie and hugged her. Both of them began to cry.

"Amalie are you all right?"

"Yes, Anna. I am." She looked Anna in the eyes and then hugged her again. "Are you?"

"I am now that you and Erik are safe."

Amalie crawled over to Erik. His face was bloody and he had several slashes across his arms and chest from the knife.

"Erik, my love, are you still with me?" She caressed his cheek.

"Yes, Amalie, I'm here…..but I don't think…… I'm doing too well."

"I'll get my bag. Anna, please get me some towels from the kitchen and some water."

She retrieved her bag from the sitting room closet and then hurried back to him. She began cleaning his wounds and then assessing which one's would need to be sewn up. His wounds were not life threatening as long as she could get the bleeding under control. It seemed that it would be possible to do so. Anna returned with the towels and water. She began cleaning his wounds and helping Amalie put bandages on the one's that were not deep.

"Aren't you glad…. that I made you…. keep your medical bag?" he asked with bated breath as he tried to find the humor in the moment.

"Don't talk Erik, just rest. This is no time to make light of the situation. You're seriously injured."

"Well, I know that I'll be all right…..because my wife…. is a doctor."

"You're impossible Erik Geraurd and that is why I love you."

"I love you too."

"Anna, could you bring me the brandy from the cabinet?"

Anna retrieved the brandy and gave it to her. She lifted Erik's head and made him drink.

"This will help with the pain when I sew up the gash in your chest."

She continued to work on stitching up Erik's wounds for two hours. He finally had passed out which allowed her to work much faster on his wounds. Anna stayed, not because she needed to but because she wanted to help. She never once looked at her husband after she shot him. She was glad that he was gone and would never hit her again or any other woman for that matter.

As Amalie and Anna were putting more pillows under Erik's head to make him more comfortable Isabel and Peter walked into the house with their many Christmas packages in hand. Anna motioned for

Amalie to stay with Erik and she exited the study and met them in the foyer. Isabel knew that something was wrong as soon as she saw Anna standing there with blood on her hands and a dazed look on her face. Isabel dropped her packages and ran to her sister-in-law.

"Anna, what happened? Why do you have blood all over you? Whose blood is it? Are you all right?" Isabel's questions seemed to fall on deaf ears. Anna stood in silence not responding for a few seconds and then finally she spoke.

"He's dead Isabel. I'm so sorry but he's dead." Her face was emotionless and calm but had tears streaming down it.

"Who's dead Anna? Erik?" Peter asked.

"No, Frederic. Frederic is dead and I'm the one that killed him."

Isabel grabbed her by the arms and shook her. "You're not making any sense Anna. Why would you kill Frederic?"

Amalie heard the interrogation going on in the foyer and decided she couldn't leave Anna to face them alone. She opened the door to the study and left it open.

"She killed him to save me and Erik." Amalie appeared outside the study door. Her face was bruised and her left eye was black. She limped slightly on her right foot. As she walked toward them she collapsed onto the floor. The adrenaline that had kept her going had finally come to an end. Isabel ran to her, picked her head up and laid it on her shoulder as she sat on the floor. Peter retrieved a wet towel from the kitchen and gave it to Isabel to place on her forehead.

"Amalie, Amalie....wake up Amalie." Her eyes opened and then she threw her arms around Isabel and hugged her.

"Isabel, I'm so sorry about Frederic."

"What happened here Amalie? Who did this to your face?" Isabel asked with tears in her eyes.

"Frederic did this to my face and he tried to kill Erik." Amalie looked at Peter and motioned for him to help her up. She stood but not without help.

"I think you need to go lie down," Peter said as he helped her stand.

"Not without Erik. Please, Peter, could you help get him up to our room? He's lying on the floor in the study. I couldn't carry him." Amalie broke down sobbing uncontrollably.

"Yes, Amalie, I'll carry him to your room."

Peter entered the study and couldn't believe what he saw. Frederic's corpse was lying on the floor in a pool of blood and Erik was lying on the floor with his body covered with bandages and his face exposed. He'd never seen Erik's hidden face and now that he had it didn't make any difference to him. It was quite a sight to behold but in comparison to what Frederic had done to the rest of him, it didn't seem so terrible. He noticed the mask on the floor and picked it up. The leather had been cut and wouldn't be of any use until it was mended. He placed it on the desk. Anna walked in to offer her assistance in getting him to his room.

"Erik, are you awake?" Peter asked as he lightly touched his shoulder.

"Yes, Peter, I'm awake."

"Do you think you can walk with our help if we can get you standing?"

"I'll try but I'm not making any promises."

Peter knelt down and pulled his right arm over his shoulder and Anna knelt down and pulled his left arm over her shoulder. They slowly raised him up. They began walking him out of the study and to his room. Isabel had already taken Amalie up to the bedroom and changed her into her nightgown and robe. Anna and Peter lowered Erik onto the bed. Then Isabel and Anna left the room. Before leaving the room Peter helped Amalie get him out of his clothes and settled into the bed.

Amalie kissed his swollen lips gently and caressed his cheek with her hand. "I love you Erik."

"Amalie, is the baby going to be all right?" Erik asked with tears coming from his eyes.

"As far as I know, the baby is fine. Frederic only hit my face and I was careful to make sure that I never fell forward onto the baby. Only time will tell, Erik. If it is in God's plans then this baby will be born when it is supposed to be born and worrying about it won't change anything." She smiled at him and held his hand. "All I want you to do now is focus on getting better so that you can help finish the nursery."

He reached up and touched her cheek that was badly bruised. "I'm sorry I didn't come home sooner."

"My face will heal, but more importantly I'm alive and that is because of you."

"How is Anna?" Erik asked.

"I'm not sure. I believe she is in shock. I'll need to have one of them get the authorities. We will need to explain what happened here."

"Are you worried Amalie?"

"I don't think anyone will question what happened here especially after I tell them what Frederic confessed to me."

"And what was that?"

"He said he killed my mother. He made it look like she committed suicide to cover it up. Honestly that makes more sense than my mother doing it of her own free will. He claimed that my mother was going to expose his secret life of affairs and violent tirades on women to his parents. She had also made him promise that he'd break off the engagement to me or she would tell the authorities."

"I'm sorry Amalie. It must be hard for you to hear that he was responsible for her death."

"Yes, but I know that she and Father are together with God now and I can't be sad about that. Besides if she was here I may have never met you." She smiled at him with her eyes.

"I wonder what your mother would've thought about me. If she disliked someone like Frederic so much, think about what she would've thought of me."

"It's hard to say what she would've thought, but you know that my father would've advocated for you. Besides you're nothing like Frederic. You've changed Erik and you recognized a long time ago that you needed to in order to have the life you wanted. Frederic thought he was above having to change. His unwillingness to humble himself was ultimately the action that led to his own destruction." She kissed his hand and placed it on his chest. "No, my love, you are nothing like him and never will be." She rose from the bed and covered him up. "Get some sleep now. I will check on you in an hour or two."

Erik grabbed her hand as she started to walk away. "Tell Anna thank you for me. Help her with whatever she needs Amalie. We owe her our lives."

"I will. I promise."

She left the room and walked down the stairs. She was met by two members of the local law from the village and the local doctor. Peter had ridden into the village to retrieve them as well as his in-laws. Chester and Meg were not surprised at the scene that greeted them. They knew that it was a good possibility that someday their son would do something that would not end well. The officers had reviewed the scene and began their investigation. They hadn't begun interviewing anyone but as soon as they saw Amalie and the damage to her face, they assumed that whatever had taken place had to have been a situation that called for self-defense.

Chester and Meg greeted Amalie with a hug and many kisses. They inquired about what had happened and as she told them the horrific details of her afternoon, excluding the confession of his murdering her mother, the officers also listened. They wrote down all that had happened. After interviewing Anna and then briefly speaking with Erik, which Amalie had allowed only after she was able to wrap the portion of his face that was disfigured with a bandage so that they could not see his birthmark, the officers concluded that Frederic's death was caused by the bullets from Anna's gun which was discharged in order to save the lives of Amalie and Erik. There would be no further inquiry into his death or the incident that happened that afternoon. The local doctor took Frederic's body back into the village to prepare him for burial at the request of Chester and Meg. They would hold a private service in the church and bury him in the family burial plot behind their home.

Meg and Chester were devastated by what Amalie had told them but they were not surprised. They knew that their son had changed but never would have thought he'd be capable of the terrible things that were being brought to light.

Amalie walked over to Anna and hugged her. She led her to the sofa in the great room and sat with her. "Erik wanted me to thank you for him. We owe you our lives." She looked at Amalie, her face showing no emotion. "What I don't understand is how you knew he'd come here."

"I followed him. He thought I was taking a nap but I wasn't. I saw him put a knife in his boot, which I've never seen him do before. I didn't know for certain but I had a feeling he was about to do something that wouldn't end well. After he left the house and I was sure that he was gone, I found Chester's revolver, loaded it and then sat on the end of the bed trying to decide what to do. I sat thinking about all of the things I'd been through with him and I knew that I couldn't let him do to you, what he had done to me."

"What did he do to you Anna?"

"I had become pregnant a year after we married but Frederic didn't want children." She began to sob. "I didn't know that he was violent. He'd never shown me any reason to believe that he would be. But the afternoon that I told him I was pregnant; he lost all control of his actions. He beat me so badly that I lost the baby and was unable to leave the house or have visitors for three months. He had his own private physician tend to me and he paid him to keep quiet. I knew that he hated Erik and the fact that you were having his child made him hate not just him but you. I'll never understand why he didn't want you to have a child, just as I never understood why he didn't want me to have our child. To have that much hatred stored up inside of you for a child that is so innocent, it doesn't make any sense."

"No one knows what makes a person change or think the way they do Anna. Some things aren't easily explained." She squeezed Anna's hand and then brushed the tears from her cheek.

"You're probably right but I'll always wonder why."

"I know, Anna. I will too."

"I decided that I'd come to your house to see if he had come here. I had hoped I was wrong but somehow knew that I wouldn't be. When I arrived, Erik was laying underneath Frederic on the floor and you were standing with your revolver pointed at his head. After he threatened you, I fired hoping that if you fired and missed that my bullets would hit him. I had to stop him and now I'm just as horrible as he was." She began to cry again.

"No, Anna, you're nothing like him." Amalie took her in her arms and consoled her. Meg, Chester, Peter and Isabel gathered around. They were moved by her story and knew that she had no choice but to do what she had done.

Chester sat beside her on the sofa, putting his arm around her. He kissed her forehead and then looked at her tear covered face. "Anna, you did what was necessary and no one in this room thinks any less of you. It took courage to live all of these years in silence but it took more courage to do what you did here today. I only wished I'd known what my son was doing. Maybe I would've been able to help him."

"You did try to help him; many times." Anna let a half smile cross her lips as she hugged her father-in-law. "He just didn't want to change. He never thought what he was doing was wrong and when you can't see your need to change then it's harder to make the changes."

"Thank you Anna and I want you to know that you're always welcome at our house. You will always be our daughter-in-law."

"We feel the same way too Anna. You will always be a part of this family." Isabel knelt down in front of her and held her hand. "I'm sorry I didn't know what Frederic was doing. I'm sorry that I didn't know you needed my help."

"It wouldn't have mattered if you knew. Frederic would've just denied it and then you would've been on his list of people to take revenge upon too. I purposely never told anyone because I didn't want them to fall prey to his tirades, especially anyone who had children like you and Peter do. I was always glad to be a part of this family; it was unfortunate that he couldn't see the value of having such a loving family."

Chester and Meg helped Anna to the coach and then took her to their house. Meg helped her clean up and put her to bed. Anna was moved by the understanding that they gave her in light of the fact she had killed their only son. She had always wondered how they'd treat her if they had found out about the way he had abused her. She had thought they'd blame her and believe him. She had misjudged them and underestimated their capacity for discerning the truth from lies.

"Thank you, Meg, for being so nice to me."

"Don't be ridiculous child; there is no reason for me not to be nice to you." Meg sat on the bed next to her and held her hand. "I'll miss Frederic. He was my son and I loved him. However, I have learned through the years that everyone has a path that they choose. When they choose their path they also choose the consequences or the blessings that go along with their choices. It was no different for Frederic. He made his choice and he suffered the consequences of that choice. I would say that I forgive you for killing him but there is nothing to forgive. He would have died at someone else's hands, perhaps Amalie's or Erik's, if it wasn't by yours. I only wished he would've seen that his behavior was destroying more than his enemies; it was destroying him. Hate and anger are not weapons that only inflict pain on the intended victims; they are weapons that slowly kill the person that carries them around in their hearts. I told him this many times. He just couldn't find it in his heart or mind to really hear my words.

Anna leaned forward, put her arms around her and they both cried. "I loved him too Meg. I know you may not believe this but I'll miss him too. He wasn't always violent and at times I could see the man I fell in love with, the man of honor and kindness that made me love him."

"I believe you. You must have loved him very much to protect him for all of these years."

"At first it was love but eventually it was fear Meg. Fear of dying, fear of losing him; fear that he'd hurt someone else. I just learned how to keep him from unleashing his rage upon me. It stopped for a while and then after he met Erik it began again. I didn't understand the reason for him hating someone he'd just met but for some reason he was determined to punish him just for being alive."

Meg held her hand tightly and put her hand on her cheek. "I'm not sure why he disliked Erik so much. I can only guess that it was jealousy and then again it may have just been that Frederic couldn't see the man behind the mask. Insecurity and fear breed lots of things. Amalie took a risk when she introduced the two of you to Erik but she was convinced that everyone would accept him as we all did. The fact is we'll never really know why he disliked him so much. However, disliking someone does not give cause or reason to do physical harm to them."

"I'm sure you're right Meg. Frederic was a complex man and even after being married to him for five years I don't think I really knew who he was. I don't think he wanted me to know."

"He was my son and I barely knew who he truly was but I'm not going to dwell on what I did or didn't know. He's gone now and there is nothing more that I can do for him. My only concern now is you, my dear. I think it is time for you to get some rest. I'm sure it will be hard to sleep but try." Meg kissed her on the forehead turned her lamp down and walked out of the room.

Chester sat at the dining room table with his Bible. Although, he didn't have any answers as to why this happened he felt comforted by the words that he read. Frederic was his first child and his only son. They had worked so hard to make sure they taught him their values and beliefs and to provide him the best opportunities that life could offer and yet, it didn't seem to have been enough. Although he despised the actions of his son he would always love him. Somehow Frederic had lost sight of what was important and let his selfishness distort his views. It was something that all of them would have to accept. Meg put her arms around him and they wept together. Their son was dead.

Love.....Always

Three months had passed since the incident at the house. The Persian and Darius had stayed on at the house to help Amalie care for Erik after Frederic's death but they were soon to leave once Meg and Chester returned from Paris where they were helping Anna relocate to her parent's house. They were expected back any day. Isabel and Peter went back to London afterward where they returned to their lives.

All of Erik's wounds had healed and he was back to playing the piano every evening and helping Amalie with the final touches in the nursery. He had crafted a new mask but rarely wore it now. All of his friends had seen him without it for so long while he was recuperating that he had grown comfortable not wearing it when they were around. Amalie never told anyone but Erik about Frederic's confession of killing her mother. She knew that it would just hurt Meg, Chester and Isabel even more and telling them wouldn't bring her mother back. So, they promised each other that they would never tell anyone. They rarely went to the study anymore. When they went to the cave they would either walk or ride out to the entrance in the clearing instead of taking the secret door. The blood stained floor was covered with a beautiful new rug and Amalie had rearranged the furniture to give the room a different look in the hopes that it would make the horrible images of what had taken place in the room disappear.

Her belly had grown bigger as her due date approached. She was glad that her pregnancy managed to survive the pushes and shoves that Frederic had exerted upon her. She had experienced labor pains the night of the altercation but was able to get through it without delivering early. She could only attribute that miracle to being a blessing from God. There were many nights that she didn't sleep after that and she knew she shouldn't worry but she did. Now it was almost time for the baby to be born and she was nervous, anxious and excited, as was Erik.

It was a cool morning in April in which Amalie awoke to her first labor pains. Erik was still sleeping soundly next to her. She knew that her labor could take hours so she didn't wake him. Instead she busied herself in between the pain by pacing up and down the hall. After an hour of doing so her pains began to come faster and more often. She alerted him to her situation which alarmed him. He immediately picked her up and put her into the bed. He brought her a glass of water and then fussed with the pillows trying to make sure that she was comfortable. She tried to reassure him that the pain was to be expected when a woman was about to give birth and that there was no need to worry but he continued to nervously pace back and forth. He had never been around such things so he had no knowledge of what to expect.

"Erik, I'd like for you to go get Meg and tell Chester that he needs to go get the mid-wife from the village."

"But I can't leave you here alone Amalie. What if something happens?"

"Meg and Chester only live a short distance from us. It won't take you long. Besides, I don't think you are qualified to deliver this baby. I don't think you would want to... now would you?"

"You're right. I'll be back as quickly as possible." He kissed her on the forehead and then made his way down the stairs and out the front door. She laid in her bed breathing as best she could through each contraction. In between the pain from the contractions she would pray. She prayed that she'd be a good mother and Erik would be a good father. She prayed for God's strength and guidance in raising their child. She prayed that if this child did bear a birthmark such as Erik's that the world wouldn't be as cruel to it as it had been to him. It had been only thirty minutes since he had left and her contractions were almost unbearable now. She had almost given up on anyone arriving before the baby made its way into the world when Meg walked through the door. She was beginning to not be able to resist the urge to push any longer.

"I'm....so glad....you're here....Meg." She said with bated breathe. "I think the baby is ready to come."

Meg hurried over to the bed and checked her. She was right; the top of the baby's head was visible. "Do you have scissors and twine, Amalie?"

"Yes....Meg...they... are....in my...medical bag...." Amalie screamed in pain and then continued "....on the dresser."

Meg found the bag and pulled what she needed out of it.

"Are you ready to push?"

"Yes!"

Meg instructed her to push and she did as she was told. After two pushes the mid-wife arrived. Meg began readying a towel in which the baby was to be placed. She gave three more pushes and then the tiny cries of a baby could be heard outside the bedroom door where Erik anxiously waited with Chester.

"Amalie," Meg whispered to her, "it's a girl; a beautiful, perfect, little girl." Amalie began to cry. She was overcome with joy but she was exhausted. The mid-wife continued to perform her duties as Meg cleaned the baby up to be presented to Amalie. Meg handed Amalie her daughter. She kissed the baby's forehead and whispered, "You're beautiful my little angel."

"What are you going to name her?" Meg asked.

"Erik and I decided that if it was a girl, her name would be Louisa Adeline Geraurd."

"I think it is a wonderful name." Meg kissed her forehead. "I'd better go tell Erik that he's a father."

"Meg?"

"Yes, Amalie?"

"Why don't you take her to him? He's been so worried. Take her and let him see his daughter." She handed Louisa to Meg.

Meg walked to the door and opened it. Erik and Chester were looking over the banister into the great room. When they heard the door open they looked to see Meg holding a tiny infant in her arms. Erik met her in the doorway.

"Is this….?" He could hardly speak for there were no words to explain the emotion that he was feeling.

"Yes, Erik, this is your daughter, Louisa Adeline Geraurd."

"She's beautiful, isn't she?" he said with a smile as he looked at her. "She looks like her mother."

"Yes, but she has your eyes Erik," Chester said as he put his hand on his shoulder.

"Would you like to hold her, Erik?" Meg asked him as his smile turned to an uncertain grin. "She won't break. I promise." Meg handed her to him. She began to cry and instinctually he began singing a lullaby and her cries quieted. He'd forgotten that he wasn't wearing his mask but as he sang to her she seemed to be studying him with her eyes; the eyes that were said to be like his. She wasn't frightened by his appearance. He realized in that moment that prejudice and fear were not born *to* man but taught *by* man. He would do his best to raise his daughter not to judge or fear people because of their appearance. He would try not to let his past influence his daughter's life. He'd do everything in his power to teach her all the things her grandfather had taught him about friendship and trust.

The mid-wife came out and informed Erik that he could see Amalie now. He took their daughter into the room and sat on the bed facing her.

"She's beautiful Amalie, just like you."

"But she has your eyes; those gorgeous, irresistible blue eyes." Amalie smiled at him and put her hand on his arm. "She seems to be in love with you already Erik. Look at the way she's looking at you."

"It's only because I was singing to her. She seems to like music."

"I don't think it's the music, I think it's your voice. You've always been able to calm me with your voice and your love."

"I'm so glad that she doesn't have....." his eyes began to fill with tears and he couldn't form the words to complete his thought. Amalie touched his arm again and said, "I'm glad too but even if she had we'd still love her just as much as we do now."

He smiled at her and then he looked at Louisa's blue eyes, kissed her forehead and whispered in her ear, "You'll always be loved. I promise."

CPSIA information can be obtained at www.ICGtesting.com
Printed in the USA
LVOW011700241011

251845LV00001B/14/P